BOOKS BY JAMES PATTERSON
FEATURING NYPD RED

NYPD Red

NYPD Red 2

NYPD Red 3

A complete list of books by James Patterson is at the back of this book. For previews of upcoming books and information about the author, visit JamesPatterson.com, or find him on Facebook or at your app store.

LARGE PRINT

NYPD RED 4

JAMES PATTERSON
AND MARSHALL KARP

LITTLE, BROWN AND

LARGE PRIN

Copyright © 2016 by James Patterson
Excerpt from *Private Rio* copyright © 2016 by James Patterson

Little, Brown and Company
Hachette Book Group
1290 Avenue of the Americas, New York, NY 10104
littlebrown.com

First Edition: January 2016

Little, Brown and Company is a division of Hachette Book Group, Inc. The Little, Brown name and logo are trademarks of Hachette Book Group, Inc.

The publisher is not responsible for websites (or their content) that are not owned by the publisher.

The Hachette Speakers Bureau provides a wide range of authors for speaking events. To find out more, go to hachettespeakersbureau.com or (866) 376-6591.

8-0-316-40706-9 (hc) / 978-0-316-28870-5 (large print)
Congress Control Number: 2015953819

2 1

States of America

For Jody and Harold
—MK

PROLOGUE

THE RED, RED CARPET

ONE

LEOPOLD BASSETT FLITTED across the room to where his brother, Maxwell, was quietly nursing a glass of wine.

"Max, I just heard from my spotter in the lobby," Leo said in a giddy half whisper. "Lavinia is on her way up. Can you stop brooding for twenty minutes?"

"I'm not brooding. I was just enjoying this absolutely *exquisite* Sancerre and trying to calculate how much this latest junket of yours is costing us."

"You can stop calculating," Leo said, "because now that I know Lavinia is coming, it's worth every dime. She's the only one we really care about."

"Then why did *we* pay fifteen thousand dollars for the Royal Suite at the Ritz-Carlton, and what are the rest of these freeloaders doing here besides pigging out on caviar and swilling champagne?"

"Max, I don't tell you how to design jewelry, so don't go lecturing me on how to plan a *soirée de publicité*. If Lavinia walked into an empty room, she'd walk right out. These people are cannon fodder. I papered the house."

"For one lousy gossip columnist?"

"*Gossip?* Try *fashion guru*. People hang on every word this woman writes, every photo she prints. She's a tastemaker, a trendsetter."

The door to the suite opened, and Lavinia Begbie entered.

"Well, well," Max said. "Judging by the arched eyebrows and frozen forehead, it looks like the hot new trend is Botox jobs gone horribly wrong. Her face looks like she had a stroke."

"I hate you," Leo said, and hurried across the room to greet the new arrival and her entourage: a photographer, an assistant, and a West Highland white terrier that Lavinia was cradling in her arms.

She set the dog on the floor, air-kissed Leo, and headed straight for Max. "Maxwell Bassett—jeweler to the stars," she said, shaking his hand. "A pleasure to finally meet you. You're quite the recluse."

Max smiled. "Leo is a tough taskmaster. He keeps me locked up in my studio designing baubles for bold-faced names."

"Locked up, indeed," she said. "The last time I spoke to Leo you were somewhere in Namibia hunting white rhinoceros."

"Please don't print that," Max said, folding his hands angelically against his chest. "PETA hates me enough as it is."

"Leo, be a dear and fetch me a double bourbon, neat," Lavinia said.

"Done," Leo said. "How about your dog? Can I get her a bowl of water?"

"Don't bother. Harlow loves cocktail parties. She'll wait until someone drops a bit of food, then she'll gobble it right up. I call them floor d'oeuvres." She turned her attention to Max. "Let's talk."

"It took months," he said, launching into his canned presentation, "but I finally found twenty perfectly matched four-carat emeralds—"

"Please," she interrupted. "Spare me. Your publicist emailed me all the details, and my photographer will get a shot of Elena Travers on her way to the red carpet. I'm here to talk about the rumors."

"They're all true," Max said. "Leo is gay. I told him you were onto him."

"I've heard you're planning to get into bed with Precio Mundo," she said.

"Precio? The big-box store? How could they possibly market a brand like Bassett? Mark the hundred-thousand-dollar bracelets down to eighty-nine thousand and put them in an endcap display?"

"Don't be coy, and don't sidestep the question. According to my sources, they want you to create a line of—"

"Ladies and gentlemen, may I have your attention, please." Sonia Chen, Leo's publicist, stood outside the bedroom door. "I've met a lot of leading ladies, but none more stunning or more gracious than the young woman who will be walking down the red carpet tonight at the premiere of her latest film, *Eleanor of Aquitaine*. It is my honor to present Elena Travers."

The actress stepped through the door wearing a strapless white Valentino gown that was perfectly set off by Max's latest masterpiece. The guests applauded, cameras clicked, and from the other side of the room Leo Bassett called out, "At long last—I have found the girl of my dreams."

The crowd laughed, and Leo rushed toward Elena, his arms spread wide. "Darling," he cooed, commanding the room, "you look ravish—"

As soon as his foot connected with the West Highland white terrier, Leo's body pitched forward. Harlow squealed, Leo shrieked, and hands reached out to break his fall. But nothing could stop his momentum until he crashed into a buffet table and landed on the rug, covered with sea bass ceviche.

A waiter helped him to his feet, and Sonia immediately materialized with a handful of napkins and began to brush the fish and salsa from his tuxedo.

Leo waved her aside and stood center stage. "First rule of show business," he said, playing to the crowd. "Never work with kids or dogs."

Nervous laughter from the guests.

He smiled at Lavinia. "And how's little Harlow?"

"She's upset, but she'll be fine," Lavinia said, cuddling the Westie in her arms. "Leo, I'm so sorry—"

He held up a hand and turned toward Elena. "My dear, I'm afraid you'll have to find another escort."

"Oh, Leo," Elena said, "nobody cares about a little cocktail sauce. Come on. We'll have fun."

"For God's sake, Leo, go." It was Max. "Nobody's going to be looking at you anyway."

"No," he said, lashing out at his brother. "Leo Bassett is not walking down the red carpet smelling like a fucking fish stick."

He turned, stormed into the bedroom, and slammed the door.

Max stole a glance at Lavinia Begbie, wondering how she'd react to Leo's theatrics. But her face had been injected with so much wrinkle-numbing botulinum toxin that it was impossible to tell.

TWO

IAN ALTMAN SCANNED the people standing behind the velvet ropes at the Ziegfeld Theater, looking for someone to shoot, but there was nobody interesting.

In fact, there was practically nobody at all. The carbon arc searchlight beams that crisscrossed the sky were doing a piss-poor job of attracting a crowd to the premiere of Elena Travers's new movie.

That was the problem with having these red carpet events in New York, Altman thought. In L.A., the glitterati showed up. In New York, anything that blocks the sidewalk is just another freakin' inconvenience.

As if to prove his point, a man trying to skirt the police barrier crashed into him, practically knocking the camera out of his hands.

"Asshole," the pedestrian yelled. "You people think you own the streets?"

Altman had been trained to avoid run-ins with the public. "Not *own*, sir," he said. "I'm with the TV crew, and we do have a permit that allows us to—"

The unmistakable thunderclap of a gun blast cut through the air, and Altman instinctively swung his camera in the direction of the sound. In the same instant, a dozen officers from the best-trained urban police force in America kicked into full emergency response mode.

Guns were drawn, radios came alive, and orders were shouted. A second shot followed, and the cops fanned out—some heading west in pursuit of the shooter while the rest tried to herd the stampeding crowd in the other direction.

Bullets didn't scare Ian Altman. He'd done two tours in Afghanistan as a combat photographer with the air force. He dropped to one knee and pointed his camera toward the action.

Through the lens, he could see it coming. A white stretch Cadillac careened out of control down West 54th Street, sideswiped a cop car, ricocheted off an NYPD traffic van, and plowed head-on into the pair of eight-hundred-million candlepower searchlights that had been lighting up the night.

Xenon bulbs exploded, and a hail of sparks and glass showered down on the cameraman as he zoomed in on the driver's side window, where a body was slumped over the steering wheel.

The first wave of cops advanced on the limo, barking at the occupants to come out with their hands up.

Altman wheeled his camera around in time to catch a young man, his shirt covered in blood, stumble from the back door. Cops came at him from all sides screaming, "Down on the ground! Now, now, now!"

The man fell to his knees, threw his hands in the air, and screamed back, "She's been shot! Get an ambulance!"

A sergeant yelled a command, and two cops approached the limo, peered inside, and then holstered their guns. The female cop crawled into the backseat while her male partner ran around the vehicle and entered it from the opposite side.

They slowly eased Elena Travers out of the car and set her down under the marquee—a rag doll, the front of her white gown as red as the carpet beneath her. The female officer knelt down and gently cradled Elena's head.

The actress tried to speak, but all that came out was a pained whimper. The cop leaned in close, and Altman moved in tight enough to read her lips. *It's going to be okay. It's going to be okay.*

It wouldn't.

Ian Altman's pulse was racing, but his hands were steady as he framed the tableau in his viewfinder.

The actress and the cop, their eyes locked in an unfathomable bond. And then Elena took one last breath, and the light in her eyes went out.

Altman had captured death on video before, but it had always been surrounded by the horrors of war. This was almost peaceful, but at the same time so much more gut-wrenching.

Out of respect, he began to widen his lens, pulling back until he could compose his final shot, one that was going out on the air live, and would eventually go viral and be seen by hundreds of millions of people around the world: Elena Travers, flawlessly beautiful, even in death, except for the deep gouges on her skin where Maxwell Bassett's one-of-a-kind, eight-million-dollar masterpiece had been ripped from her chest.

PART ONE

LONG DAYS.
SHORT NIGHTS.

CHAPTER 1

NOTHING ATTRACTS A crowd like a dead celebrity.

By the time Kylie and I arrived at the crime scene, a wave of humanity had descended on the Ziegfeld Theater, bearing candles, flowers, stuffed animals, and, of course, pictures of the late Elena Travers.

The *Daily News* would sum it up with one word in their morning edition.

FANDEMONIUM!

"Zach! Zach Jordan!"

I looked up and saw Stavros Kellepouris walking toward us. Sergeant Kellepouris was old-school, tough on his officers and even tougher on himself, which is why cops who work for him either respect him, hate his guts, or both.

"Zach, I knew they'd kick this one up to Red," he said, shaking my hand. He turned to Kylie. "And you must be Detective MacDonald."

"Kylie. Good to finally meet you, Sergeant. And for the record, it didn't get kicked up. It came down from on high. What have you got so far?"

"A dead movie star, a limo driver in the OR with a bullet in his back, two perps in the wind, and a video which won't give you much to go on."

"You're right," she said. "We've seen it."

"The whole damn city has seen it," Kellepouris said. "There were maybe fifty, sixty people here when they thought she was showing up alive. But stretch her out in a pool of blood on the sidewalk, and an army of vultures shows up with their camera phones hoping to capture a piece of Hollywood history."

"Give us a rundown of what went down before the shots were fired," I said.

"Quiet night, just the usual paparazzi you have to wrangle and keep behind the ropes, but it was no problem. I had more cops than I needed."

"Why's that?"

"It's all part of the Hollywood bullshit game. Travers was wearing this zillion-dollar necklace, and somebody in PR thought it would look better with twelve cops to guard her instead of four. The studio pays the city for the security, so they can hire as many as they want. We were all just props in blue uniforms, until the shit hit the fan."

"Tell us about the man who was in the car with her."

"Craig Jeffers. He's her personal trainer, but from what he told me, they had another kind of personal relationship going on that they kept under wraps."

"What can you tell us that we didn't see on the video?"

"It looks like it started out as a simple snatch-and-grab. Two mooks with guns stopped the limo. I don't think they had any intention of hurting anyone. They just wanted to heist some bling."

"What went wrong?"

"It was Jeffers. He's a bodybuilder—macho to the core. He decided to go all Jason Statham and wrestle the gun away from one of the perps. It didn't work out the way he planned."

Kylie shook her head. "Men are such assholes," she said.

Kellepouris grinned at me. "You got lucky, Zach. I like this one. She sounds a lot like my wife."

"Anything else?" I said.

"I got stripes, Zach, no shield, so I didn't dig very deep. Also, Jeffers seemed too devastated to handle a lot of questions. What he did was beyond dumb, but you've got to feel sorry for him. That poor bastard will have Elena Travers's blood on his hands for the rest of his life."

"That's what I like about you, Stavros," I said. "You never hold back on your opinions."

"I hate to disappoint you, Detective, but that's not my opinion. Those are Craig Jeffers's words, not mine."

CHAPTER 2

WE WALKED PAST the sandwiched remains of the limo and the searchlight truck and made our way to the red carpet, where Chuck Dryden was kneeling next to the body of Elena Travers.

Dryden, who has all the charisma of a medium security prison, looked up. His normally stoic facial expression softened when he saw Kylie, but he was still all business, no foreplay. "She took a 9mm slug to the abdomen," he said. "She bled out."

"Thanks," Kylie said, giving him her practiced you're-my-favorite-crime-scene-investigator smile.

"It's my job," he said, and returned to the work at hand, signaling that his report was over.

We entered the Ziegfeld, which was empty except

for a few cops and a man sitting on the floor, his back to the wall, his head in his hands.

"Mr. Jeffers," Kylie said softly.

He raised his head. His eyes were red, his face contorted with pain. "I told her I was sorry," he said. "Before she died, I held her in my arms and told her I was sorry. She didn't say anything, but I know she heard me."

Kylie knelt beside him. "We're going to find the men who did this."

"*I* did it," he said. "It was my fault as much as anybody else's."

"Can we talk?" Kylie said, standing up.

Jeffers stood. He was blond, six two, with wide shoulders, a thick neck, and bulging pecs that strained against his bloody shirt.

It's possible that he'd hit the genetic jackpot, but I'm enough of a gym rat to know a steroid user when I see one. The disproportionately developed upper body, the bulging veins on his hands, and the prominent acne told the story. Craig Jeffers was a juicer.

"We were at a red light," he said. "Two guys with guns came out of nowhere. They forced the driver to roll down the windows, and one of them pointed his gun at Elena. I'm sure she would have given him the necklace if he asked, but no—he had to dig his fingers into her chest and yank it off. The bastard drew blood. He hurt

her, and she screamed. That's what set me off—
the scream."

"What do you mean, set you off?" Kylie asked.

"I snapped. I went for his gun. I know they tell
you not to, but you don't think when the adrenaline
kicks in like that. I had one hand on his wrist, and
I was about to punch him with the other when the
gun went off."

I'd heard it before. A man, armed with nothing
more than an overabundance of testosterone, de-
cides to try his luck at hand-to-gun combat. It
might work for Jackie Chan in the movies, but it
failed for Craig Jeffers in real life.

"And then what?" Kylie asked.

"He fired another shot. I found out later that it hit
the driver. But everything else is a blur. All I could
focus on was Elena."

"Can you describe the two men?" Kylie asked.

"They had their faces covered with green surgical
masks, and they were wearing black knit caps. The
one who reached in the back wasn't wearing gloves,
so I could see his hands. He was white."

"What was your relationship with Elena Travers?"
I asked.

"I loved her."

"You were also her personal trainer?"

"That's how it started, but six months ago I asked
her out on a date. I never thought it would go anywhere, but it did. I couldn't believe it. Elena could

have had any guy in Hollywood, but she only wanted to be with me. I was ready to spend the rest of my life with her. And now…"

He shook his head. The interview was over, but Kylie and I gave the man a few moments to reflect on his loss.

The three of us stood there in the vast open space of the Ziegfeld lobby, red carpet beneath us, crystal chandeliers glittering above, half a dozen larger-than-life-size pictures of Elena Travers assaulting our senses from every angle. Finally, Jeffers broke the silence.

"It's all my fault," he said. "If Elena had gone with Leo like she was supposed to, she would still be alive."

And just like that, the interview was no longer over.

"Who is Leo?" I asked.

CHAPTER 3

LEO, IT TURNED out, was someone Kylie had met.

"I doubt if he'd remember me," she said when we were back in the car.

"How is that possible? You're the most unforgettable cop on the force."

"I wasn't a cop that night. It was an industry party, and I was there as Mrs. Spence Harrington. Leo was so starstruck he barely said hello to me. People like him don't waste their time talking to the *wives* of people who make movies."

We found Bassett's number in Elena Travers's cell phone. I called him and told him we had a few questions.

"My brother and I have some questions of our own," he said. "Can you meet us at our place?"

By the time we got there, the street was clogged with news trucks, paparazzi, and the usual assortment of homicide junkies. Two squad cars and a pair of traffic agents wearing Day-Glo yellow vests had been dispatched to the scene to help maintain sanity.

Working for Red, I get a firsthand look at how the other half lives. Of course, the Bassett brothers weren't exactly the other half. They were more like the 1 percent of the 1 percent, and their "place" was more like a palace.

Back when New York was in its industrial heyday, lower Manhattan was peppered with loft buildings intended for commercial or manufacturing use but off-limits for residential. In the early eighties, the law changed, and the smart money gobbled up the cold, bleak, rat-infested buildings for next to nothing.

The Bassetts got in early and transformed a six-story warehouse on West 21st Street into two spectacular triplex apartments. Leo occupied the lower half of the building, and Kylie and I took the elevator to the third floor.

The door opened into a vast room with vaulted ceilings, massive windows, and museum-quality furniture. The two men who were waiting for us looked nothing like brothers.

One was big and burly, with a smoky-gray beard and icy blue eyes. He was wearing faded jeans and a nondescript T-shirt. "Max Bassett," he said.

The other was short, with soft, doughy features and ink-black hair that could only have come from a bottle. His outfit, a red smoking jacket over deep-purple silk pajamas, looked like it was right out of Hugh Hefner's closet.

"I'm Leo," he said. "Thank you for coming. We are devastated, and there's no real information on television. Please tell us what happened."

We sat down, and I gave them the highlights.

"I don't understand," Leo said. "We've been robbed before. Jewel thieves almost never get violent. Why did they have to shoot her?"

"You're not listening," Max said. "They shot her because her idiot boyfriend grabbed for the gun."

Leo lashed out. "So you're saying it's all my fault?"

Max came right back at him. "Jesus, Leo, how the hell did you manage to make this about you?"

"Because *I* was the one who was supposed to go with her. If someone stuck a gun in my face, I'd have said, 'Take the necklace, take my wallet, take what you want—just don't hurt us.' But I didn't go, and now she's dead."

"Why *didn't* you go?" I asked.

"It was a stupid accident," Leo said. "I was—"

"More like a stupid decision," Max said. "He didn't go because he got *cocktail sauce* on his jacket. Elena didn't care. She asked him to go anyway. But he said no."

Leo stood up. "Thank you, Max. Because I didn't

feel bad enough as it is." He turned to me. "I'm not feeling well. If you have any more questions for me, I'll be happy to talk to you in the morning. Alone."

He didn't wait for an answer. He just turned and walked out of the room.

"There you have it, Detectives," Max said. "My brother's MO. Grand entrances and even grander exits. He's a total drama queen even when the drama isn't about him. This is a terrible tragedy. How can I help you find the people who killed Elena?"

"Can you describe the necklace?" I said.

"Seeing as I designed it, yes. There are twenty emeralds—absolutely superbly matched stones, four carats apiece. Each one is surrounded by a cluster of round and pear-shaped diamonds. They're tiny, five points each, but the effect was dazzling. She looked gorgeous."

"Who knew she'd be wearing the necklace?" I asked.

Max shook his head. "Everybody. It was one of Leo's misguided publicity initiatives."

"It sounds like you don't see eye to eye with your brother," Kylie said.

"Not remotely. Maybe once upon a time you could trot Marilyn Monroe or Elizabeth Taylor down the red carpet wearing an eight-million-dollar necklace and hope that the stunt would cast some kind of magic halo effect over the brand. But not anymore. I told Leo he was still living in the second half of the twentieth century. The hype would be all about Elena, and no one would even remember she was wearing an original Max Bassett. Well, I was wrong. Now everyone will remember me as the man who designed the necklace Elena Travers died for."

"Mr. Bassett, whoever took the necklace is going to try to sell it," Kylie said. "We need to get pictures and laser inscriptions to the JSA and the FBI as soon as possible."

"Our publicist, Sonia Chen, will have it for you within the hour," he said. "I'm impressed. Most cops aren't familiar with the Jewelers' Security Alliance."

"We've had a bit more experience in this area than most cops," Kylie said. What she didn't say was that when you're assigned to Red, stolen jewelry is as common as shoplifting.

CHAPTER 4

UNDER NORMAL CIRCUMSTANCES, getting home five hours after my shift ended wouldn't be a problem, but for the past twenty-four days my life had been anything but normal. Cheryl and I were living together.

Or at least we were trying to, but I was doing a lousy job of holding up my end of the living arrangement. This was the fifth night I'd come home late since she'd moved in, plus I'd been called into work two out of the past three weekends.

I'd met Dr. Cheryl Robinson about four years ago. I was on the short list of candidates for NYPD Red, and she was the department shrink assigned to evaluate me. I know it's what's on the inside that counts, but it's impossible to meet Cheryl and not be dazzled by the outside. Most of her family is Irish, but it's the DNA of her Latina grandmother that gives her the dark brown eyes, jet-black hair, and glorious caramel skin that turn heads. I was instantly smitten.

She had only one drawback: a husband. But good things come to those who wait, and about a year ago, Cheryl's marriage to Fred Robinson crashed and burned, and we went from friends to lovers to whatever it is you call it when two people start living together but hang on to both apartments because they're not so sure it's going to work out.

"Hurry up," she said as soon as I opened the front door to my apartment.

"I'm sorry I'm late," I said. "I was—"

"I know, I know," she said. "It's coming up on the eleven o'clock news."

She was on the sofa wearing black running shorts and a turquoise tank top, her hair tied back in a ponytail. She patted the cushion next to her, and I sat down.

"You must be starved," she said, leaning over and giving me a kiss.

I was, but you don't come home five hours late and ask what's for dinner. I didn't have to. Cheryl had set a plate of cheese, olives, salsa, and chips on the coffee table along with a bottle of wine and two glasses. I dug into the food as a somber anchorman led off with the murder of Elena Travers.

The report was interspersed with film highlights of Elena's career, the limo crash, her body on the red carpet, and a still shot of the missing necklace. And since Kylie and I had been involved in three high-profile cases in the past year, the reporter thought it was newsworthy to point the cameras at us and mention us by name as we entered the Ziegfeld to question Craig Jeffers.

The piece ended with a shot of a teenage girl, tears streaming down her face, kneeling down to add a bouquet of flowers to the makeshift memorial.

"It's terrible," Cheryl said, her own eyes watery and ready to spill over. "I'm glad you and Kylie are on the case. You'll solve it."

"It won't be easy," I said. "It seems like a robbery gone bad, so there's no direct link between the killer and the victim."

"Don't look so down. You've cracked tougher cases."

"I know, but it's going to mean working overtime. I'm sorry."

"Stop it," she snapped.

I didn't know what I'd done, but clearly it wasn't good. "Stop what?" I said.

"Apologizing."

"I thought women liked apologies," I said, turning on my boyish smile. "Especially if they're accompanied by flowers or jewelry."

She muted the TV. Not a good sign. "I don't know

what other women like, Zach, but the woman you're living with doesn't like you apologizing on spec."

"I'm not sure what that means."

"It means you just apologized to me *in advance* for working overtime. It's manipulative. You're trying to preempt any negative reaction I might have the next time you come home late."

"I thought I was taking responsibility for my actions."

"And I think you're asking for a free ride. *'How can Cheryl be mad? I told her this would happen.'*"

"What can I say? I feel guilty for all the times I've worked late."

"Why? You're a cop. I know you keep crazy hours. In fact, you may remember that I'm one of the people who helped you land this job."

"So what's my best course of action here, doctor?" I said. "Should I retract the apology, or should I get down on my knees and beg your forgiveness for having made it?"

That cracked the code. She laughed. "I have a better idea," she said. "We've both spent the whole night focused on death. Let's do something that reaffirms life."

She took me by the hand and led me to the bedroom. She dimmed the lights to a warm golden hue, and we undressed slowly, deliberately, not touching, leaving just enough space between us for the anticipation to build.

"Not yet," she whispered as I stood there naked, clearly ready. It was agonizing and tantalizing at the same time. I waited as she pulled back the sheets and lay on the bed.

"Now," she breathed softly.

I lowered my body gently to meet hers, let my tongue caress her breasts, and slid effortlessly inside her.

And there in the soft light, entwined with the woman I was growing to love more and more every day, all the harsh realities of carrying a badge and a gun melted away. My anxieties about the past and my fears of the future disappeared.

There were no words. Just the calming peace of being with the only person in the world who really mattered. It truly *was* life affirming.

CHAPTER 5

I GOT TO Gerri's Diner the next morning and settled into my favorite booth. Gerri herself came out from behind the counter and brought me coffee.

"I saw you on the news last night," she said.

"How'd I look?"

"You looked like you could use a good night's sleep, but from the way you dragged your ass in here this morning, I'm guessing you didn't get one. Breakfast will help," she said. "What would you like?"

"Eggs over easy, bacon, toasted English."

"Would you like anything else with that?" she asked.

"No, thanks."

"It doesn't have to be on the menu," she said. "I take special care of my special customers."

"Oh, for crying out loud, Gerri," I said as soon as I realized I was being snookered.

Gerri Gomperts is a take-no-prisoners, abide-no-fools Jewish grandmother who serves up home cooking along with a side order of her sage but snarky wisdom on what makes relationships work.

"Do I look like I need therapy?" I asked.

"Who said anything about therapy?" she asked, all wide-eyed and innocent. "All I know is that Cheryl moved in with you three weeks ago, last night you didn't get home till God knows when, and then you showed up this morning looking more stressed out than a virgin at a lumberjacks' convention. So I'm going to go out on a limb and say that your troubled mind is more troubled than usual. If therapy would help, then you've come to the right diner."

"You couldn't be more wrong," I said.

"Sounds like I struck a nerve. I'll be right back."

She returned with my breakfast, topped off my coffee, and sat down. "You do this all the time," she said. "You show up with that needy-guy look on your face, I offer to help, and you play hard to get. Either tell me what's going on, or I'll find someone else who appreciates what a woman with my life experience brings to the table."

I told her.

She shrugged. "So you're busy. It goes with the territory. Cheryl's not going to move out because you're on a high-profile case and have to work late."

"Don't be so sure," I said. "I know too many cops whose relationships imploded because they put the job first."

"Your job isn't the problem, Zach."

"Then what is?"

She picked up the sugar packet dispenser and dumped it on the table.

"What are you doing?" I asked.

"It's the diner version of a PowerPoint presentation."

She picked up a pink packet of Sweet'N Low and a blue packet of Equal. "The blue is you, and the pink is Cheryl," she said. "And here you are, together at home." She put both packets back into the empty dispenser.

"Over here is work," she said, picking up a salt-shaker and putting it on the other side of the table.

"Now, every day, you go to the salt mines," she said, moving the Zach packet from home to work, "where you are joined by a lot of your fellow men in blue." She surrounded the saltshaker with Equal packets.

"And your ex-girlfriend Kylie." She added a single pink packet to the blue pile. "Then you and Kylie go off and spend the next ten to fourteen hours together." She moved the Sweet'N Low and an Equal to a vacant spot on the table.

"So," she said, "do you still think it's about working overtime, or are you apologizing to Cheryl for spending those late nights with Kylie?"

"I hope you're not charging me for this," I said, "because your entire analysis is based on old news. I've moved on. Kylie is the past. Cheryl is the future. The Zach Jordan soap opera is over."

"I'm sure you believe that, but you forgot one thing. When you moved in, you and Cheryl went from dating to cohabitating. You're living with her now, and I'll bet that every night you're out late playing cops and robbers with your past, you're haunted by the fact that your future is all alone in the love nest waiting for you to come home."

She handed me the dispenser with the solo pink Sweet'N Low packet in it. "Mull it over," she said.

Before I could respond, my phone vibrated and a text popped up. It was from Captain Cates.

Gracie Mansion. Now.

"Gerri, I've got to go," I said, standing up.

"Wait a minute," she said, pointing at the packets of artificial sweetener scattered all over the table. "Are you going to just leave this mess here?"

"Since when is that my job?" I said.

A victory smile spread across her face. "It's all part of the therapy, Zach. It's your life. You clean it up."

CHAPTER 6

MURIEL SYKES HAD been mayor of New York for only three months, but Kylie and I were already on her speed dial. We had done her a real solid when she was a candidate, and as good fortune would have it, the new mayor believed in reciprocity.

The brass at Red, who knew the benefits of being in bed with the politicians in power, loved the fact that one of their teams had become the mayor's go-to cops. So when Cates's text came telling us to go to Gracie Mansion, we didn't waste time prioritizing. Mayor Sykes *was* our priority.

Kylie was waiting for me outside the One Nine.

"Do you know what the mayor wants?" I asked as soon as I got in the car.

"No," Kylie said. "I was in the office when Cates got the call. There were no specifics. She just told me to roll."

"Did you fill Cates in on where we are on the Elena Travers case?"

"It's more like I filled her in on where we aren't. We got nothing. All I could tell Cates is that these guys weren't high-end jewel thieves. They're a couple of mooks who are in over their heads and will try to unload the necklace fast. I told her we put the word out on the street, and we're hoping to get a hit from our extensive CI network."

"Extensive? We've got a call in to three CIs. She didn't buy that bullshit, did she?"

"Of course not. But it did get a laugh."

Two minutes later, we arrived at Gracie and let the guard at the gate know we were there to see Mayor Sykes.

"You better hurry," he said. "She's going to be wheels up in less than a minute."

The mayor's black SUV was parked in front of the mansion. I recognized her driver.

"Charlie, what's going on? We just got a call that the mayor wanted to see us."

"And she just got a call that the governor wanted to see her. We all have to dance for someone, Zach."

Kylie and I walked up the porch steps just as the front door flew open, and Muriel Sykes stormed out. She was wearing a warm purple coat and a cold, hard scowl.

"Good morning, Madam Mayor," I said.

"America's sweetheart was murdered in my city on my watch. What the hell is good about it?" she said. "Where are you on the case?"

"We've got nothing of substance to report yet," I said.

"*Nothing of substance* seems to be the theme of my day," she said. "I'm on my way to Albany to be lied to."

She walked down the porch steps and headed for the SUV. Charlie opened the rear door as she approached.

Kylie and I followed. "Mayor Sykes," I said, "you sent for us. Was it just to get an update on the Travers case?"

"Hell, no. I knew you had nothing because nobody from Red called to say you had something."

She climbed into the backseat of the car, and Charlie closed the door. Sykes rolled down the rear window. "I called for something else. It's a nasty can of worms, and I can't trust anyone to deal with it but you."

"Thank you," I said. "Do you have time to give us the details?"

"Detective, I don't have time to wind my watch. Howard can give you the details. He's waiting for you inside."

She rolled up the window, and the SUV took off for the 145-mile trip to the state capital.

"I've never seen her in such a foul mood," I said. "I wouldn't want to be Charlie."

"Hell," Kylie said, "if this is the real Muriel Sykes, then I wouldn't want to be Howard."

That got a laugh out of me. Howard Sykes was the mayor's husband. We went back up the porch steps to find out what nasty can of worms he was about to entrust us with.

CHAPTER 7

MURIEL SYKES WAS a scrappy kid from the streets of Brooklyn who worked her way through law school, was appointed U.S. attorney for the Southern District of New York, then crushed a sitting mayor in her first run for office. If she had one defining quality that propelled her along the way, it was grit.

Her husband was neither gritty nor scrappy. A privileged child raised on New York's affluent Sutton Place, Howard Sykes had navigated his way from the city's private school system to the Ivy League and ultimately to Madison Avenue, where his white-bread good looks and well-bred patrician manner made him a natural fit in a world where image was often more valued than substance.

But there was a lot more to the man than a proper golf swing and a gift for captivating his dinner guests with advertising war stories. Howard was a virtuoso at orchestrating marketing campaigns that won the hearts of consumers and sweetened the bottom lines of his clients. He retired at the age of sixty to manage his wife's political campaign and was credited with being the force behind making her the first female mayor of New York City.

And to top it all off, he was a hell of a nice guy. Kylie and I had met him at several charity functions, and he had a way of always making us feel as important as any billionaire in the room.

He was waiting for us in the living room of the First Family's private residence. "Zach, Kylie, thanks for coming," he said, ignoring the fact that it was a command performance.

"How can we help?" I asked.

"I'm on the board of trustees of two hospitals here in the city," he said. "A month ago some medical equipment disappeared from Saint Cecilia's."

"What kind of equipment?"

Ever the consummate adman, Howard had prepared visual aids. He opened up a folder and pulled out a photo of a contraption that looked like an iPad on steroids.

"That's a portable ultrasound machine used for cardiac imaging. It weighs ten pounds, which means the tech can walk it to any bedside in the hospital."

"But this one walked out of the hospital," I said.

"This and two more just like it. They cost twenty thousand a pop. My first thought was that that's the downside to making these machines so compact: they're easy to steal. However"—he pulled out the next picture—"this one disappeared about the same time."

It looked like R2-D2's taller brother.

"It's an anesthesia machine. Fifty thousand dollars, and at four hundred pounds, you can't exactly slip it into a backpack. And yes, it has wheels, but it also has an electromagnetic security device embedded in it, and the hospital has guards at all access points. But it still went out the door."

"Did Saint Cecilia report the thefts?" Kylie asked.

"No. We had no proof that anything was *stolen*, and we didn't report them missing. The hospital decided to write it off and chalk it up to bad security."

Kylie and I said nothing. Because so far nothing made sense. A low-level crime that the victim didn't report, and yet the mayor, knowing we were caught up in the Elena Travers murder, asked us to drop everything and get involved.

Howard finally dropped the other shoe.

"I'm also on the board at Mercy Hospital, and two days ago it was hit. This time they got away with a hundred and seventy thousand dollars' worth of equipment. I don't believe in coincidences, so I did some digging, and I found out that nine hospitals had been robbed in two months. Total haul, close to two million dollars." He handed me a printout. "The specifics are all here."

"And you'd like us to find out who's behind the thefts," I said.

"Yes, but not in your usual style."

"I didn't know we had a style," Kylie said, looking at me. "He's going to have to tell us what it is so we don't keep doing it."

Howard smiled and pulled a newspaper clipping from the folder. It was a picture of Kylie and me leaving the Bassett brothers' house.

"The media loves you," he said. "It's one thing to be on the front page when you solve a major crime, but last night you interviewed the people whose necklace was stolen, and you made page five of the *Post*. You guys get ink wherever you go, and my goal—and Muriel's—is to keep a tight lid on this investigation. She called the PC this morning, and he's on board."

"This is a pervasive crime spree, but it's the first time we've ever heard of it," Kylie said. "Why is it so hush-hush? And why not tell the public what's going on? Sometimes they can be our best source of leads."

"If you ask the head of any one of these hospitals, he'll tell you that the secrecy is for the well-being of the patients. People want to feel safe when they check in, but if they hear that criminals have stolen a piece of equipment the size of a refrigerator, they're going to worry. *What else can these villains take? My wallet? My laptop? My newborn baby?* The prevailing wisdom at the hospitals is that it's better to keep it quiet. Less stress for the patients."

"What's the real reason they don't want to go public with the thefts?" I asked.

"Because if this shit gets out," Howard said, a wide grin on his face, "it would put a serious crimp in their fund-raising."

CHAPTER 8

"CHANGE OUR STYLE?" Kylie said as soon as she pulled the car out of the mayor's driveway. "Is he serious? One of the reasons we get press is because we solve crimes. Riddle me this, Batman: how are we supposed to crack this case if we can't put out any feelers to the public?"

"Because we can solve anything, Girl Wonder. That's why the mayor of Gotham City picked us," I said. "Why don't we start by talking to the people we're actually allowed to talk to? Get on the Drive, and let's shoot down to Mercy Hospital and talk to their security people."

She turned left on 79th, and we headed south on the FDR.

"There's only one way to get two million dollars'

worth of hospital equipment from New York to whatever third world buyer is willing to pay for it," Kylie said. "Big fat shipping containers."

"Good idea," I said. "Let's give Howard's list to Jan Hogle and see if she can run it against the manifests of cargo ships that sailed within a few days of each heist. She can cross-check by weight. If they stole x pounds of equipment, she can flag every shipment that weighs about the same."

"That wasn't my idea," Kylie said. "I was thinking we could go down to the shipyards and talk to the dockworkers. Those guys have eyes and ears everywhere, and a few of them owe us."

"Sounds like a plan," I said. "And then our pictures would be in the paper as the first two cops fired by the Sykes administration."

Kylie's cell phone rang. We were doing fifty on the Drive, so she tapped a button and the call went directly to speaker.

"This is Detective MacDonald," she said.

"This is Mike Danehy at Better Choices," the voice on the other end said. "Is Mrs. Harrington there?"

She grabbed the phone and took it off speaker. "This is Mrs. Harrington."

She dropped her voice after that so that I could barely hear her end of the conversation, but I could tell by the look on her face that it was bad news. Something was going on with Spence.

A lifetime ago, when Kylie and I were new at the academy, we had a throw-all-caution-to-the-wind sexually liberating affair that lasted twenty-eight days. And then, like the lyrics to a bad country song, her boyfriend got out of rehab, all shiny clean and sober, and she dumped me and married him.

For eleven years, Spence Harrington didn't pick up a drink or a drug. But then he did. Since then he'd been in and out of rehabs trying to get the monkey off his back. Connecticut, Oregon, and now Better Choices, a day program right here in New York.

"Mike, I know the rules, but they suck," she said, getting louder as she got more frustrated. "Surely I can do something. Anything."

She obviously didn't like Mike's answer because her response was to hit the gas and blow her horn at the yellow cab in front of her.

"I'm sorry, Mike, but that's not *enabling*," she said. "It's called being his wife."

The taxi in front of us refused to move over, so she swerved around him on the right, almost running him into the divider.

"Okay, thank you," she said. "Keep in touch."

She hung up the phone.

"What's going on?" I said.

"Wrong number," she said, pulling the car off the Drive at the East 53rd Street exit.

It took less than a minute for us to get to Mercy

Hospital on First Avenue. She parked in a no standing zone, killed the engine, turned to me, and said, "Spence is missing."

It didn't quite process. "What do you mean, missing?"

"That was his counselor, Mike Danehy. Spence hasn't shown up at rehab for three days."

"Did they try calling him?"

"Oh yeah. They called to kick him out of the program, but they couldn't find him to tell him, so they finally called me."

"What do they want you to do?"

"Oh, Mike was very explicit. He told me to do nothing. He said Spence has to hit rock bottom before he can find his way back up."

"That's good advice," I said. "But of course you're not very good at taking good advice."

She gave me half a smile.

"Do you want help?" I said.

She didn't answer.

"Kylie, your drug addict husband is missing. Do you want help?"

"Yes, goddamn it, Zach, but I'm too stubborn to ask."

"That's okay," I said. "You don't have to."

CHAPTER 9

WALKING INTO HIS office, you'd never know that Gregg Hutchings was a hero. I'd worked with him and knew he'd racked up a chestful of medals, but here at Mercy Hospital, there was no trace of his service with NYPD.

"Hutch," I said, "where are all the pictures of PCs hanging ribbons around your neck?"

"This is corporate America, Zach. Nobody cares about my past glories. They're more interested in my golf scores and how many hundred thousand dollars' worth of equipment I let slip through my fingertips over the weekend."

"We heard you had a little incident," I said. "How can we help?"

"For starters, let me give you a little insight into

theft prevention," he said. "If this was a supermarket, and people were stealing frozen peas, I'd set up a video cam in the frozen pea section. But at Mercy, if I want to keep a watch on the expensive hardware in my dialysis unit, I can't put my cameras in there. HIPAA says no surveillance in any room where there are *identifiable patients.* It's like running a museum and telling the guards not to watch the people who are looking at the paintings. How long do you think it will be before the Picassos start walking out the door?"

"But you've got cameras in the public areas," Kylie said. "If someone tries to walk off with a piece of equipment, you'll see it in the hallway."

"You think?" He turned to a bank of CCTV monitors on the wall. "It looks like a lot of coverage, but I've only got eyes on 20 percent of the complex. Even then, the hospital doesn't want to come off like Big Brother, so instead of putting cameras out in the open to act as deterrents, we have to hide them in air vents, or behind exit signs and smoke detectors."

He pointed at a monitor. "You see that technician? He's rolling an X-ray unit from Radiology to Recovery. And here's a guy with an EKG machine waiting for the elevator. And see this food cart? Who's to say if someone slipped an ultrasound unit in with the salmon croquettes? Everything is on wheels. I can watch it move through the public space, but I can't tell if it winds up back in the treatment rooms or it gets smuggled out the door."

"Tell us about the most recent theft," I said.

"We bought six state-of-the-art dialysis machines and locked them up till the manufacturer could run our techs through some training. All six disappeared. Whoever took them knew the keypad code to the room and how to get them out of the hospital without being tagged by a single camera."

"So they had someone on the inside," Kylie said.

"We have thousands of doctors, nurses, patients, visitors, and delivery people going through here every day," he said. "But I might have gotten lucky."

He opened a drawer, took out a file, and spread it out on his desk. "Her name is Lynn Lyon," he said, pointing at a picture of a woman in her thirties. "She's a volunteer in our gift shop, but a guard caught her taking pictures in the room with the dialysis machines."

"How'd she get in?"

"She told him the door was open, but I don't buy it."

"Did you change the code on the keypad?" Kylie asked.

"I would have, but the guard didn't think it was important, so he didn't mention it until after the horse was out the barn door."

Kylie's cell rang.

Our boss liked to micromanage, so I figured she was checking up on us. "Cates?" I asked.

Kylie shook her head and stepped out to take the call in private.

I skimmed Lynn Lyon's personnel folder. "Have you talked to her since the robbery?" I asked.

"She's not on the schedule this week," Hutchings said, "and I can't just bring her in for questioning. I have no jurisdiction."

"But we do," I said.

"Look, I know this is below your pay grade, and you're only here because Howard Sykes drafted you. But I'm glad he did. I need all the help I can get."

Kylie stepped back into the office. "I'm sorry, Gregg, but Zach and I have to go," she said.

"We'll take a run over and talk to Ms. Lyon," I said, grabbing the folder.

"Thanks," Hutchings said. "These dialysis machines will go for top dollar on the black market outside the U.S. See if you can get something out of her before they make their way to Turkmenistan."

I followed Kylie out the door. "Who was on the phone?" I said.

"Shelley Trager. He's waiting for us at Silvercup Studios."

Trager was Kylie's husband's boss. "Is this about Spence?" I asked.

"Oh yeah."

"Did they find him?"

"No," she said, "but when they do, I'm going to kill him."

I knew enough not to ask any more questions.

CHAPTER 10

IT'S HARD TO make it to the top in the entertainment business. It's even harder to do it in Queens, three thousand miles from the heartbeat of the industry in Hollywood. But Shelley Trager, a street-smart kid who grew up on a tenement-lined block in Hell's Kitchen, had pulled it off. Now, at the age of sixty, he was the head of Noo Yawk Films and part owner of Silvercup Studios, a sprawling bread factory in Long Island City that had been converted into the largest film and television production facility in the Northeast.

Added to the Trager mystique was the fact that the success and the power never went to his head. According to BuzzFeed, he was one of the best-liked people in show business. He was also the driving force behind Spence Harrington's stellar career.

Spence was only six months out of rehab when Shelley took him on as a production assistant. A year later he gave him a shot as a staff writer on a failing show, and Spence turned it around. The young golden boy then pitched his own idea, Shelley bankrolled it, and the team had their first hit. A string of winners followed until Spence went out on drugs, and it all blew up.

Shelley responded with tough love and banned Spence from the set till he finished rehab.

Kylie pulled the car into the Silvercup parking lot on Harry Suna Place. Carl, the perennially chatty guard at the front gate, recognized her immediately.

"Good morning, Mrs. Harrington," he said, stone-faced. "Mr. Trager is waiting for you at Studio Four."

He waved her into the lot. No banter. No jokes. No eye contact.

"This is worse than I thought," Kylie said. "Carl won't even look at me. Maybe I shouldn't drag you into this."

"Into what?" I asked.

"Somebody broke into the studio last night and trashed some sets."

"You're not dragging me into anything," I said. "It's a crime scene. It's what we do."

"Only this time I'm married to the person who did the crime."

"Do they have proof?"

"No, but whoever broke into the lot went straight to Studio Four and destroyed two standing sets at *K-Mac.*"

I winced. K-Mac had been Kylie MacDonald's nickname back in the academy. I still used it. Spence had shanghaied it. He had created a show about a female detective named Katie MacDougal who had serious boundary issues. The fictional K-Mac was a lot like the one he was married to.

Audiences liked the show. Kylie hated it.

"I'm going with you," I said.

We entered the lot and made our way past a man with a bloodied knife in his chest, a burned-out city bus, and two nuns on a smoke break. As unreal as it all was, nothing prepared us for the devastation inside Studio Four. It looked like someone had taken a wrecking ball to it.

Shelley was waiting for us inside the soundstage. "For the record, I'm not going to report what happened," he said to Kylie. "You're not here as cops. I called you because you're his wife."

"Thank you," she said. Then she walked slowly through the shattered glass and splintered wood that had been the squad room. Desks were overturned, computers smashed, and the ultimate insult: the NYPD shield on the wall had been spray-painted red. I'm sure the choice of color was not lost on her.

She crossed the room to the other set—Katie MacDougal's bedroom—stepping over the shards of broken mirror and glass bottles that had been on the vanity, steeling herself as she approached K-Mac's bed, where the sheets, the pillows, and the mattress had all been slashed.

She finally turned away. "Shelley, I'm so sorry," she said. "I know he's mad at me because I wouldn't take him back into the apartment, but..."

"I kicked him out too. He's mad at both of us, and he's sending us a message."

Kylie shook her head. "What kind of message is this?"

Shelley didn't answer.

Whatever the message was, there was no nuance to it.

CHAPTER 11

"I'M INVOKING THE DWI rule," I said as Kylie and I walked back to the parking lot.

A faint smile crept across her face. When she gets riled up, Kylie drives like a NASCAR champion, so we have an agreement: no Driving While Infuriated.

"Come on, Zach," she said. "I haven't wrecked a car since way back in…"

"January," I said. "You're almost ready to get your three-month chip."

The smile turned into a grin, and she tossed me the keys.

It was only a fifteen-minute drive from the studio to Lynn Lyon's apartment on West End Avenue, and Kylie talked nonstop. The topics ranged from the Elena Travers case to the hospital robberies, and finally to how my new living arrangement with Cheryl was working out. The only thing Kylie didn't talk about was the elephant in the car: her drug addict husband.

But I'm sure that was what she was thinking about. By now she had dismissed the advice she had gotten from the counselor at the rehab. Kylie was an action junkie, and, while Spence may not have hit rock bottom yet, after seeing the destruction he'd left at Silvercup, she was no longer capable of doing nothing.

We pulled into a parking lot at Lincoln Towers—eight high-end buildings spread across twenty landscaped acres in the middle of Manhattan's trendy Upper West Side. Not exactly where I'd expect to find someone selling stolen medical equipment on the black market.

The head shot Hutchings showed us of Lynn Lyon hadn't done her justice. She opened the door wearing jeans, a gray sweatshirt, and a sauce-spattered apron. Even with no makeup and her hair caught up in a blue bandanna, I got that rush men get when they're suddenly face-to-face with a naturally beautiful woman.

We ID'd ourselves and told her we had some questions to ask her.

"I'm right in the middle of something," she said. "Can you come back later?"

"No, ma'am," Kylie said. "It can't wait."

"Neither can my risotto," she said. "We'll have to talk in the kitchen."

She didn't wait for an answer. "I'm a food blogger, and I'm working on my next post," she said, leading us into a cluttered kitchen, where I picked up the earthy smell of mushrooms.

"My take on porcini-asparagus risotto," she said, picking up a wooden spoon and stirring a shallow pot. "What's this about?"

"There's been a robbery at Mercy Hospital," I said.

"Well, that's hardly a big surprise," she said. "I warned them." With all the poise of a TV chef, she turned to the oven and took out a loaf of fresh-baked bread, set it on the counter, and picked up a camera.

"What do you mean you warned them?" I said.

"Some of these volunteers will leave the gift shop and run off to grab a cup of coffee," she said, clicking off a few photos of the bread. "Instead of locking the place up, they hang a sign that says 'Back in five minutes.' They're too trusting. It was bound to happen."

"It wasn't the gift shop, Ms. Lyon," Kylie said. "They stole six new dialysis machines."

"Six...I don't understand," she said, ladling broth from a stockpot onto the risotto. "I work in the gift shop, but...Oh my God—I was in with the new dialysis machines last week."

"Taking pictures," Kylie said, gesturing at the camera.

Most people—guilty or innocent—would respond with indignation: *Are you calling me a thief?* Not Lyon. She put the hand that wasn't stirring the risotto to her mouth. Her eyes watered up, and a tear rolled down her cheek. "This is so embarrassing," she said.

"What were you doing in a restricted area?" Kylie asked, all bad-cop body language and tone of voice.

"It didn't say Restricted, and the door wasn't locked. I have a friend who is a dialysis nurse upstate. I was telling her about this new equipment Mercy bought, and she asked me to send her a picture, so I did. That's all. It was harmless. I can't believe you're accusing me of stealing."

"Nobody is accusing you of anything," Kylie said. "I'm just asking a few routine questions."

"If you knew me, you wouldn't ask things like that. I don't steal. Cooking and volunteer work are my passions. My soul needs redemption, and I get that from both."

The tears were gone now. "I have a few questions of my own," she said. "How am I supposed to get six dialysis machines out of the hospital? And what would I do with them if I had them? It's not just embarrassing; it's insane. Unless you're planning to arrest me, please leave."

We left.

"You bought her act?" Kylie said once we were back in the car.

"How do you know it was an act? You hit her with some circumstantial evidence, and she had a plausible explanation."

"Oh please: pretty lady, at home in the kitchen, turns on the waterworks. Guys fall for it all the time."

"So all of a sudden I'm a *guy?* I thought I was a cop."

"I'm a cop too, and the first thing I thought of was, if I were going to send someone to case a hospital, I'd send someone who could fly under the radar. She fits the bill."

"Well, right now we have nothing to go on," I said.

"So why don't you humor me? Let's look at the other hospitals that were hit and see if Lynn Lyon volunteered at any of them."

Kylie and I have similar instincts, and we're usually in sync when we question someone. I was pretty sure I was right on this one, but this time her anger at Spence spilled over, and she took it out on Lyon.

"Fine with me," I said. "You want to call the other hospitals?"

"Absolutely. Police work is my passion, Zach, and my soul could use a little redeeming," she said. "Also, I try to never miss out on an opportunity to prove I'm smarter than you."

CHAPTER 12

UNTIL LAST NIGHT, the most expensive thing in Teddy Ryder's tiny two-room apartment on the Lower East Side was a JVC TV he bought for two hundred bucks on Overstock.com. It was now out-shined by the emerald and diamond necklace sitting on his coffee table.

Teddy hadn't slept since the robbery. The guns had just been there to make a point. Nobody was supposed to get killed. His partner, Raymond Davis, had pulled the trigger, but he swore up and down that it wasn't his fault. He blamed it all on the guy in the back of the limo who had grabbed for the gun. Then Raymond had stretched out on the bed and slept like a brick till seven that morning.

Now Raymond was out trying to renegotiate the deal with Jeremy.

"Fifty thousand is bullshit," Raymond had said once they'd watched the news and found out the necklace was worth eight million. "We're upping the price to half a mil."

It was late afternoon by the time Raymond finally got back from his meeting with Jeremy. One look at his face, and Teddy could tell that the negotiations had gone down the toilet.

"Jeremy is an asshole," Raymond said.

"How much did you get?" Teddy asked.

"More than the original deal, but less than I was hoping for."

"How much?"

"Ninety thou."

"Apiece?"

"No. Ninety for the whole enchilada."

"Is he crazy?" Teddy said. "We're not asking for cigarette and beer money. We need enough so we can disappear."

"Don't you think I said that already?"

"Well, then go back and tell him we know how much the necklace is worth, and if he doesn't give us fair market value, we'll find a buyer who will."

"Yeah, I said that too. He laughed in my face. Told me the dead actress makes it too hot to handle." Raymond took the necklace from the coffee table and held it up to the light. "He's right. I asked around. Nobody will touch it."

Teddy could taste the panic welling up in his

throat. His heart was racing, and he wanted to scream *"The dead actress was your fault,"* but he was having too much trouble breathing to waste his breath on Raymond.

He lowered his body to the armchair he'd salvaged from a curb after he'd done his last stretch at Rikers. "So now what do we do?" he asked.

"I've got it all worked out," Raymond said. "Jeremy is coming over tonight. We pack up, give him the necklace, and leave for Mexico as soon as we get the money."

"I'm not going anywhere till I say good-bye to my mom," Teddy said. "As soon as I get my share, I'm going to go over to her place, spend the night, and ask her to make me a stack of cottage cheese pancakes for breakfast."

"And how much will that cost you, Teddy boy? Five grand? Ten? How big a chunk will you be giving Mommy?"

"What I give her is none of your business."

"It's my business if we go to Mexico, and I've got forty-five thousand dollars, and all you've got is a belly full of cottage cheese pancakes. I'm not supporting you, Teddy. Or your mother."

"Don't worry about me," Teddy said. "What time did Jeremy say he'd be here?"

Raymond shrugged. "He didn't give me a time. He just said tonight. Wake me when he gets here. I'm going to take a nap."

CHAPTER 13

I WAS AT my computer when a message from Kylie popped up on the screen.

I have an update on the Happy Homemaker. Stop by my office if you want to hear more.

Kylie loves to be right. She loves it even more when I'm wrong.

Her *office* is the desk directly behind mine. I swiveled my chair. "It sounds like you have something to gloat about," I said.

"Me?" she asked, gloating. "I just thought you'd want to hear the latest on the hospital robberies. I did a little research, and it seems your favorite risotto lady volunteered at four of the nine hospitals that were robbed."

"Does she have a rap sheet?"

"She's clean as a whistle. In fact, three of the volunteer coordinators I spoke to said she was one of the best they've ever worked with, and they wished they had a dozen more like her."

I waited for the *but*.

"*But*," she said, "I did find something interesting. Her father was a petroleum engineer. As a kid she moved around the Middle East. After college, she went to India for three years and worked for a charity that provided medical treatment for street children."

"And that's interesting because...?"

"You heard what Gregg Hutchings said. Where do you think all this high-tech equipment is going to wind up? Lyon is a do-gooder, and she spent years surrounded by third world deprivation. My guess is she's not even getting paid. She's not only doing volunteer work for the hospitals; she's doing volunteer work for the people who are ripping them off."

"That's brilliant police work, Detective MacDonald. The woman has no criminal record, but she's seen poverty, so she's decided to do her part for the underprivileged by helping a bunch of black marketeers traffic stolen goods," I said. "Why don't you run that by Mick Wilson at the DA's office and see how long it takes him to kick you out on your ass?"

"That's not the apology I was hoping for," she said.

"So she worked in four of the hospitals. If I were a

lawyer, I'd call it more circumstantial evidence. But as a cop, I'm willing to admit there's more to like about Ms. Lyon than her porcini-asparagus risotto."

"Are you willing to go back and bring her in for some serious questions?"

"No."

"Why not?"

"Because I'd rather let her think we've lost interest, then put a tail on her and see if she can lead us to someone higher up the food chain."

"That's the first intelligent thing you've said since you were suckered in by that teary-eyed Martha Stewart act. There's hope for you yet, Jordan."

My cell rang, and I picked it up. It was Cheryl.

"Hey, what are you doing tonight?" she asked.

"You tell me," I said.

"How do you feel about Italian food?"

"Fantastico."

"Can you be home by seven?"

"You bet," I said.

"Great. Love you."

"Love you back."

I hung up the phone and let what I'd just heard wash over me. My brain was thinking about the night ahead when Kylie violated my reverie.

"Zach, did you hear what I said?"

"Sorry. Run it by me again."

"I said we can't tail Lyon. I know the mayor wants us on these hospital robberies, but they're sucking up time we need for the Travers homicide. Let's talk to Cates and see if she can drum us up another team to do the legwork."

"Sure."

She got up from her desk and headed toward Cates's office. My body followed, but my head was still wrapped up in the phone call from Cheryl.

It was the first time I'd ever heard her refer to my apartment as *home*. It felt incredible.

CHAPTER 14

CAPTAIN DELIA CATES is third-generation NYPD. She grew up in Harlem, and if you ask her where she went to college, she'll smile and say, "Oh, there was a good school a mile from my house." The school, as those of us in the know can tell you, is Columbia University.

She graduated at eighteen, got a master's in criminal justice from John Jay College, and did four years in the marine corps before joining the department. She rose through the ranks like a comet, and when our previous mayor created NYPD Red, his consigliere, Irwin Diamond, tapped Cates to run it.

"It's not that I was the best cop for the job," Cates told me one night when we were having a drink. "But when most of your constituency is overprivileged white men, it's smart politics to put a black woman in charge."

The truth is, she *was* the best cop for the job, and most days I love having her as my boss. This day was not one of them.

"That's all you've got?" she said when Kylie and I told her where we were on the Travers murder. "You two haven't done squat since you met with the Bassett brothers last night."

"We've got cops canvassing the area, looking for eyewitnesses," Kylie said. "And there are at least twenty-five traffic and private security cameras at 54th and Broadway, where the shooting happened. We have Jan Hogle going through those."

"And how about that *extensive* network of CIs you told me about this morning?" Cates said. "How's that working out?"

"You're right, Captain," I said before Kylie could mount a defense. "We haven't done squat on the Travers case. No excuse."

Cates laughed. "Of course you have an excuse. It's called politics over police work. The mayor and her husband want you on these hospital robberies. You're stuck with it. But I can't take you off this homicide. Which means you have to do both."

"We can," I said with as much conviction as I could muster, "but we could use some help. We have a person of interest—a hospital volunteer who may have been the inside person on four of the nine jobs.

She may lead us to bigger fish, but we need to tail her. Do you think you can snag us another team to throw against it?"

"I'd be happy to," Cates said. "Do you think you can snag me the perps who killed Elena Travers?"

"We'd be happy to," Kylie said.

Cates ignored the wisecrack and looked at me. "You've got Betancourt and Torres," she said, waving us out of her office without another word.

Five minutes later, we were sitting down to brief our backup.

Before they came to Red, Detectives Jenny Betancourt and Wanda Torres had more collars than any team in Brooklyn South. Betancourt is a pit bull when it comes to details, and Torres—well, she's just a pit bull. Kylie and I had worked with them before, and we liked them—partly because they were new and eager to make their bones, and partly because they reminded us of us. They bickered constantly, like an old married couple.

"I agree with Kylie," Betancourt said after we briefed them. "Lyon spent her formative years watching a lot of people die because of substandard medical care. That's enough to give her a motive."

"Bullshit," Torres said. "I spent my *formative years* in the South Bronx. Five kids in my grade school died of asthma. *Asthma*, for God's sake. How's that for shoddy medical care? People who grow up in poverty steal steaks from the supermarket, TV sets, maybe—not medical equipment."

I told them to hash it out on their own, reminded them how critical the case was to the mayor's husband, and turned them loose.

"What are your plans for the night?" Kylie asked me as soon as Betancourt and Torres left.

"Cheryl and I are going out for Italian food," I said. "How about you?"

"Oh, I don't know," she said. "It's been a long day. I think I'll go home, take a bubble bath, order up some dinner, open up a bottle of wine, and watch anything with Mark Wahlberg in it."

"Sounds like a restful night," I said.

"That's my plan," she said. "Rest up."

She was lying through her teeth. I had no idea what her plan was, but I knew one thing for sure: a bubble bath, a bottle of wine, and a Mark Wahlberg movie had nothing to do with it.

CHAPTER 15

I GOT HOME at 6:52, eight minutes under the deadline. Cheryl was in the kitchen, spreading a pungent buttery mix on both sides of a split loaf of ciabatta.

"What's going on?" I said.

"I'm making garlic bread."

"My keen detective instincts picked up on that," I said. "But I thought we were going out to dinner."

"Who said anything about going out? I asked you how you felt about Italian food. You said *'Fantastico,'* so that's what I'm making. There's a lasagna in the oven. It'll be ready about seven thirty."

"This is amazing," I said.

"It's not amazing," she said. "It's called dinner. Normal couples do it every night."

I came around behind her, cupped her breasts in

my hands, and let my lips and tongue nibble the back of her neck. "And what do normal couples do if they have thirty-five minutes to kill before their lasagna is ready?"

"Keep your pants on, Detective Horndog," she said, wriggling away. "At least until after dinner. For now, why don't you open a bottle of wine and turn on the TV? It doesn't get any more normal than that."

I put my badge, my gun, and my cell phone down on the breakfast bar that separated the kitchen from the dining area, pulled a bottle of Gabbiano Chianti from the wine rack, and poured two glasses.

I found the TV remote, flipped on *Jeopardy!*, and sat down on the sofa. Five minutes later, Cheryl joined me, and the two of us spent the next half hour vying to see who was the fastest at coming up with the right answer. It was a lopsided contest. She trounced me.

It was pure, unadulterated domestic boredom, and I loved it.

"Loser does the dishes," she said, heading back to the kitchen.

I turned off the TV and went to the bathroom to wash up. I was looking in the mirror when my eye caught the pink bathrobe hanging next to my white one on the back of the door. Cheryl was not the first woman I had lived with. But this was the first time in my life that I wasn't having second thoughts.

By the time I got back, the overhead lights in the dining area were dimmed, two flickering candles lit the room, and dinner was on the table: a steaming pan of lasagna, a salad bowl filled with greens and cherry tomatoes, and a basket of garlic bread.

"Are you sure this is normal?" I said. "Because it looks pretty *fantastico* to me."

Cheryl was standing next to the breakfast bar. "Don't sit down," she said. She had my cell phone in her hand. "It rang while you were in the bathroom."

"Whoever it is, tell them I'm eating dinner. I'll call back."

"It's your partner," Cheryl said, her voice flat and devoid of emotion. "She needs a cop."

I took the phone. "Kylie, unless someone has a gun to your head, it'll have to wait."

"Zach, I'm at a gas station up in Harlem."

"Doing what?"

"I tracked down one of Spence's dealers."

"Why? After everything the counselors at the rehab told you, why the hell would you—never mind, I know why you do the crazy shit you do. What I don't know is why you'd go up there on your own without any backup."

"Because I thought I could handle it on my own."

"But you can't." I looked at Cheryl and mouthed the words "I'm sorry." I turned back to the phone. "Okay, just tell me what's going on."

"The dealer's name is Baby D. I confronted him

and told him I was looking for my husband. He said he hasn't seen Spence in months, but he's lying. I know because he's wearing Spence's new watch."

"You can't bust him for that, Kylie."

"For fuck's sake, Jordan!" she yelled. "Are you going to give me a lecture on all the things I *can't* do? I thought you said you'd help. Forget it."

She hung up.

I stood there, seething.

"What's going on?" Cheryl said.

"Same old, same old. She's in over her head, she's out of control, and she needs help."

"Did you tell her to call for backup?"

"She can't. It's not police business. It's her own crazy shit. I don't know what I'm going to do," I said, tilting my head at Cheryl, hoping she'd pick up the baton.

"Don't give me that puppy-dog look," she said. "You know exactly what you're going to do. You're just hoping I'm the one who tells you to do it. Well, it's not going to happen."

Of course it wasn't. I pressed the Recent Calls button on my phone and tapped the top one.

Kylie picked up on the first ring. "What?" she demanded.

"I told you this morning that I'd help, and I meant it."

"Fine. Then get your ass up to the BP station on 129th and Park as fast as you can."

"Give me twenty minutes," I said, looking straight

at Cheryl. "In the meantime, don't do anything stupid."

"Okay, okay," she said. "And, Zach?"

"What?"

"Bring cash."

I hung up the phone.

Cheryl walked over to the table, blew out the candles, then turned on the lights.

I grabbed my gun and badge from the counter, threw on my jacket, and went out the door.

Neither of us had said a word, which, in hindsight, was probably the smartest thing we could have done.

CHAPTER 16

I MANAGED TO flag a taxi as soon as I stepped out of my apartment building. The bad news was that it turned out to be a Prius—a great little car for the environment, with the emphasis on *little*. There was no time to look for another cab, so I jammed my six-foot frame into a backseat designed for five-footers, and we headed uptown.

I sat there, cramped, hungry, and fuming mad. I was pissed at Kylie for manipulating me the way she had, and I was even more pissed at myself for buying into it. The visual of a candlelit dinner gone south and the look on Cheryl's face when I walked out the door was burned into my brain, and I tried to shake it out of my head.

The cabdriver didn't say a word. I couldn't blame

him. Nothing says "keep your distance" like a nervous white guy dashing out of an Upper East Side apartment building and asking to be taken to a sketchy street corner in Harlem.

It was even sketchier than I expected. Harlem has changed dramatically in my lifetime. The stigma of street crime and urban decay has been replaced by trendy restaurants and designer boutiques, but the gentrification had not yet reached the corner of 129th and Park.

The avenue was dominated by the Metro-North train tracks that ran overhead. The street below was dotted by vacant lots, a fenced-in parking lot, and a combination BP station/twenty-four-hour food mart. The area around the pumps was well lit, and the driver pulled over and dropped me off there.

As soon as I squeezed my body out of the environmentally friendly little yellow box, I saw Kylie's car parked on 129th Street. I got in the passenger side, and she started driving.

"Where are we going?" I said.

"Baby D has several offices around town. One of them is a chicken-and-waffles place a few blocks away, on Lexington."

"How'd you know where to find him?"

"Because I'm a cop, and my husband is an addict. I tailed Spence on a couple of his drug runs just in case anything like this ever happened."

"You *tailed* him?"

"Don't judge me, Zach."

"Tell me about this Baby D," I said.

"Real name is Damian Hillsborough. Forget everything you know about these stereotype ghetto dealers hanging on the street corner, covered in tats and chains, peddling eight balls, and packing nine mils. Baby D is clean-cut, college-educated, and totally nonthreatening. He's carved out a nice little niche for himself in the upscale Caucasian market."

"Does he have a rap sheet?"

"No. He's smart. He did a year at NYU law school before dropping out to go into a more profitable line of work."

"And what's my role in all this?"

"I want you to score some blow. As soon as you make a buy, I'll step in."

"Sounds like a great plan," I said. "Except for that nasty little entrapment law the defense attorneys love to throw in our faces."

"I thought you were done lecturing."

"Kylie, it's not a lecture. It's Police Procedure 101. I've worked undercover. The criminal has to initiate the offense. A cop can't induce someone to commit a crime and then arrest him."

"I didn't say I was going to arrest him. I'm trying to find my husband, and I need some leverage."

We got to 126th Street and Lexington Avenue, where there was a cluster of storefronts: a McDonald's, a Dunkin' Donuts, a check-cashing place with the corrugated metal gate pulled down and locked, and a yellow awning that said "Goody's Chicken and Waffles." We got out of the car and walked up to the window.

"That's him over there, the one with the green sweater," Kylie said, pointing at a young black man sitting alone at a table, his fingers resting on the keyboard of a laptop.

"You want my take on your plan?" I asked.

"Go ahead."

"It's piss-poor. You think this guy is going to sell me drugs? If he's as smart as you say he is, he wouldn't sell me an aspirin if I got hit by a bus."

"Hey, I'm trying to figure this out as I go along. Do you have a better idea?"

"I've got something in my head, but it's going to take two of us, and I don't know if you're up to it—it's not going to be easy."

"Don't be an idiot, Zach. Of course I'm up to it. I'll do whatever it takes. What's your idea?"

"I'll go inside the chicken place and work on Baby D. You stay outside."

"And do what?"

"Nothing. Don't call me. Don't hand-signal me. And since I can't stop you from watching me through the window, don't barge in and tell me I'm doing it wrong."

"So you just want me to hang outside and do nothing?"

"Hey, I told you it wouldn't be easy. I'm going in. Don't screw it up."

She hesitated.

"Kylie, do you want my help or not?"

"Go ahead," she said. "Do it."

I walked through the front door of Goody's before she had time to change her mind.

I had no plan, no idea what I was going to do. All I knew was that it would be a hell of a lot easier to do it without her.

CHAPTER 17

THE FIRST THING I noticed about Goody's was how incredible it smelled. There were at least thirty people having dinner, and a few more at the counter, waiting to order.

Baby D was the only one not eating. And despite the fact that his fingers were resting on his keyboard, he was not typing. He was watching me.

Kylie was right. He didn't look anything like the stereotypical drug peddler you see in the movies or, for that matter, in real life. He looked more like a model who had stepped out of a J. Crew catalog. Tan chinos, tattersall shirt, and a V-neck sweater with the sleeves rolled up past his wrists. He was about twenty-five, clean-shaven, and damn good-looking.

I walked up to his table.

"Good evening, officer," he said.

"What makes you think I'm a cop?" I said.

"You don't exactly fit the profile of the neighborhood clientele."

"Neither do you," I said.

"Point taken," he said. "And what can I do for New York's Finest this evening?"

He may just as well have said "Checkmate." He had made me for a cop, he understood the laws of probable cause, and he knew there was nothing I could do except stand there like a rookie and ask him questions he didn't have to answer. The smug look on his face said it all. I was his entertainment for the evening. I hated him.

"You look hungry, officer," he said. "You know what you might like? Goody's Barnyard Platter." He flashed me a self-satisfied smile. "It's all *white-meat chicken*."

That did it. I snapped. My brain hadn't come up with a plan, so my testosterone took over. I grabbed him hard and pulled him from his chair. It shocked the hell out of both of us.

"You have no right to grab me like—"

"Shut your mouth, D bag." I bent his left arm back and pulled the gold watch from his wrist.

My heart was pounding in my chest. I've been trained to deal with people who are rich, famous, and used to getting their asses kissed. If a cop wants to make the cut at Red, he's got to be even-tempered, self-disciplined, emotionally stable. Kylie can sometimes cross the line, which is why Cates teamed us up. I was the voice of reason. But suddenly, without warning, I had become Dirty Harry.

I flipped the watch over and read the inscription. "Who's Kylie?" I said.

"I don't know."

"The back of your watch says she loves you always," I said, twisting his arm.

He yelped. "I bought it in a pawnshop."

I shoved him back down in his chair. "Let me see the receipt."

By now most of the people in the restaurant had looked up from their food and were watching the angry white guy push around the preppy-looking black kid. None of them looked like they were contemplating getting involved, but I flashed my shield just in case, and they quickly went back to the all-important task of filling their bellies and hardening their arteries.

Then I held the shield up to Baby D. "Detective Zachary Jordan," I said, sitting down directly across from him.

"You just broke every rule in the Boy Scout handbook, Jordan."

"Well, now you know what kind of cop you're dealing with. Where's Spence Harrington?"

"I already told the lady cop—"

"Her name is Kylie. Like it says on your watch." I handed it back to him.

"I already told her. I don't know where her old man is."

I unsnapped my handcuff holster and pulled out the cuffs.

"What's that for?" Baby D said.

"I'm arresting you for selling drugs."

He laughed. "Dream on, Detective. Do you think I'm stupid enough to be holding?"

"I haven't quite figured out how stupid you are yet, Damian, but I'm the one who's holding. I've got a baggie with an eight ball of booger sugar right here in my jacket pocket, and when I take you in, I'm going to say you sold it to me."

"Bullshit. That's a goddamn lie."

"You're right." I leaned forward and whispered, "I borrowed it from the evidence clerk at my precinct, but I'm going to swear you sold it to me. So either step outside and talk to my partner, or an hour from now your pretty little baby face is going to bring joy to the hearts of a lot of lonely men in a holding cell at Central Booking."

Drug dealers don't give up their customers' whereabouts to the cops. It can be bad for their business. Or their health. Damian stared at me. Was I lying? Or did I really have cocaine in my pocket that I'd say was his?

I gave him my best Clint Eastwood stare back, but I didn't have the balls to say, "Do you feel lucky? Well, do ya, punk?"

He blinked. He stood up and closed his laptop, and I walked him out to Lexington Avenue.

"Mr. Hillsborough has had a change of heart," I said to Kylie. "Ask him anything."

"When did you last see my husband?" she said.

"He didn't tell me he was married to a cop."

"Answer the question," she said.

"Yesterday. He was on a shopping spree, but he was a little low on cash, so we negotiated, and I got this handsome timepiece, and he got...well, you know what he got." Damian held out Spence's watch. "Take it. It's yours."

Kylie shook her head. "No. Technically, it's yours. Where is Spence now?"

"Look, lady, I'm a dope dealer, not a travel agent," he said, putting the watch back on his wrist. "I don't know where to find your husband, but he knows where to find me. And the way that boy was fiending, trust me: he will."

Kylie pulled her card out of her pocket and handed it to him. "Here's your get-out-of-jail-free card, Damian," she said. "Don't lose it."

CHAPTER 18

"WHAT THE HELL was that all about?" Kylie said as soon as we were back in the car.

I shrugged. "I don't know. He pissed me off. I guess I lost my shit."

"You could have lost your job, Rambo. You're lucky Damian is a dope dealer. If he was Joe Citizen, he'd lawyer up and call you out on police brutality."

"I'm not worried. The definition of police brutality is the use of excessive force by a cop when he's dealing with a civilian."

"It looked pretty damn excessive to me."

"Yeah, but I wasn't a cop. I was off duty."

"So that must have been your off-duty shield you flashed," she said, laughing.

"Are you finished yet, Judge Judy?"

"Almost. I've got one more thing to say." She stopped the car at a light on 116th Street. She turned to me, and a generous smile spread across her face. "Thanks, partner."

"I was wondering when you'd get around to that."

"My timing sucks, but I mean it, Zach: thanks. When I tracked Baby D down, I thought I'd ask him a few questions, and that would be it. I didn't know he'd be such a hard-ass. It threw me off. That's why I called you. I couldn't have done it without you."

"Anytime, partner," I said. "The problem is I don't know how much it's going to help. All he told you was that Spence scored some coke yesterday. I'm sure you must have figured that out this afternoon when you were standing ankle-deep in the wreckage at Silvercup."

"It helps a lot more than you think," she said. "Spence pulled five thousand dollars out of our bank account yesterday morning, which means he had enough cash to buy a quarter of a key."

"I don't get it," I said. "If he had that much money, why did he pay Baby D for the drugs with his watch?"

"For the same reason he busted up those sets. He was sending me another message."

"Which is...?"

"If it has anything to do with me, he's going to destroy it or get rid of it."

"Ouch," I said. "That hurts."

"It sure does," she said. "That's why he's doing it."

The light turned green, and we rolled south on Lexington. I pulled my phone out of my pocket. It was after nine. At this point calling Cheryl wouldn't cut it. I put the phone in my lap and stared out the window.

Kylie must have read my body language. "Do you want me to call Cheryl and apologize for screwing up your dinner?"

"Absolutely not."

"From the look on your face, I'm guessing she was pissed that you had to leave."

"Let's just say she wasn't happy."

"She better get used to it, Zach. She's living with a cop now. It's the nature of the beast. We get called out day and night."

"She works for the department, Kylie. I'm pretty sure she knows what being a cop is all about."

"So what's her problem?"

"This wasn't a cop call," I said.

I could see Kylie connecting the dots in her head. Knowing her, this had been all about NYPD putting the squeeze on a bad guy. She'd completely forgotten that the entire operation was personal.

"Oh," she said. "Right. It won't happen again."

I doubted it.

We were at 86th and Lexington, nine blocks from my apartment, when the phone in my lap went off.

"You see?" Kylie said. "She can't be that mad if she's calling you."

I looked at the caller ID. Private caller.

"It's not her," I said. I answered the phone. "This is Detective Jordan."

"My man, Zach," a familiar voice on the other end said. "This is Q. You looking for a couple of scrubs who are holding a necklace so hot they're almost ready to pay someone to take it?"

"Everybody is looking for them," I said, "and I'm at the top of the pile."

"That's why I called you first. I'm upstairs at the Kim."

My adrenaline was pumping. "We're less than five minutes away," I said.

"*We're* less than five minutes away?" he said. "Does that mean you're with that knockout partner of yours?"

"Yes, I'm with Kylie."

"At this hour? Sounds like you two are pulling the night shift. I hope I'm not interrupting any under-cover work," he said, following up with a lecherous laugh just in case I didn't get the joke.

"You're a pig."

"That's funny, Zach," he said, still chuckling. "First time a cop ever called *me* a pig. I'll see you in five."

He hung up, and I turned to Kylie. "Change of plans. We're meeting Q Lavish at the Kimberly Hotel."

She hit the gas, and we sped past a familiar brick building on 77th and Lex. My apartment is on the tenth floor.

I craned my neck, looking up, trying to see if the lights were still on, but we were going too fast.

"What are you doing?" Kylie said.

"Nothing. I'm just checking to see if Cheryl's home."

"Of course she's home. Do you think she moved out because you bailed on one dinner?"

"No. I'm just antsy. We're still working out this living together thing."

"Zach, it's going to work out just fine. And Cheryl's not going anywhere. She's a smart woman. She knows the score."

"Yeah, she does," I said.

Old girlfriend, one. New girlfriend, zero.

CHAPTER 19

QUENTIN LATRELLE, A.K.A. Q Lavish, is our best confidential informant. And our least expensive. I've worked with him for two years and have never paid him a dime. That's because Q isn't in it for the money.

Q is a pimp. But it's a word he never uses. "It would be like calling Yo-Yo Ma a fiddle player," he says. "I'm a purveyor of quality female companionship for gentlemen of breeding and taste."

Many of those gentlemen traveled in the same social circles that Red was created to protect and serve. That's where Kylie and I came in. Q knew that if any of his elite clientele got arrested in flagrante delicto, he had someone on his speed dial who could make the unfortunate incident go away.

If that sounds like the wealthy horndogs have an unfair advantage over the average johns, they do. But if Q could help us find the perps who murdered Elena Travers, I'd be happy to help out some Wall Street power broker who got caught with his pants down.

The Kimberly, on 50th between Lexington and Third, is an upmarket hotel that manages to combine traditional European elegance with trendy New York nightlife. Q was waiting for us at Upstairs, the Kim's opulent-to-the-max rooftop bar with a spectacular 360-degree view of Midtown.

Fluent in the language of fashion, Q knew how to dress whether he was having dinner at a four-star restaurant or hanging at a dive bar. Tonight he was wearing a pearl-gray suit and an open-collar navy shirt. Not very clubby, but perfect for the business-casual code at the Kim. Bottom line: he fit right in.

We sat down at his table, declined a drink, skipped the foreplay, and told him to get straight to business.

"Teddy Ryder and Raymond Davis," he said. "They were cellies at Otisville, and they've been bunking together ever since. Not gay, just a couple of underdogs who threw their lot in together, hoping that the whole would be greater than the sum of its parts."

"And is it?" I asked.

"If they were remotely competent, would I be

here?" he said. "I'll start with Teddy. He's white, midthirties, comes from a family of grifters. His mom and dad sold swampland in Florida back in the eighties, and over the years they've probably run every scam in the con man's bible. They were good, Annie and Buddy Ryder. He died a few years ago, and Annie's about seventy, so she's basically out of the game, but I wouldn't be surprised if she still kept her hand in by bilking the blue-haired granny crowd out of their bingo winnings.

"Sadly for Annie and Buddy, whatever criminal acumen was in their DNA skipped a generation. Their only progeny, Teddy, has zero street charisma. The poor boy couldn't sell a five-dollar cure for the clap if it came with a four-dollar coupon. Also, he's never been arrested for carrying a piece. Jacking a limo at gunpoint is so far out of his league I'm surprised he didn't shoot himself."

"How about the other one?" I said.

"Raymond Davis is fortysomething, biracial— mom was white, father was African American, both long gone. He's about as smart as a turkey sandwich, and to prove it he was scouting the bars uptown looking for a buyer for some hot jewelry. He tried to keep it vague, but that lasted until he was pressed for a description, and he all but held up a picture of that diamond necklace that was on the front page of the morning paper. Raymond's done two stretches for armed robbery, so if I were a betting man, I'd say he was your shooter."

"Do you know where we can find these two?" Kylie said.

"No, but I bet you've got someone down at One P P who can help you out."

That got a laugh. "Wiseass," she said. "We can take it from here. Thanks. You got anything else?"

"Not for NYPD. But I might have something for you. Something more…personal."

Q Lavish might joke with me about working the night shift with Kylie, but he'd never get smarmy with her. He was too much of a gentleman. Plus, the look in his eyes said he was dead serious.

"Go ahead," Kylie said.

"I heard you're looking for your husband."

"Jesus, Q," she said. "I know you're wired, but how did you—"

"I have clients in the TV business. They talk. I listen. I don't know where he is right now, but I know he's been over the edge. It's not my place, but if you need an extra pair of eyes and ears…"

"Oh God, yes. Thank you."

"Don't thank me yet. Just tell me whatever you think might help."

She recapped the last few days since Spence went missing. Q didn't say anything until she told him about our run-in with Baby D.

"Drug dealers are the worst," he said. "And that

pretty boy is as bad as the rest of them. He wouldn't call you if Spence came over to his house and shot his mother. Giving him your card was just a waste of paper. But now that I know he's one of your husband's contacts, I'll keep him on my radar."

Kylie stood up, shook his hand, and thanked him again. Even if Q didn't come up with a single lead toward helping us find Spence, she knew that his offer was genuine. And if he ever reached out to her for help getting one of his overprivileged clients out of a jam, she'd reciprocate in a nanosecond.

In the New York criminal justice system, it's all part of the circle of life.

CHAPTER 20

AS RELIABLE AN asset as Q Lavish might have been, the State of New York didn't think he was reliable enough. We couldn't arrest Davis and Ryder solely on the word of an informant. We needed an arrest warrant, and finding a judge to sign one at this hour of the night would take time. Time we didn't want to waste.

Parole officers, on the other hand, had a lot more latitude than cops. They could show up at a parolee's house anytime. No warrant. No warning.

"Call RTC and find Davis's PO," Kylie said as she barreled up Third toward the One Nine.

The Real Time Crime unit worked out of One Police Plaza, and they could tell you in a heartbeat just about anything you needed to know about anyone in their databases. I called them, and in under a minute, I had Davis's address and the cell number of Brian Sandusky, his parole officer.

My next call was to Sandusky. "Brian," I said, "this is Detective Zach Jordan. One of your boys, Raymond Davis, was fingered as the shooter in the robbery-homicide at the Ziegfeld Theater last night, and I need you on scene to get me inside so I can bypass a warrant."

"Davis? Elena Travers?" Sandusky said. "Holy shit, count me in."

Some POs hate being dragged out at night to make a house call, but Sandusky was young and eager to help out on a high-profile case. I told him to meet us at the precinct.

Then I called Cates, gave her a top line, and asked her to call in an ESU team to help us bring in Davis and Ryder.

Seventy minutes after we left the Kimberly Hotel, Kylie and I were in our car, followed by two Lenco armored trucks from Emergency Service Squad 1, in lower Manhattan. PO Sandusky was in the backseat.

"Fourteen heavily armed cops in full body armor ready to take down two bungling low-level criminals," he said as Kylie led the convoy across town, toward the FDR Drive. "Your average taxpayer might think that's excessive."

She looked over her shoulder at him. "That's

because your average taxpayer's never been shot at," she said.

Davis and Ryder lived downtown, on Rivington Street. We parked our vehicles around the corner on Suffolk and met up with one of the cops from the three units we'd dispatched as soon as we had the address.

"That's the building, over there," he said, pointing to a five-story gray-brick building. The facade from the second floor to the roof was covered with a cluster of metal fire escapes that probably dated back to the first half of the twentieth century. There was a storefront at street level, but it was boarded up, and the window had become a canvas for a graffiti artist who had done a remarkably good likeness of the Notorious B.I.G.

"Nobody in or out since we got here," the cop said.

I gave a hand signal, and a dozen cops poured out into the street, weapons at the ready. The team leader opened the front door and stopped.

"Blood," he whispered. He threw a light on the floor, and I could see it. A trail of blood leading to the inside door. He turned the knob. It didn't give.

One of his men took a Hooligan Tool and cracked the lock like it was an egg.

There were more bloodstains on the stairs. We followed the trail to Davis's apartment door, on the third floor.

"We've got probable cause to enter," I whispered to Sandusky, pointing at the bloody floor. "Leave the building. Now."

He looked both relieved and disappointed, but he didn't argue. He left.

"Open it," I said to the team leader.

One of his men had a universal skeleton key: a thirty-five-pound steel battering ram. One swing and the wooden door splintered.

There was a man sprawled facedown on the floor, and I held a gun on him as the team stormed the apartment. They checked the bedroom and the closets, and within seconds I heard a volley of "Clear, clear, clear."

I holstered my gun. The man on the floor was unmistakably dead.

"Roll him," I said.

Two of the cops flipped the body over.

It was Raymond Davis, his face ashy gray, his eyes bugged open in wide surprise, a single bullet hole in the middle of his forehead.

PART TWO

BEST. MOM. EVER.

CHAPTER 21

IT WAS THE kind of crime scene that nerds like Chuck Dryden live for. A dead murder suspect with a bullet in his brain, a second bullet embedded in the pockmarked plaster on the opposite side of the room, and a wall covered with bright red high-velocity blood spatters that were the clues to the dirty little details of Raymond Davis's last moments on earth. For Chuck it was the equivalent of forensic porn.

Kylie and I left him to his fun and went out to canvass the area.

We went back to the bloody trail that had led us to the apartment and followed it down the stairs, out the front door, and onto the street. A half block from the building it ended abruptly.

"He must have figured out he was leaving bread

crumbs," Kylie said. "You think Teddy Ryder is our bleeder?"

"I doubt if he's our shooter," I said. "These guys were BFFs."

"It wouldn't be the first relationship that was dissolved by a bullet."

"But Teddy is gun-shy. His parents were con artists. In their line of work the only reason to carry a piece is if you're hoping for a stiffer sentence when you get busted. Besides, we know that Raymond was trolling the bars, looking for a buyer."

"I guess he found one," Kylie said. "So, two shots fired in apartment 3A. How many of the tenants do you think heard anything?"

I laughed. New Yorkers in general are reluctant to come forward and get involved—especially in a crime of violence. And I was willing to bet that Raymond Davis's neighbors would be even less inclined to talk to the cops. With twelve apartments in the building, at least somebody would have to have heard the two gunshots. And yet no one had called 911. We went through the motions anyway and knocked on every door in the building. As expected, nobody heard a thing.

We went back to the apartment, where Chuck was waiting to give us his top line impressions.

"Be careful where you sit," he said as soon as we got through the door.

"Gosh, thanks, Dr. Dryden," Kylie said, "but they taught us crime scene etiquette back at the academy."

"I'm sorry, Detective MacDonald," Dryden said. "Let me rephrase that. This place is riddled with bedbugs. Be careful where you sit."

We stood.

Dryden went through his usual series of disclaimers reminding us that some of his conclusions were not yet scientifically chiseled in stone. Then he launched into the scenario the way he saw it.

"If you two are correct, and Davis and his partner killed Elena Travers and stole an eight-million-dollar necklace, then this is where they tried to unload it. But, as you well know, there is no honor among thieves. Davis was dropped where he stood, but his partner managed to get out with what is most likely a flesh wound. The slug that caught him was in the wall. It's a .38."

"And where's the necklace?" Kylie asked.

Dryden smiled. "Where indeed?"

"But you searched the place."

"Top to bottom."

"Did you find anything?"

"Yes, I did," he said, his expression totally deadpan. "Bedbugs."

Kylie rewarded him with a smile. "Let me rephrase that," she said. "Did you find anything that might help us in our investigation?"

"Possibly," he said. "Mr. Davis had a gun. He

didn't get to use it tonight, but it's a 9mm—the same caliber as the murder weapon that killed Elena Travers. I'll run it through ballistics and get back to you tomorrow."

I looked at my watch. "It's already tomorrow," I said.

"Oh, good. In that case, I'll have it for you today."

"Last question," Kylie said. "Do you have anything on the shooter? A partial print? Hairs? Fibers? Anything?"

"Sorry. He was either very good or very lucky, but I've got nothing except for the two .38 slugs he left behind."

"Then there's only one way we're going to catch him," Kylie said, looking at me.

"What's that?" I said.

"Find Teddy Ryder."

CHAPTER 22

I CALLED THE office and asked the desk sergeant to get out a BOLO on Teddy Ryder. "And I need a hospital check," I said. "He took a bullet."

Within minutes, Ryder's picture would be distributed citywide, and every precinct would send out a team to check the local hospitals for a gunshot victim.

Then I called Q. I thanked him for leading us to Davis and asked if he knew where we could find Ryder's mother.

"Sorry, Zach," he said. "You know how grifters are. Annie Ryder is like a gypsy. She could be in any one of fifty states, although I'd probably eliminate Alaska and Hawaii."

It wasn't what I was hoping to hear, but at the

same time, I was relieved. If Q had an address, Kylie and I would have had to follow up on it immediately. When the case is this hot, sleep is not an option.

"Here's a thought for you, Zach," Q said. "Try running her name through NCIC."

The National Crime Information Center is an electronic clearinghouse of crime data that can be tapped into by any criminal justice agency in the U.S. Q's advice was the cop equivalent of telling a civilian to Google it.

"Thanks a heap," I said. "I just thought I'd try you first. I figured you had a better database."

I hung up and walked over to Kylie, who was still talking to Dryden.

"Good news," I said. "Q has no idea where to find the mom. We can punch out now."

I didn't have to tell her twice. We said good night to Dryden and left the apartment.

We were halfway down the stairs when Kylie stopped and tapped her forehead.

"Son of a bitch," she said.

"What's going on?" I said.

"Remember what Gregg Hutchings told us about those hidden security cameras at the hospital? Look up."

I tipped my head toward the stairwell ceiling. I saw it immediately. There were two smoke detectors mounted on the cracked plaster. One was centered directly over the stairs just the way the building code required. The other was tucked into a corner.

"This second smoke detector is too close to the wall to be effective as a smoke detector," I said. "But it's a damn good place for a camera."

"And I'll bet it's not the only one," Kylie said.

We walked the building from the lobby to the roof and found three more.

"All wireless," Kylie said. "The question is, whose apartment is the signal going to?"

"There's probably a sophisticated high-tech way to find out without waking up the whole building," I said.

Kylie grinned. "But sophistication has never been our strong suit. Let's rattle all their cages," she said, banging on the door of apartment 5A.

The same tenants who weren't happy to see us the first time we canvassed the building were even less happy this time around. Especially since Kylie confronted every bleary-eyed one of them with a bad-to-the-bone snarl and a few choice words. *We found your surveillance cameras. Show us the monitor. Now!"*

The standard responses ranged from dumbfounded stares to an angry "What the fuck are you talking about?"

We pissed off everyone on the fifth floor and two people on the fourth, but the next apartment was the charm.

CHAPTER 23

ELLIOTT MORITZ, THE tenant in 4C, was about sixty, mild mannered, and by far the least confrontational of all the tenants we had met. He quickly admitted that the cameras were his.

"And who authorized you to install them?" Kylie said.

"They're not exactly *authorized*," Moritz said, backing up a step. "I sort of have unwritten permission from the landlord."

"Unwritten permission won't hold up in court, Elliott," Kylie said.

"Court? Wait a minute, officer, I'm not the criminal here," Moritz said. "It's the woman in 5B. She's a flight attendant. She sublets her apartment whenever she's out of town, and the people she rents to are noisy and dirty, and you can smell the marijuana through the air vents. So I complained to the building management. They said they can't evict her without proof. So I said I would get some, and they said okay."

"You're right, Elliott," Kylie said. "What she's doing is illegal. But so is spying on your neighbors. If this were any other night, I'd arrest you, but I've got a homicide to deal with, and you may be able to help, so I'm going to let you decide how we handle this. Option one: I wake up a judge, get a warrant to impound your equipment, and book you on charges of video voyeurism. Option two: you show me and my partner your video feed, and I'll give you the name and cell number of an inspector in the city's Buildings Department who hates illegal subletters even more than you do."

Moritz wisely chose option two.

He had a quad monitor with one camera pointed at the flight attendant's apartment on the fifth floor. The other three only covered the stairwells. At 9:37 a man had trudged up the stairs to the third floor.

"That's our guy," Kylie said when he didn't show up on the fourth-floor camera.

There was no audio track, so we didn't get to hear the gunshots, but at 9:44, Teddy Ryder stumbled down the stairs, bleeding. A minute later, the man who had lumbered up the stairs raced down. The image was poor quality, but we could tell that our suspect was white, about six feet tall, and no more than thirty-five years old. It wasn't much, but it was a start.

Kylie downloaded the video onto her cell phone. We took it back to the precinct, found a tech to pull some screenshots, and got them out to every cop in the city.

It was almost two a.m. when Kylie dropped me off at my apartment. Angel, my favorite doorman, was on duty.

"You look beat, Detective," he said.

"Fighting crime isn't as glamorous as it looks," I said.

He laughed and said good night. I got in the elevator. It had been hours since I'd walked out on Cheryl without saying a word, and I wondered if she'd still be there when I got upstairs.

Angel probably knew. But I was too embarrassed to ask him if my new live-in girlfriend had moved out with all her stuff while I was away.

CHAPTER 24

ANNIE RYDER WAS a night owl. As her husband, Buddy, loved to say, "Annie never goes to sleep on the same day she wakes up." So when her cell rang at ten minutes after midnight, she didn't panic. She just figured it was one of her insomniac neighbors who wanted to stop by for a cup of tea and an earful of gossip.

The screen on her iPhone said Private Caller, but that didn't bother Annie either. Caller ID was a two-way street, and since she always blocked her name and number from popping up, she couldn't fault anyone else. She muted the TV and answered the phone with a crisp "Hello. Who's this?"

"Ma," a weak voice on the other end said.

She stood up and pressed the phone to her ear. "Teddy, are you all right? What's wrong?"

"I got shot."

"Oh Jesus. Where?"

"In my apartment, but I'm not there now. I ran like hell."

"Teddy, no—not where were you when you got shot. Where did the bullet hit you?"

"Oh. He shot me in the stomach."

Annie was good in emergencies, but this was a crisis. She instinctively moved over to the sideboard and rested her hand on Buddy's urn for strength.

"Listen to me," she said. "Get yourself to a hospital. Now."

"Ma, are you crazy? I go to the hospital with a gunshot wound, and they call the cops."

"Teddy, I'd rather visit you in jail than identify your body at the morgue. A bullet to the abdomen can be lethal. God knows how many of your organs got torn up. Get your ass to an ER before you bleed to death internally."

"My organs are fine," Teddy said. "You're thinking like I got shot in the belly button. That's not what happened. It's more like the bullet went through the fat parts that hang off the side."

"Love handles?" Annie said.

"Yeah. That's not so bad, right?"

"Of course it's bad. You want to get an infection

and die of sepsis? We have to treat it right away. Where are you?"

"I just got off the subway. I'm standing outside the station."

Annie gritted her teeth. *The* subway. *The* station. Teddy had never mastered the art of spelling out details. "*Which* station?" she demanded.

"Yours, Ma. I took the N train to Astoria Boulevard. I'm right here under the el by the Pizza Palace on 31st Street."

"Jesus, you're right around the corner?"

"Yeah, but I didn't want to just come up to the apartment in case the cops are watching it."

"Smart thinking, kiddo," she said.

The catchphrase was a throwback to Teddy's grade-school days, when he was a permanent fixture in the slow learners' class.

Early on, Buddy came up with a plan. "The kid may not be too bright," he said, "but we can't be the ones to reinforce it. Our job is to con him into thinking he's smarter than he is."

From that day forward, whenever Teddy did or said something that would be normal for an average kid, Annie and Buddy rewarded him, sometimes with a sweet treat, sometimes a little gift. But the positive feedback that always made Teddy the happiest was those three little words: *Smart thinking, kiddo.*

It still worked. "Thanks, Ma," Teddy said. "So what do I do now?"

"I'll come for you," she said, lifting the lid of the trunk where Buddy had kept the tricks of his trade. "First I've got to find something for you to wear so nobody recognizes you. Now just promise me you'll stay out of sight till I get there."

"I'm starved."

"Promise, damn it."

"Okay, okay, I promise."

She hung up the phone. "The boy is in deep shit this time, Buddy," she called out to the urn containing the ashes of her dead husband as she rifled through the wigs, props, and collection of uniforms that had helped the con man pass as anything from a meter reader to an airline pilot.

Two minutes later, she had what she needed, raced out of the apartment, and then checked every parked car on Hoyt Avenue. Twenty-four minutes after that, Teddy Ryder walked through the front door of his mother's building in plain sight.

Annie was positive that there were no cops watching, but even if there were, she doubted they'd realize that the man with shoulder-length blond hair wearing a bright orange safety vest and carrying a red insulated pizza bag was the one every cop in the city was looking for.

CHAPTER 25

TEDDY PUT THE pizza box on the kitchen counter, pulled out a slice, and grabbed a can of Bud from the refrigerator.

"Alcohol dehydrates you," Annie said, snatching the beer out of his hand and dumping it into the sink. She opened one of the bottles of orange Gatorade she'd brought home from the Pizza Palace and handed it to him.

Teddy inhaled half the slice and took a swig of the neon-colored drink. "You ever patch up a bullet wound when you were a nurse?" he asked.

"*Nurse?* I was a candy striper. I learned a few things from watching the nurses, but mostly I stole morphine ampoules to sell to the junkies in my neighborhood. Now take off that stupid wig and strip down to your shorts. I'm going next door to borrow a few medical supplies."

She took a tote bag from the hall closet and left. By the time she got back, Teddy was three slices into the pie, and his jeans and shirt were on the floor.

"That's the beauty of living in a building full of old people," Annie said, setting down the tote bag. "It's like an all-night pharmacy. They have everything you need for a do-it-yourself gunshot wound repair kit."

She handed him a bottle of pills. "Amoxicillin," she said. "Take four now, and then we'll space them out, four a day."

Teddy didn't argue. He popped four of the antibiotics and washed them down with Gatorade. Annie spread a sheet on the sofa and pulled a bottle of Smirnoff vodka from the tote bag. "It's not the pricey stuff," she said, "but it'll do."

"I thought you said no alcohol," Teddy said.

"This isn't for drinking. Lie down so I can see where you got hit."

Teddy stretched out on the sofa, and Annie studied his bloodied left side. "You're lucky," she said. "It's a clean shot. The bullet went in the front and out the back, but I'm sure it dragged pieces of fabric from your dirty shirt along with it. We have to kill the bacteria before it spreads. Bite down on that throw pillow."

"Why?"

"Because it's going to hurt like hell, and I don't want you to wake up the neighbors when you start screaming."

"Ma, I'm not going to scre—"

She poured the eighty-proof Smirnoff disinfectant on the wound, and Teddy let out a piercing shriek that he managed to stifle with the pillow.

"Next time maybe you'll listen to your mother," Annie said, dabbing his skin with a soft cloth. "When I tell you it's going to hurt, it's going to hurt. And when I told you Raymond Davis was no good for you, I was right. But no, you had to wait for him to shoot you before you took my word for it."

"Don't talk bad about Raymond, Ma. He didn't shoot me. He's dead. The guy who shot me shot him first."

"Jesus, Teddy. What the hell were you two involved in that someone would want to kill you?"

"This guy Jeremy hired us to steal some shit, so we did, and then when it was time to pay us off, he decided to kill us instead."

Annie reached into her tote bag and took out a box of adult diapers. She opened one and placed the absorbent fabric so it covered both sides of the wound. "Stand up and hold this so I can wrap it," she said.

Teddy did as he was told.

"What did you steal?" Annie asked as she began wrapping an ACE bandage around Teddy's waist.

"A diamond necklace."

"I can't believe it. You robbed a jewelry store?"

"No," Teddy said, his head down. "A limo. There was this actress in the back, and Jeremy knew she'd be wearing this expensive necklace, and—"

"Oh my God. Elena Travers?"

Teddy didn't answer. He didn't have to.

"You killed Elena Travers?" Annie said.

"I didn't shoot her, Ma. Honest. Raymond did."

"But you had a gun."

"Yeah."

"And what's the one cardinal rule that your father taught you?"

"No guns."

"And now that poor actress is dead, and you're facing life in prison. Who is this Jeremy, anyway? What's his last name?"

"I don't know. Raymond did all the up-front work. Tonight was the first time I saw him. He was supposed to give us ninety thousand for the necklace, but Raymond didn't trust him, so when Jeremy shows up, Raymond tells him we're not giving him the necklace until he hands over his gun."

"And of course he did," Annie said. "No arguments."

"Right. So then I go and get the necklace and put it on the coffee table."

"And just like that," Annie said, "Jeremy pulls out a second gun that he had tucked in the back of his pants."

"It was an ankle holster. He drilled Raymond right between the eyes. He turned on me, and I head-butted him just as he pulled the trigger. He went down hard, and I ran for my life."

"The cops will be looking for you. Sooner or later, they're going to be knocking on my door. You can't stay here."

"Ma, I've got no place else to go."

"I'm cat-sitting for the couple next door while they're on a cruise. You can stay there for the next ten days."

She taped down the ends of the ACE bandage. Then she picked up his shirt and helped him into it. "You can put your pants on by yourself," she said.

Teddy stepped into his jeans, buttoned the fly, and cinched the belt. "Hey, Ma," he said, digging his hand into his pocket. "I brought you a present."

He pulled out the diamond and emerald necklace and handed it to her.

"Oh my God," she said. "Teddy, it's…it's exquisite. I thought Jeremy took this."

"He did, but when I knocked him down, he hit his head. He was kind of groggy, so I figured I'd grab the necklace while I could, and maybe one day you and me could find a buyer on our own."

Annie Ryder stood there, watching the light refract

off the eight million dollars' worth of stolen jewelry in the palm of her hand. At first she was dumb-founded, unable to speak. And then she found the words that always brought joy to the face of her slow-witted but good-natured son.

"Smart thinking, kiddo."

CHAPTER 26

I OPENED THE door to my apartment. It was pitch-black. I'm from the school of "I'll leave a light on in the window for you," so this was not a good sign. I tapped the switch on the wall and breathed a sigh of relief. Cheryl's purse, keys, and department ID were sitting on the hall table.

I made my way to the dining room, flipped on a light, and there it sat: the romantic dinner for two was exactly where it was when I walked out. Still on the table, untouched, and, by now, incredibly unromantic.

I didn't have to wonder how Cheryl felt. Nothing says "You're not getting laid tonight" like cold clotted lasagna and rock-hard garlic bread.

But in case I had any doubts, the bedroom door

was shut, and my blanket and pillow had been dumped on the sofa.

I carried the perfect dinner out to the incinerator room, cleaned the kitchen, then tossed and turned on the sofa until five forty-five. The bedroom door was still shut, and I knew I'd be smarter to leave and shower at the precinct.

But first I stopped at the diner to talk to my therapist.

"The doctor is in," Gerri said, bringing me coffee and a bagel, then sliding into the booth across from me. "What the hell did you do wrong now?"

"That's the thing," I said. "I'm not sure I did anything wrong."

I filled her in on the details of last night. She didn't say a word till I was finished.

"Let me start with a question," she said. "Do you really want this relationship with Cheryl to work out?"

I didn't hesitate. "Of course."

"Then why would you leave her and go up to Harlem to be with Kylie?"

"Wait a minute—I didn't leave her to *be with Kylie*. Kylie needed help. That's the nature of who I am. When there's a damsel in distress, I—"

Gerri erupted. "*Damsel in distress? Kylie?* News flash, Zach: Kylie MacDonald is a pistol-packing, ass-kicking, ball-busting hellcat. The day she's a damsel in distress is the day I'll be on the cover of the *Sports Illustrated* swimsuit issue."

"Okay, okay, you're right. *Damsel in distress* was a poor choice of terms."

"More like a profoundly stupid choice of terms."

"What I should have said was, Kylie is a loose cannon. She went up to Harlem—on her own, without backup—an off-duty cop on a harebrained mission to find her husband's drug dealer and then strong-arm him into telling her how to find Spence."

"So to sum it all up, you made a choice. You chose Kylie over Cheryl."

"You're oversimplifying."

"Then let me undersimplify. Let's say I have magic powers, and with one wave of my hand, I can guarantee you a happy life with the woman of your choice. Who's it going to be?"

"Cheryl."

"You know that for sure?"

"Yes."

"Does she know that for sure?"

"Cheryl knows that I love her, and hopefully she understands why I bailed on dinner last night."

"Zach, I'm not sure you understand why you did what you did last night."

"What is that supposed to mean?"

"Nothing." She stood up. "I'm a short-order cook, not a shrink. I'm sorry I said that."

"Well, it's too late to unsay it. What do you mean, I don't understand what I did last night?"

She sat down. "When my daughter Rachel was

nineteen, she had an affair with a married man who was thirty-six. A year later, he got divorced, and a few months after that, he asked Rachel to marry him. I told her I was against it."

"Because of their age difference?" I said.

"No. Because the guy cheated on his wife. I said to Rachel, 'If he'll do it *with* you, he'll do it *to* you.' She married him anyway. Five years later, she caught him in bed with another woman. She was devastated. She left him and moved back home with me. I felt terrible for her, but deep down inside, a little piece of me felt vindicated…justified. I told her that he was no good for her, and I was right. So here's my final question of the day, Zach. Did you go up to Harlem to protect Kylie from getting in trouble, or did you go to help her pick up the pieces of a marriage you've been hoping would crash and burn?"

I didn't answer because I didn't know the answer.

Gerri stood up again. "Are you okay?"

"I'm fine, but I think I may need a second opinion."

"Good idea," she said. "Try the Metro Diner on Broadway. Even if you're not impressed with the therapy, you'll love the mac and cheese."

CHAPTER 27

I WALKED AROUND the corner to the One Nine and headed straight for the locker room. I looked like a man who hadn't spent the night in his own bed, and the last thing I needed was for Kylie to see me and badger me for an explanation.

I showered, shaved, put on clean clothes, and walked into the office looking as fresh as a gangbanger wearing a brand-new suit to his court date.

"I've been trying to call you for the last fifteen minutes," Kylie said, not remotely interested in my appearance. "Let's go."

"Let's pretend we're equal partners, and I get a vote," I said as I chased her down the stairs. "Where are we running off to?"

"Murray Hill Medical Center. They got hit last night."

"What'd they steal this time? Bedpans? Kylie, we've got a double homicide on our hands. Why don't we send Betancourt and Torres to take statements so we can focus on the Travers case?"

"Because our new best friend, Howard Sykes, called to inform us that an already delicate situation just became even more delicate. He's at Murray Hill now waiting for his two star cops to show up and handle the situation with the utmost diplomacy."

I followed her outside. "I don't get it. We've been keeping this case under wraps since we started. What got stolen that makes it even more delicate?"

"It's not what got stolen. It's who witnessed the crime."

"We have a witness?"

"Two. But I doubt if they're going to cooperate. Get in the car. I'll fill you in on all the ugly politics on the way over."

I got in the car.

"The room where the equipment was stored had a keypad lock on it, but the perps knew the key code," she said as we headed south on Lexington. "Guess what they found inside when they opened the door."

I shrugged. "Unless it's Teddy Ryder, I'm not sure I care."

"A doctor shagging a nurse," she said.

"Okay, I care."

"And he's not just some randy intern. This doc generated over two million for Murray Hill last year."

I've been attached to Red long enough to figure out why Howard wanted us at the scene. "So it's politics over police work," I said. "Howard expects us to keep the doctor's name out of the investigation."

"As Howard put it, he's a witness, not a criminal," she said.

Five minutes later, we pulled up to the hospital entrance on East 33rd Street. One of the mayor's aides escorted us to an office in the admin section, where Howard Sykes was waiting for us with our reluctant witness.

"This is Dr. Richard," Sykes said.

"Detectives, I seem to be in a spot of bother here, but Howard assures me I can rely on your discretion," he said in that proper British accent that immediately cloaks the speaker with an aura of erudition and culture.

He was fiftyish, tall, trim, with silvering hair and what the Brits call bearing. Having spent a lot of my time with men of means, I calculated that his worsted wool Armani suit and his Gucci ostrich-skin loafers would run me at least a month's salary. There was a gold band on the fourth finger of his left hand.

"Yes, sir," I said. "Tell us what happened."

"Unbeknownst to me, there is a band of brazen thieves stealing hospital equipment," he said. "Had I been aware of the crime wave, I would not have been so quick to choose the room where the new spirometry equipment is being housed. I'm rather mortified to admit that I was in there for a late-night dalliance with a member of the nursing staff, whose name I shall not reveal unless I am remanded to do so by the courts."

"I assure you that won't happen," Howard said, speaking on behalf of the entire criminal justice system. "Just tell the detectives what you can."

"It was shortly after midnight. They opened the door, and I must say, they were as surprised to see the two of us as we were to see the four of them. They were all wearing scrubs, so I assumed they were staff, but then one of them pulled out a gun."

"Did you see their faces?" Kylie asked.

"Yes, and my first thought was, *Now that I can identify them, they're going to kill me.* But upon closer inspection, I could see that they were wearing masks. Not your typical Halloween fare, but skintight Hollywood-quality silicone. Ingenious disguise, actually."

"And then what?" I asked.

"The one with the gun spoke. He was very calm, very polite—had a bit of a Texas accent, a little like Tommy Lee Jones. He assured us that we wouldn't be hurt if we complied. Then two of them bound our hands and feet and covered our mouths with duct tape while the other two put the equipment on a gurney and covered it with a sheet. They were in and out in less than two minutes, but it was six in the morning before my companion and I were found."

Lucky for us, someone found him. If he had managed to get out on his own, we wouldn't have had a witness. We thanked him, and he left in a hurry.

"Even though they wore masks," I said to Howard, "we'd like to check the security footage to see what vehicles they used."

"There is no security footage," he said. "They wiped the hard drive."

"These guys are ninjas," Kylie said. "Do you know if the hospital backs up their video to the cloud?"

"I'm afraid they don't. From what I understand, an upgrade is scheduled for next fiscal year, but I'm not on the board here. I only stepped in because the mayor and I are personal friends of the doctor and his wife."

"Do you want to tell us Dr. Richard's real name?" Kylie asked.

Howard smiled. "No. Like they used to say on *Dragnet*, the names have been changed to protect the innocent."

"Is there any chance we could get to interview his *companion*, this member of the nursing staff?" Kylie said.

"I certainly can't help you there, Detective," Howard said. "*I* don't even know her name."

"Based on the doc's choice of words and his avoidance of pronouns," Kylie said, "I don't even know if it's a *her*."

CHAPTER 28

"SO WHO DO you think wound up with the necklace?" Kylie said as soon as she started the car. "Teddy or our phantom buyer?"

It was a simple enough question, but something about the offhand way she asked it set me off.

"Wait a minute," I said. "Are we back on our primary case now? Because my head is still jammed up with this drop-everything hospital mission you decided was so critical, and I'm having trouble keeping up every time you change gears. It would really help me if you handed out a schedule first thing in the morning to let me know how you plan to orchestrate my day."

She turned off the engine and swiveled her body

around to square off with mine. "You got a problem with me, Zach?"

I hardly ever get in Kylie's face, and with her husband running wild, this was definitely not the best time to vent. But it was too late. I lost it.

"Yeah. You're not my boss. You're my partner. I understand you can't always say no to city hall, but next time, check in with me before you say 'I'll be right there' and then drag me along like I'm your pack mule."

"I did try to call you, *partner*, but you were too busy licking your wounds, so I made a judgment call."

"What wounds?"

"Oh please. I walked by the diner this morning, and there you were, wearing last night's rumpled clothes, pouring your heart out to Gerri. I figured you had a major blowup with Cheryl when you got home. And then a half hour later, you walked into the office looking fresh as a daisy. Did you think I wouldn't pick up on it? You and I went at it pretty heavy back in the day, so I know what you smell like after you shave and shower, I know that's the backup shirt you keep in your locker, and I know when you're pissy because your love life is off the tracks. Plus, I'm a detective with New York's Finest. A little credit, okay?"

"Fine," I said, doing my best to spin the word so that it sounded more like "Go fuck yourself."

She slid back behind the wheel and started the car.

"You want to tell me where we're going?" I said.

"We're driving to the Bassett brothers' to see if they recognize Raymond Davis or Teddy Ryder from their mug shots," she said. "And if we're really lucky, maybe they can ID the guy who chased Ryder down the stairs. Does that meet with your approval, Detective—"

"Teddy!" I said.

"Teddy what?"

"Teddy has the necklace."

"Fifty-fifty chance that you're right, but how come you sound so sure?"

"You just said it. 'The guy who *chased* Ryder down the stairs.' I think if our mystery man had the necklace, he'd have left the building nice and casual so as not to attract any attention. But this guy went tear-assing down the steps. He was after Teddy, and my best guess is that he never caught him, or we'd have gotten a call informing us that our double homicide has been upgraded to a triple."

She thought about it for a few seconds. "Y'know," she said, "you're pretty smart for a pack mule."

"We still have to nail both of them," I said, "but we have a better shot at finding Teddy. Any word from NCIC on Annie Ryder?"

"As of an hour ago, they haven't yet come up with a viable hit on her. She has a three-year-old

Maryland license with a Baltimore address, but she hasn't lived there in more than two years. Since then, she got a speeding ticket in Nashville and another one on the Jersey Turnpike. She's not easy to pin down."

"For all we know she got those tickets on purpose, just to throw the bloodhounds off the scent," I said. "Q was right. She doesn't want to be found."

"Oh, we'll find her," Kylie said. "In the meantime, let's go see if Leo Bassett has had the cocktail sauce removed from his jacket and the broom removed from his ass."

CHAPTER 29

ON THE WAY downtown, I got a text from Chuck Dryden.

"Good news," I said to Kylie. "We've got ballistics back on Raymond Davis's Walther. It's a 100 percent match with the gun that killed Elena. Of course, there's no way we can prove that Raymond was the shooter."

"No, but on the plus side," Kylie said, "we don't have to bring him to trial."

West 21st Street was back to normal. The media vans and the paparazzi were gone, most likely in hot pursuit of the crime du jour.

Leo buzzed us in and was anxiously waiting for us when the elevator doors opened. "Detectives," he said. "I'm so glad you're back. I must apologize for my little hissy fit the other night, but I was beyond distraught about Elena."

"We understand perfectly," Kylie said. "There have been some developments in the case, and we have some pictures we'd like to show you."

"What kind of developments?"

"First, we'd like you and your brother to look at some photos."

"Suspects?" he said, tapping his fingertips together as if he were applauding.

"Persons of interest," I said.

"Oh, I love that term," he said. "Let's do it. I'll get Max."

We sat down at the dining room table with both of them and laid out six mug shots, two of which were Teddy and Raymond.

"I've never seen any of them in my life," Max said immediately.

Leo took his time. He picked up one of the pictures and stared at it. "Oh, of course," he said.

"You recognize him?" I asked.

"I thought I did, and then I finally figured it out. He looks like a young Richard Widmark."

"The actor?" I said.

"Yes, but the early years. Like when he played Tommy Udo in *Kiss of Death*," he said. "I'm sure this is absolutely no help at all, but at least *I'm* taking a few minutes to put a name to the face."

"I didn't *need* a few minutes," Max said, looking

directly at me, although the dig was clearly aimed at his brother. "I've never seen any of them. Leo said you had some developments in the case. What are they?"

"There was a shooting on the Lower East Side last night. This man is dead, and this one is wounded and on the run." I pointed to Raymond's mug shot, then to Teddy's. "We have good reason to believe they stopped the limo and killed Elena Travers."

"Who are they?" Max said.

"Raymond Davis and Teddy Ryder. Do either of those names ring a bell?"

They both shook their heads.

"They're career felons, but this crime is way above their pay grade," I said. "They may have been turning over the necklace to the person who hired them when the shooting went down."

"Did you recover the necklace?" Max said.

"No, but we were hoping you might be able to identify the probable shooter."

I handed Max the fuzzy surveillance screenshot we pulled out of Elliott Moritz's security video.

He studied it. "The lighting is terrible. It could be anybody. It's certainly nobody I recognize...from life *or the movies*," he added as he handed the screenshot to Leo.

Leo looked at it and shook his head. "Can you get us a better picture? A different angle? Or maybe do some of those crazy computer tricks to make it less blurry, like they do on the TV shows?"

"I'm sorry, Mr. Bassett," I said. "It is what it is. We knew it was a long shot, but we had to ask."

"What do we do now?" Leo asked.

"Nothing," I said. "We just wanted to touch base with you and let you know we're making progress. We'll get back to you soon."

Leo escorted us to the elevator, and Kylie and I rode down without saying a word. Only when we were back in the car and out of range of their security cameras did Kylie break the silence.

"What's your take on those two?" she said.

"Max is a coldhearted bastard who cares more about the missing necklace than about the dead woman who was wearing it. And Leo, who doesn't understand the difference between the movies and real life, acts like he's starring in a jewelry heist film, and the two of us are extras who play cops. What's your take?"

"You know me, Zach. I suspect everybody of everything. The problem is, Max seems too smart to hire a couple of bozos like Teddy and Raymond, and Leo seems too dumb to put an operation like this together. So based on what we know about them, it's hard to connect them to the crime."

"Then maybe the real problem is, we don't know enough about them," I said, taking out my phone. "Yet."

CHAPTER 30

LEO BASSETT STOOD behind the drapes, peeked out the window at West 21st Street, and watched as Detectives Jordan and MacDonald drove off.

"They're gone," he said.

"They'll be back," his brother said.

"Two or three more times, maybe," Leo said with a toss of his hand. "The last time around the cops barely bothered to talk to us. Don't worry. These two will give up soon enough. They always do."

They always do. Max closed his eyes and marveled at how blissfully ignorant his brother could be.

Over the past twenty-two years, the Bassetts had been the victims of three previous robberies. Each one had been flawlessly planned by Max and executed by professionals. None of the cases had been

145

solved, and the claims, each one filed with a different insurance company, were paid in full—a total of nineteen million dollars. Max then recut the stolen gems and sold them as loose stones.

"Leo," Max said patiently, "these two cops will not give up. They will be back again, and again, and again. You want to know why?"

Leo shrugged.

Max exploded. "Because they've got a dead fucking movie star on their plate. I told you this was a bad idea from the get-go. Banta and Burkhardt are in prison for the next thirty years, and what did I say to you? I said let's not press our luck. Let's not try this with somebody new. But no: you swore that Jeremy could pull it off, and he'd bring in two top-notch replacements. Top-notch? One is dead, the other is on the run, and the cops have a surveillance picture of your boy toy. You better find Jeremy *and* our necklace before they do, or we're in deep shit. I don't know why I let you talk me into this."

"Talk you into it? Don't lay this on me. What choice did we have? We're hemorrhaging money. Do you know how much you've spent on your over-the-top African safaris and your insane deep-sea expeditions?" Leo demanded. "And God knows how many millions you've poured into the lake house."

"While you, on the other hand, are as frugal as a church mouse on a pension."

"I've worked hard all my life, Max. I've earned my little taste of la dolce vita."

Max snorted. "Little taste? You are the most narcissistic, hedonistic person on the planet. You flew thirty people to Paris in September, put them up in a five-star hotel for four days, paid for their food, their wine, their—"

"Shut up!" Leo screamed. "It was my sixtieth birthday, and yes, I spent a lot of money, and no, I have no regrets. *Non, je ne regrette rien, mon frère.* I'm spending my money now, while I'm alive, and if I don't have enough, I will go out and get more."

"You want more money, Leo? All you have to do is sign the goddamn contract with Precio Mundo, and you'll have all the money you ever need to feed your face until the day you die."

"Never! Leo Bassett is a jeweler to the stars, not a flunky for a bunch of cut-rate, low-rent, bargain-basement Mexican whores."

"*Flunky?* You'd be in a partnership with one of the wealthiest corporations in the world. And they're not cut-rate. They're mass-market. Which means half a million women could be wearing our jewelry instead of one dead actress."

Leo took a step back. "What are you implying, Max?"

"I'm not *implying* anything. I am flat-out saying that it's your fault she's dead. You were supposed to be in the backseat with her. You were supposed to keep her calm and get her to hand over the necklace without an argument. It may have been the single most important thing you've ever had to do in your life, Leo, and you blew it off because you didn't want to walk down the red carpet smelling like a fish stick."

"I'm sorry about Elena, but stealing the necklace was the right call."

"Why don't you put that in a little handwritten note to Elena's parents? *'Dear Mom and Dad. Sorry about your daughter, but I needed the money. Signed, Leo Bassett, jeweler to the stars.'"*

Maxwell Bassett knew where his brother's buttons were, and he knew this was the last one he had to push.

Leo threw him the finger, turned, and stormed out of the room.

Poor Leo, Max thought. *Did you really think I would let you and Jeremy be in charge of stealing an eight-million-dollar necklace?*

He smiled. This was going better than he'd planned.

"The same goes for me, Leo," he whispered softly. *"Non, je ne regrette rien, mon frère."*

CHAPTER 31

"ONE DEAD PERP is a good start," Captain Cates said after we brought her up to speed on the Travers murder, "but it's been almost forty-eight hours. Elena was an international star. Half the world is waiting for answers."

"Then you might want to tell half the world that we'd have more answers if we didn't get sidetracked every time another body-probe machine went missing."

"I feel your pain, Jordan," Cates said, "but this is NYPD Red, and nothing is redder than whatever is troubling Mayor Sykes and/or her husband. I gave you a backup team, but you two are still on the front line till these hospital robberies are solved."

"Even if it takes time away from our primary case?" I said.

"You have *two* primary cases, Detective. What you don't have is a personal life. Do I have to say 'That's an order'? Because if I do, consider it said. Now, is there anything else I need to know?"

"We did a quiet background check on the Bassett brothers," Kylie said. "This is the fourth time they've been robbed in twenty-two years."

"The bodega in my neighborhood has been robbed four times since July," Cates said. "Give me a perspective."

"The JSA stats say there were about fifteen hundred jewelry robberies last year—about four a day," Kylie said. "So for the Bassetts to get hit four times in twenty-two years isn't enough to put up a red flag. But this robbery smacks of being an inside job, and since Leo and Max are as inside as you can get, we wanted to know more about them."

"I've met them," Cates said. "Leo is a charming old queen. Dumb with a capital Duh. He was caught in a compromising position in a men's room at a movie theater a few years ago, but that's the extent of his criminal history. If you ask me, Max is the real felon."

"His name didn't pop up in the database," I said.

"That's because our penal code turns a blind eye to what he does. Max Bassett spends millions of dollars to hunt in private compounds where exotic animals are bred so they can be legally slaughtered. African elephants, lions, rhinos, polar bears—the man has a trophy room filled with the heads and carcasses of some of the world's most endangered species."

"That's disgusting," Kylie said.

"And expensive," Cates said. "Max may be wealthy, but he doesn't have unlimited resources. If he's addicted to killing rare animals, stealing an eight-million-dollar necklace would pay for more than a few safaris."

"It sounds like a motive, boss, but Zach and I interviewed someone today who told us the Bassett brothers are about to get very, very rich very, very soon."

"Who told you that?"

"Lavinia Begbie."

"The gossip columnist?"

Kylie's phone rang. She checked the caller ID. "I think this is the call we've been waiting for. Let me take it at my desk. Zach, tell the captain what Lavinia told us."

She stepped out of the room.

"We talked to Lavinia Begbie because she was at the Bassett brothers' cocktail party the night of the murder," I said. "Leo was supposed to be in the limo with Elena, but he bailed out at the last minute, which seemed a little convenient to us. But Begbie said that Leo tripped over her dog, took a header into the buffet table, wound up covered with goop, and was in no shape to make a public appearance."

"So his alibi for not being in the limo holds up," Cates said, "but I'm much more interested in the part about the Bassetts coming into big money."

"Begbie said they're about to make a zillion-dollar deal with Precio Mundo to mass-market their brand."

"I didn't go to business school," Cates said, "but that sounds to me like winning the ultimate big-box-store lottery."

"Exactly. So why would they risk it all to steal a necklace?"

Kylie came bursting through the door. "Good news, Captain. NCIC has a lead on Annie Ryder. Zach and I have to run."

"Go," Cates said. "Keep me posted."

For the second time that day, I chased Kylie down the stairs and out the door, but this time we weren't heading off to another hospital. I was convinced that Annie Ryder was the linchpin to cracking the Travers case, and I was psyched.

"Where is Annie holed up?" I asked Kylie as I got into the car.

She put it in gear and pulled out. "I have no idea."

"What the hell are you talking about?"

"That wasn't NCIC who called me. It was Shelley Trager. His cleaning lady showed up at the corporate apartment and found Spence smoking crack with two other men."

"That phone call was about Spence? But you told Cates we just got a major break in our biggest case. Are you out of your mind?"

"Oh, I'm definitely out of my mind, Zach," she said, nearly running down a pedestrian in case I had any doubts.

"How in God's name could you lie to our boss like that?"

"Zach, she just put a freeze on personal time. How in God's name could I tell her the truth?"

"And did you think about telling *me* the truth before you dragged me into this train wreck?"

"I didn't exactly have time to come up with an elaborate game plan, Zach," she said, zipping through another red light. "Besides, you would have tried to talk me out of it, and I don't have time for that either. I need to do this, and I need you with me."

"For what?"

"You're the only one I can trust to help me talk some sense into my drug-addled husband."

"Spence's counselor specifically told you—you have to let the man hit rock bottom. You can't save him, Kylie."

Kylie almost never cries, but I could see that she was fighting to hold back the tears behind that strong MacDonald wall of resolve. She almost never curses either, but she wheeled around and hurled an f-bomb at me.

"Fuck Spence's counselor! I'm his wife. I'm also a detective first grade with the most elite police unit in this city, and I'll be damned if I'm going to sit around and watch my husband pull a ten-year stretch for crack possession."

CHAPTER 32

SHELLEY'S APARTMENT WAS only a five-minute drive from the precinct. With Kylie behind the wheel, I figured I had half that time to bring her down from DEFCON 1 to a more manageable state of hothead with a short fuse.

"Do you have a plan?" I asked.

"You know me, Zach. I'm methodical to a fault. That's why they call me the queen of departmental procedure."

"Listen to me," I said. "You're a cop. You can't just storm into the apartment—"

"I'm not storming. Shelley left me a key. What he should have done was change the lock after he put the place off limits, but he trusted Spence to play by the rules. Big mistake to trust a junkie. Spence had

155

a key, the doormen all knew him, so he apparently just waltzed right in with Marco and Seth."

"You know his drug buddies?"

"I've seen them around Silvercup. Marco works for the catering company that services Spence's productions. He's a decent guy—married, goes to meetings when he's clean—but he relapsed about a year ago and never bounced back. Seth is a total asshole. He's a kid, maybe twenty-four, went to NYU film school, works on and off as a production assistant, acts like he knows it all, and when he's hopped up, he knows even more. Neither of those two guys has enough money to feed his habit, which is why they glommed on to Spence."

"Let me repeat the question," I said as she pulled up to the building on East End Avenue. "Do you have a plan?"

"No. Do you?"

I didn't answer. My only plan was to keep her from going ballistic.

The concierge at the front desk barely looked at us. He handed Kylie a set of keys, then busied himself with paperwork. Clearly he'd spoken to Shelley.

I've been to crack houses, but never to one on the tenth floor of a luxury building with a magnificent view of the East River. The smell hit us as soon as Kylie opened the door, and while the place hadn't been destroyed like the studio sets, it looked like the aftermath of a frat party. No wonder the cleaning lady bolted. Spence had turned Shelley's multimillion-dollar corporate apartment into a three-bedroom, three-bathroom drug den.

There were two men in the living room, one sprawled on the sofa, one on the floor, neither of them Spence. Kylie and I searched the place. He was gone.

We went back to the living room. The man on the floor had managed to pull himself to a sitting position, his back against a coffee table littered with drug paraphernalia, his legs stretched out on the rug.

"You got a warrant, Detective Harrington?" he said. "Or are you just not familiar with the Fourth Amendment?"

"It's Detective MacDonald, Seth, and I'm here because the owner of this apartment reported a break-in."

"And I'm here because your crackhead husband was having a boys' night out, and he invited me over."

"I'm going to make this easy on you, Seth," Kylie said, standing over him. "Tell me where to find Spence, and I'll let you walk."

"*Let me walk?* I can walk anytime I want to. You busted in here without cause. But if you want to haul me in, fine. I'll tell the DA that the cop who arrested me is married to my drug dealer."

"I'm trying hard to be nice to you," she said, her

voice calm and composed. "Last chance, Seth. Where's Spence?"

"You want to know where Spence is? Sure thing," he said, looking up at her and spreading his legs even wider. "But first, suck my dick."

And that was all it took for the woman without a plan to come up with a brilliant strategy. She kicked him right in the balls.

Seth curled up into himself, screaming in the kind of excruciating pain that only some men have ever experienced, but all men dread.

I grabbed her just in case she thought she hadn't made her point, and for the next three minutes we watched Seth writhing on the floor, gasping for air, and fouling Shelley's hand-knotted one-of-a-kind Persian rug with vomit.

Relief came eventually, and Seth finally settled into a teary whimper.

"Marco," Kylie said to the man on the sofa, her voice barely above a whisper. "Did you see what just happened? Your friend here said, 'I can walk anytime I want to.' Does it look like he can walk?"

Marco shook his head, his eyes wide with fear. He sat up, knees pressed tight against each other, hands cupped over his nuts. "I swear on my daughter's life, I don't know where Spence went. Him and me, we're friends. I don't have a lot of money, but I always know where to get the good shit, so we make a good team."

My phone rang. I picked up.

"Did you find Annie Ryder yet?" It was Q.

"NCIC is still working on it."

"Then you were right," Q said. "I *do* have a better database than they do. Annie's back in New York. She's got a place in Astoria."

He gave me an address on Hoyt Avenue. I hung up and nodded at Kylie. "We've got a twenty on Annie."

"We're done here," she said to Marco. "Take this worthless piece of shit with you."

Marco dragged Seth to his feet and practically carried him out the door.

Kylie locked up and texted Shelley to send for a cleaning crew and a locksmith.

"Thanks," she said once we were back in the car. "I was pretty crazy when we left Cates's office. Having you there helped calm me down."

I smiled. All things considered, she had been pretty calm. But I doubted if Seth would agree.

CHAPTER 33

"ED KOCH OR Robert F. Kennedy?" Kylie asked before we pulled out into traffic.

I laughed out loud. Annie Ryder lived in Queens, and we were in Manhattan, on the opposite side of the East River. There were two ways to get across, neither of them any faster than the other. But having butted heads with me about her need to run the show, she was now turning the next critical decision over to me: which bridge to take.

"Haven't you busted enough balls for one day?" I said. "Just get me there alive."

We took the RFK.

Ryder lived on the seventh floor of a newly constructed fifteen-story tower that had been designated as affordable housing for seniors. Kylie rang the bell in the lobby.

"Ms. Ryder," she said. "NYPD. Can we ask you a few questions?"

"Only if you have identification," the voice came back. "I can't open the door unless you show me proof that you really are the police."

Kylie gave me a grin. Annie was playing the little old lady afraid to open the door for muggers. The charade continued outside her apartment until we proved that we were legit, and she finally let us in.

Annie had been charged twice with fraud, and even though nothing stuck, her picture was still in our database. But the person who opened the door looked nothing like the steely-eyed, stern-jawed, fiftysomething grifter whose mug shot I'd studied. This Annie was twenty years older, and with her gray hair pulled back in a bun and a warm crinkly smile on her face, she looked like the woman you'd cast to play the farmhouse granny in a Hallmark commercial.

"How can I help you, officers?" she asked.

"We're looking for your son, Teddy," I said.

"Then you should get in touch with his parole officer. That fella always knows where Teddy is better than his own mother," she said, capping it off with a roll of her eyes that looked like it had been lifted from a fifties sitcom.

"When did you last see him?" Kylie asked.

Annie tapped her chin and thought about it for a bit. "Oh, I remember," she said. "He came here for dinner Monday night. I made a meat loaf. Then the two of us watched TV while we had our dessert."

"What was on that night?" Kylie said, asking the standard cop follow-up question.

"Well, I love to watch the celebrities get all dolled up, so we turned on the show where they were doing live coverage of a Hollywood premiere. It was horrible. Here's me and Teddy, just sitting there eating our Chunky Monkey ice cream, watching to see who's the next one to walk down the red carpet, and all of a sudden, this limo crashes and out tumbles that poor actress who got shot."

We hadn't asked her for Teddy's alibi for Monday night, but she'd decided to get it on the record. Her bogus story had just the right amount of detail, and she wrapped it up by gracing us with a warm grandmotherly smile, which I'm sure was the exact same one she'd lay on the jury when she perjured herself on her son's behalf.

"Can you tell me what's going on that you want to talk to Teddy?" Annie said. "He's made some mistakes, but he served his time, and now he's back on the straight and narrow."

Normally, it's not a question we'd answer, but she already knew why we were there. "We're investigating a homicide," I said. "A man named Raymond Davis was shot in his apartment."

Annie covered her mouth with both hands, reeling from the horror of it all. "I hope you don't suspect Teddy. He and Raymond were best of friends. Besides, my son would never, ever hurt a soul," she said, her eyes watery. "It's how he was raised."

"Did Teddy ever talk to you about Raymond?" I asked. "Like, do you know if anyone had a grudge against him?"

"I wish I could help, but you know how boys are. Teddy never tells me anything. Always confides in his father. They had a long talk Monday night while I was fixing dinner."

Bingo. We'd finally caught her in a lie. Q had told us that Buddy Ryder was dead, and NCIC had confirmed it.

"Then maybe his father can help us out," I said. "Can we talk to him?"

She put her hand on my arm and led me over to a sideboard. "You can talk to him all you want," she said, pointing to a bronze cremation urn with Buddy Ryder's name engraved on it. "Just don't expect him to talk back."

Game, set, match.

"The envelope, please," Kylie said as soon as we got in the elevator.

"I tried," I said. "Did I even get nominated?"

"No. She played you like a grand piano. The old girl could have done her victory lap right after the

Chunky Monkey ice cream and 'that poor actress who got shot.'"

"I know. She had all the right answers before we even asked the questions."

"Mothers lie, Zach. And Annie Ryder does it better than most."

CHAPTER 34

WE GOT BACK to the precinct three hours after we left Cates's office pretending to be in hot pursuit of Annie Ryder.

"The captain is probably wondering why we've been gone so long," Kylie said, giving me an impish grin.

Our side trip to Shelley's apartment and Kylie's throw-down with Spence's stoner buddies had wasted a serious chunk of time, and the grin was to let me know that she didn't care.

"I need five minutes before we go to her office," I said, heading up the stairs.

"What's more important than debriefing Cates?"

"Salvaging my relationship with Cheryl."

"Bad idea. Cates put a freeze on personal time," she said, giving me another grin.

I gave her the finger and double-timed my way up the stairs to Cheryl's office. She wasn't in. I bounded up another flight of stairs and got to Cates's office just a few steps behind Kylie.

Cates was in the middle of a meeting, but she dropped everything as soon as she saw us. I'm sure she said something, but I didn't process a single word. I just stood in the doorway staring at the three other people sitting in the room. Our backup team, Betancourt and Torres, and, next to them, Cheryl.

She gave me half a smile. On closer inspection, it looked more like half a frown. I eased my way into the room as Kylie gave Cates a top line summary of our visit to Annie Ryder.

"She definitely knows where Teddy is," Kylie said, "but she's too smart to lead us to him."

"I'll post a team outside her apartment anyway," Cates said. "Any intel is better than nothing at all."

"Thanks," Kylie said.

"Glad you got here," Cates said. "We've been running down where we are on the hospital robberies. Torres, catch them up."

"Lynn Lyon hasn't been anywhere near a hospital since we started tailing her," Torres said. "She's onto us."

"She's not onto *us*," Betancourt corrected. "She

knows that her cover is blown, and whoever she's working for knows it. Her scouting days are over."

"So now what?" Kylie said. "We can't wait for them to hit another hospital and hope they trip up."

"We *are* going to wait for them to hit another hospital," Cates said. "But we're going to be inside the hospital waiting for them to show up."

"There are over a hundred major medical facilities in the five boroughs," Kylie said. "We can't cover all of them."

"We only have to be at one, and Cheryl has an idea on how to zero in on the right one. I'll let her spell it out for you."

It was a sting, and a damn good one. It took Cheryl less than a minute to lay it out.

"I love it," Kylie said, "but we can't do it without Howard Sykes on board."

"Then talk to him and get back to me," Cates said. "This meeting is over."

The group broke up, and Cheryl walked past me and down the hall.

I followed. "Cheryl, can we talk?"

She let one hand sweep across the wide-open squad room filled with cop eyes and cop ears. "This is not the right place for a conversation, Zach."

"I just need to say six words."

"Fine." She gestured for me to follow her. She opened the door and started down the stairs. I thought we were going to her office, but after half a flight, she stopped, and the two of us stood in the empty stairwell. This was as much privacy as I was going to get.

"Six words," she said.

I took a deep breath and looked into her eyes. "I'm wrong. You're right. I'm sorry."

My father had taught me those words when I was seventeen, after I'd had a huge argument with my girlfriend the day before our senior prom. It had worked like gangbusters on my prom date, but it definitely wasn't flying with Cheryl.

"Is that it?" she said.

"No. An apology is just the beginning. I want to talk about what happened and then prove to you that it won't happen again."

"We can't exactly do that here," she said, pointing at the grimy gray stairs and the city-mandated fire hose hanging on the wall.

"I was thinking dinner."

"I hope you don't expect me to cook," she said.

"No, I thought I could nuke us something nice."

She cracked a smile.

"Or Gerri's Diner," I said.

The smile got wider.

"Okay. My last shot: Paola's," I said, throwing out the name of her favorite restaurant. "I can call Stefano and ask them to bake me a humble pie for dessert."

The smile exploded into an eye-rolling, this-guy-is-incorrigible laugh.

"Seven o'clock," she said. "Pick me up in my office."

She headed down to the second floor, and I went back up to the third. I wouldn't be sleeping on the sofa tonight.

CHAPTER 35

JEREMY NEVINS HAD never killed anyone before, but shooting Raymond Davis didn't faze him a bit. The arrogant bastard had it coming. First he'd botched Jeremy's biggest score, and then he'd had the balls to demand more money.

Jeremy was at a table in the Recovery Room, a plate of half-eaten Buffalo chicken wings and an untouched mug of Stella Artois in front of him. He wasn't hungry, but he needed the real estate and the Wi-Fi, and no place was deader than a sports bar at three in the afternoon. *Correction,* he thought, looking down at his eighty-thousand-dollar Audemars Piguet watch: 3:01.

The watch had been a gift—more like a signing bonus. But with an eight-million-dollar pot of diamonds at the end of the rainbow, Jeremy would have signed on for a Timex.

The plan had been perfect until Leo, his self-obsessed partner in crime, decided not to get in the limo because he didn't *look right.*

So now Elena was dead, the necklace was in the wind, and Jeremy was on his own, trying to formulate plan B.

He didn't know where the necklace was, but he was pretty sure he knew who had it: Teddy Ryder's mother. He'd never met Teddy until last night, but he knew all about him. The man had never had an original thought in his life, and now that he was wounded and scared, he'd go running home to Mama.

And Jeremy knew exactly where to find her. When you plan a crime with a scumbag like Raymond Davis, you hedge your bets. Jeremy had attached a GPS tracker to the underside of Raymond's Honda Civic just in case he decided to take the necklace and drive off with it.

But the GPS had paid off even sooner. In the week leading up to the robbery, the car made two round-trips from Teddy's apartment to Hoyt Avenue in Astoria. Jeremy's antennae went up, so on the third day he tailed the Honda to Annie Ryder's doorstep.

He knew the old con woman's history, and he knew that pulling a gun on her wouldn't produce the necklace. The only way to get it was to cut her a deal, and then get Leo to pay her price.

He tapped on his cell phone and searched Google News. There was nothing on the shooting of Raymond Davis. Either the cops made him for just another crime statistic not worth the ink, or they figured out the connection to Elena Travers and put a lid on it.

The phone vibrated in his hand, and he flinched. It was Sonia Chen. He had no desire to talk to her, but she was too connected to the Bassetts: he couldn't ignore the call.

"Hey, baby," he whispered into the phone. "How's the world's sexiest publicist?"

"Terrible. Come on over to my apartment."

"Honey, I'm busy."

"Just for an hour. Please."

"Sonia, I'm horny too, but—"

"Don't be an asshole, Jeremy. I didn't say horny. I'm scared. I'm lonely. I can't sleep. I've never been involved in anything like this. Elena's dead, and I keep thinking maybe if I made Leo go in the car with her—"

"Sonia, I'm sorry. But don't blame yourself. What happened is sad, but it wasn't your fault. It just happened."

He waited for a response. Nothing.

"Sonia…does that help, baby?"

"It would help a lot more if you came over here

and said it in person," she said, capping the plea with a loud sigh. "Just for a little while. I really don't want to be alone. Please."

Without Sonia Chen, Jeremy never would have met Leo Bassett. He didn't need her anymore, but if there's one thing he'd learned stalking prey in the valley of the rich and gullible, it was to never, ever burn bridges.

He looked at his watch. *How pathetic that your wrist is worth a fortune,* it said, *but the rest of you still isn't worth shit.*

"Of course I'll be there, baby," he said. "I'll be right over."

His face-to-face with Annie Ryder would have to wait.

CHAPTER 36

ANY WOMAN WHO *tells a man she wants to be cuddled and not fucked is either lying to herself or to the guy, or both,* Jeremy thought after he'd brought Sonia to her third frenzied orgasm in an hour and a half.

The first one had left her in tears, and he held her in his arms while she sobbed for the dead actress. The second one was much more joyful, like a good old-fashioned, no-strings-attached romp in the sack. The final one was slower, more tender at first. He took his time, teasing her with his tongue, lulling her with gentle kisses, sliding her down onto his lap, and keeping up with her gentle undulating rhythm.

And just as she began to slow down, he lifted her

up, and with her legs wrapped tightly around him, he pressed her against a wall with deep, hard, unremitting thrusts until the moans of "Don't stop" exploded into cries of surrender.

Another satisfied customer, Jeremy thought as he showered. Everybody was good at something, and he'd been blessed with the equipment and the technique to drive a lover to insane new heights.

In the end, not all of them remembered him fondly. Some despised him. Some wished him dead. But none of them would ever forget him.

Sadly, none of that charm or sexual prowess would serve him well in his next encounter. All anyone needed to go up against Annie Ryder was cunning. And he knew enough about her to know that she had more than most.

And yet when the gray-haired woman opened the door to her apartment, Jeremy couldn't help himself. "You're much younger than I expected," he said, reverting to habit.

"And you're every bit as full of shit as I expected," the old lady said, ushering him into the living room. "Have a seat."

He sat down on a rose-colored sofa, and she sat next to him, practically knee to knee. "You called me," she said. "What's on your mind?"

"Your son has my necklace."

"*Your* necklace?" Annie said. "You and I must not be on the same page, because the necklace all the

TV reporters are talking about belongs to these two Bassett brothers."

"It did. But I hired your son and his friend to procure it for me, and they reneged on their part of the deal."

Annie smiled. "And from what I understand, according to the Book of Jeremy, the punishment for reneging is a bullet through the brain."

"That was an unfortunate misunderstanding."

"What about shooting my son? Was that another unfortunate misunderstanding?"

"Mrs. Ryder—"

She rested her fingers on the back of his hand. "Please...call me Annie."

"Can we cut the crap, Annie?" he said, pulling his hand away and standing up. "I'm not one of your marks. I'm the guy who hired Raymond and Teddy to do a simple job, and they turned it into a page-one clusterfuck. Here's the bottom line: you've got the hottest piece of jewelry on the planet, and there's not a fence within three thousand miles that will handle the necklace Elena Travers died for. So unless you're wired up to the diamond mob in Antwerp or Amsterdam, you can either sell it to me or you can wear it to your next tea party and watch the rest of the old ladies wet their—"

"Get out," Annie said.

"What?"

"You heard me," she said, standing. "Get out, you

foulmouthed, disrespectful little snot. Get out before I call the cops."

"Look, I'm sorry about the language. All I want is the necklace."

"I don't have any necklace, and even if I did, I wouldn't sell it to a bad-mannered, ill-bred punk." She reached into her pocket and pulled out a small cylinder. "This is pepper spray. I've used it before, and I'll use it again. Out."

She opened the door and watched as Jeremy backed out. Then she locked it behind him.

Teddy came out of the bedroom. "Ma, you were awesome, but now we're never going to sell the necklace."

"Of course we will."

"To who?"

"Your good buddy Jeremy. He'll be back, and next time he shows up, he'll show me a little more respect."

"You think he'll be back?"

"Not back here, but he'll call me in less than an hour. Guaranteed."

"You are the coolest mom in the world."

"Thank you, sweetheart. How are you feeling? Still sore?"

"It hurts, but no big deal."

"Can I get you anything? You want some tea?"

"Sure."

Annie filled the teakettle and then set it on the

stove. Then she went to a cabinet and took down a tin of cookies.

"Hey, Ma, can I ask you one question?" Teddy said.

"Anything."

"Isn't pepper spray like a weapon?"

"It's for self-defense, but technically pepper spray can be a dangerous weapon."

"But you have a thing about no weapons, so how come you have pepper spray in your pocket?"

Annie took out the cylinder. "You mean this?" she said, holding it up.

Teddy grinned. "I got you now, Ma. How you gonna talk your way out of this one?"

Annie pointed the cylinder directly at her face, pressed the button, and sprayed it into her mouth.

"Breath freshener," she said. "Wintergreen. Any more questions?"

CHAPTER 37

"GO NEXT DOOR and take a nap," Annie instructed her son after they'd finished their tea and cookies.

"Aw, Ma," Teddy whined. "That place stinks like cat. Why can't I just stay here?"

"Because this place stinks like cop. There were two detectives here this morning. What do I do if they come banging on my door with a warrant? Tell them to come back in five minutes so I can tidy up?"

"Fine," Teddy said, sulking. "What are you going to do?"

"I've got a date," she said, her eyes smiling. "Now get out of here while I make myself as beautiful as I possibly can, considering what I've got to work with."

She opened the door, scouted the hallway, gave

Teddy the high sign, and he scurried to the adjacent apartment in seconds.

Then she went to the bedroom, opened the closet, and looked at herself in the full-length mirror. She frowned. "Needs work," she said.

So she got to work. Makeup first, hair next, and then she slipped into a seldom-worn but totally chic Carolina Herrera black cocktail dress. A pair of sensible heels, two dabs of perfume, and finally, her hands a little shaky, she put the emerald and diamond necklace around her neck.

She went back to the closet door for a second look. "Mirror, mirror on the wall," she said. "Who looks like eight million bucks now?"

She walked to the living room and stood in front of her late husband. "What do you think, Buddy?" she said, doing a full twirl. "It normally costs three thousand, but you know what a smart shopper I am. I got it for a steal at Bergdorf's."

She laughed out loud, and she could practically hear him laughing with her. She took the urn from the sideboard, set it on the kitchen table, and sat down across from it.

"I'm in over my head, Buddy," she said. "I could use some advice."

She placed a hand on either side of the urn and closed her eyes.

"The newspaper says this little bauble is worth eight mil, but I don't know beans about fencing jewelry. What do you think this Jeremy guy can get for it? Forty cents on the dollar?"

Buddy didn't respond.

"Thirty cents? Twenty-five?"

Her palms warmed when she got to fifteen. They tingled when she got to twelve.

"So if he's getting a million out of the deal, what should my cut be?"

She ran through some numbers again until the two of them zeroed in on 17½ percent.

Then they talked. Mostly about Teddy, because he was always their biggest issue, and finally she apologized for not keeping her promise. Buddy had asked her to spread his ashes up and down the Strip in Vegas, and Annie had agreed. She just hadn't said when.

"There'll be plenty of time for Teddy to spread us both. In the meantime, I need you around."

She sat there for ten more minutes, the urn cradled in her hands, until the phone rang. She put it on speaker so Buddy could hear.

"Mrs. Ryder. It's Jeremy. Look, I'm sorry. We got off on the wrong foot. Can we talk?"

"You can talk," Annie said. "I can listen."

"I originally hired Teddy and Raymond for fifty thousand. Then I upped it to ninety. I'll give you one and a quarter."

"One seventy-five," Annie said. "Take it or—"

"I'll take it," Jeremy said. "But I need time to pull

the money together. How about if I come over to-morrow around noon?"

"Good idea. Bring some chloroform and an empty trunk. What am I, stupid? This either goes down in a public place or it doesn't go down at all."

"Okay, okay. What about Central Park?"

"Jeremy, old ladies *without* any jewelry get mugged in Central Park. Meet me at 205 East Houston Street at noon."

He repeated the address. "What's there?" he asked.

"Your necklace," she said, hanging up.

She removed it from around her neck, wrapped it in an empty plastic bag from CVS, took the top off the urn, and dropped the bag inside.

"Keep an eye on this for me, Buddy," she said. "You're the only one I trust."

CHAPTER 38

"IT LOOKED LIKE you connected with Cheryl after our meeting with Cates," Kylie said, navigating the car through the usual Third Avenue rush hour logjam. We were on our way to talk to Howard Sykes at Gracie Mansion. "Did you two lovebirds finally cement the relationship?"

"*Connected* would be an overstatement," I said. "We had a brief encounter, like two ships in the night, only we were two cops on a stairwell. *Cement* is an even bigger stretch. Right now, our relationship is being held together by static cling. As for *lovebirds...*"

"I get it, I get it," Kylie said, hanging a right on 88th Street. "I'm sorry I asked."

"Don't apologize. I'm happy to have someone to

dump it on. You were right this morning about me licking my wounds. By the time I got home last night, I was relegated to the sofa, and I didn't get to see Cheryl till this afternoon. And you can't do what I have to do in a house full of nosy cops, so I'm going to try to make reparations tonight over dinner at Paola's."

"And are you telling me all this because you think I'm hooked on the soap opera you call your love life? Or is it your not-so-subtle way of telling me not to call you tonight because you're busy doing damage control?"

"What do you think, Detective?" I said.

"My finely tuned detective instincts tell me that if you're wining and dining Cheryl at Paola's, she definitely won't break up with you *before* dinner."

We crossed East End Avenue, pulled into the mayor's driveway, and ID'd ourselves at the guardhouse. An aide escorted us into Howard's study. I cut straight to the chase.

"Sir," I said, "we have thirty-five thousand cops at our disposal. That's more than enough manpower to station a unit at every single hospital in the five boroughs and wait for this gang to strike again. But..." I let it hang there.

"But," he said, filling in the blank, "you can't mobilize that many people and still expect to keep a crime wave of this magnitude under wraps."

"Exactly."

"I've worked with you two long enough to know you didn't come here to ask me to take the lid off this operation," he said. "You have a plan, don't you?"

"Actually," Kylie said, "our department shrink, Dr. Cheryl Robinson, came up with it. Zach and I like it, but we can't pull it off without a lot of help from you."

"What can I do?"

"We need you to help us set up the next robbery."

"You...you want me to help you rob a hospital?"

"No, sir. We want you to help *them* rob a hospital, but we'll be there waiting for them."

"Jesus," he said. "Maybe I watch too many crime shows on TV, but I thought I'd tell you detectives the problem, you'd dig up some clues, and then you'd track these bastards down."

"These bastards don't leave a lot of clues," I said.

"And which of our city's fine medical institutions have you selected to be the designated victim?"

"If you can convince them," I said, "Hudson Hospital."

"How'd they get so lucky?"

"Two reasons. First, there's the safety factor. These thugs are well armed. So far they haven't used their guns, but if they walk into a trap and they're faced with a SWAT team, they may not give up without a fight. Hudson is in the middle of a renovation, and we can contain the operation to the two floors where there are no patients or staff."

"And the other reason?"

"We think Hudson has something they want," Kylie said.

"They've stolen anything and everything," Howard said. "Their philosophy seems to be, if it's not nailed down, take it. How could you possibly know what they want?"

"Dr. Robinson did an analysis, and they're being much more selective than we originally thought. They've never stolen the same equipment twice."

He shrugged. "So? Stealing is stealing."

"There are nuances," Kylie said. "If somebody breaks into a department store and steals a rack of fifty fur coats, odds are those coats are going to wind up on the black market. But what if he breaks into the same store and takes two coats, six dresses, a few pantsuits, five pair of shoes—"

"It sounds like he's shopping for his wife," Howard said.

"Exactly. These guys are taking two of these, three of those, one of this. Dr. Robinson's theory is that they are slowly collecting inventory for a single medical facility."

"Jesus," he said. "You think they're stocking their own hospital?"

"Yes, but they still don't have everything they need."

"What do you think they'll be shopping for?"

"Dr. Robinson calculated that based on the medical needs of a large percentage of the population, and based on the prohibitive cost of the diagnostic equipment, they would be very tempted to go after a state-of-the-art mobile mammogram machine," Kylie said.

"And Hudson Hospital just bought two of them," I said.

"I know their CEO, Phil Landsberg," Howard said.

"And we know their head of security, Frank Cavallaro," I said.

Howard Sykes sat back in his chair and rubbed his temples with his fingertips. He closed his eyes for at least fifteen seconds and finally looked up. "Do you think you can actually pull this off?"

"Not without you on board," I said. "What do *you* think, sir? Can you help us?"

"What do I think? I think it's nuts. Totally, certifiably crazy," he said. "But I'll call Phil Landsberg in the morning and see if I can convince him to join us in our insanity."

CHAPTER 39

JEREMY NEVINS, WEARING nothing but a pair of black bikini briefs, padded across the room and explored the contents of the hotel minibar. "Do you believe the prices on this shit?" he said. "A jar of macadamia nuts and a bottle of Heineken cost more than my first car."

Leo Bassett, lying naked under the sheets, laughed and stared at the sinewy, sculpted, perfect thirty-two-year-old body standing only ten feet away.

Spending Wednesday nights in the penthouse suite at Morgans with Jeremy had become a tradition, their private little escape from the rest of the world. And with Elena's death, the robbery gone bad, and Max's craziness about selling the company name, Leo had more to escape from than usual.

"What are you thinking?" Jeremy said, popping the cap on the beer.

"How much I love you, and how much I hate Max."

"I love you too. And Max isn't so bad."

"He's insane. He wants to sell our soul to the devil. He's going to turn the Bassett brand into McDonald's."

"That would be terrible," Jeremy said. He took a macadamia nut out of the jar and seductively set it onto his tongue before easing it into his mouth. "And think of the fallout. You'd make jillions of dollars. Maybe zillions. I don't know. I'm not good at math."

"I don't care how much I can make. The name Bassett stands for the ultimate in luxury. When I introduce myself, I can see the look in people's eyes. It's as if I said my name is Tiffany or Bulgari. Do you have any idea how good that makes me feel?"

Jeremy gave him a boyish pout. "I thought making you feel good was my job," he said, setting down the beer and striking a pose.

Leo squirmed under the sheets. "Yes, it is, and you're late for work."

Jeremy tucked two fingers into his briefs' elastic waistband, licked his lips, and slowly, tantalizingly, lowered the front of the briefs.

Leo's eyes were wide, and his breathing was shallow.

They all love a good show, Jeremy thought, *and Leo is a better audience than most.*

"But first," Jeremy said, letting the waistband snap back into place, "we have some business to attend to. I found the necklace."

Leo sat up. "Are you serious? Why did you wait until now to tell me?"

"I was waiting for you to be in a receptive mood, and from where I'm standing, you look pretty damn receptive."

"Who has it?"

"The same guy who ran off with it last night—Teddy Ryder. Only he gave it to his mother, and let me tell you, Leo, this broad looks like that little old lady from *The Golden Girls,* but boy, can she play hardball. She negotiates like the head of the Teamsters union."

"How much does she want?"

"A hundred and seventy-five K."

Leo shrugged. "It's more than we've paid in the past, but it's still a drop in the bucket. We'll collect the eight million from the insurance company, and even though Max has to cut the big stones down, they'll still be worth five, six mil."

"That's what I thought you'd say, so I told her we had a deal. I have the ninety you gave me. I just need another eighty-five thousand in cash before noon tomorrow."

"No problem," Leo said. "Just don't run away with it."

"Don't worry, sweetheart. Even though you claim not to care about becoming a zillionaire, I promise I won't run away with your money."

He was being honest. Annie Ryder would wind up with the hundred and seventy-five thousand. All Jeremy wanted was the necklace. He didn't need Max to recut the stones. He had a diamond cutter lined up in Belgium and was booked on a KLM flight to Brussels tomorrow night.

"What do you think?" Jeremy said. "Enough business for one night?"

"More than enough."

Jeremy picked up the remote to the stereo, turned up the music, and spent the next five minutes artfully shedding a few ounces of nylon and spandex. When the dance was over, he stood in the middle of the room, gloriously naked and heart-stoppingly desirable.

Leo pulled back the sheets. "Come to Papa, baby."

Jeremy crawled into bed, and the fat, pasty man pulled him close, shoved a thick tongue into his mouth, and reached down between his legs.

Jeremy moaned convincingly. It was all in a day's work.

CHAPTER 40

THERE ARE THREE reasons why I love Paola's restaurant. First, there's the incomparable Italian cuisine that Paola Bottero brought to America from Rome.

Second is the unabashed hospitality that greets me every time I walk through the door. Tonight was no different. Paola's son, Stefano, welcomed us with an enthusiastic *"Buona sera,* Dr. Robinson, Signor Jordan" and warm hugs that made me feel like we weren't customers but friends invited over for dinner.

And third, it's my go-to place to bring a date after I've made a fool of myself.

"You're nothing if not predictable," Cheryl said after we'd been seated and our wine had been poured. "Every time you and I have come here, it's been for dinner and an apology."

"There's a method to my madness," I said. "If you dump me, at least I still get a great dinner out of it."

"I'm not going to dump you. I love being with you. I'm just not sure I can handle living with you."

"I'm sorry. I really screwed up last night."

"I'm not sure you screwed up. I think you were just Zach being Zach."

"But it's not the Zach you deserve. You planned this fantastic evening, and when the phone rang, I walked out on you."

"Ran out."

"In my head, I kept thinking, 'You're a cop. This is what cops do.' But it wasn't a cop call. It was…"

I stopped. This was tougher than I thought, and I was afraid I was going to make matters even worse.

"It was what?" Cheryl said.

I drank some wine. "This morning I went to the diner, and I told Gerri what I did. Her immediate reaction was, 'Why did you walk—' Sorry. 'Why did you *run* out?' And I said, 'That's what I do whenever there's a damsel in distress.'"

Cheryl laughed.

"Well, at least *you're* laughing," I said. "Gerri went batshit. She told me Kylie was definitely not a damsel in distress. And she's right. Kylie can handle herself. She kicked a guy in the balls today. The poor bastard probably won't walk straight for a week."

"I agree with Dr. Gerri. Kylie can fend for herself."

"Anyway, I thought about it, so this afternoon, when I had five minutes, I googled 'Men who try to rescue women.' I've got what you psychologists call the White Knight Syndrome."

"Oh, for God's sake, Zach. No, you don't."

"I don't?"

"Absolutely not. Would you like my professional opinion?"

"Hell yeah."

"Instead of googling everything that troubles you and then accepting as gospel whatever some idiot blogged about on the Internet, why don't you talk your problems out with a shrink?"

"I'm in luck. I've got one right here."

"Fat chance. You're going to have to find one you haven't slept with."

"Hmm...that's going to be a challenge."

She dipped two fingers in her water glass and flicked it at me. "This conversation is officially over. Let's talk about some fun stuff—like what did Howard Sykes think about my idea?"

"Nervous, but willing. Can I just say one more thing on the topic you don't want to talk about?"

"One, and that's it."

"I just want you to know I'm trying. I told Kylie we were going out to dinner and not to call me. I figured if I were trying to lose weight, I wouldn't stock the house with Oreos and Häagen-Dazs ice cream. Same principle. Out of sight, out of mind."

She didn't say a word. This time, the conversation *was* officially over.

For the next hour, we ate, we drank, we laughed, we talked—dinner was everything I could have hoped for. We were both too full to order dessert, but that didn't stop Paola from sending a mind-blowing lemon tart to our table and then joining us for five minutes to catch up on how we were doing.

As of that moment, we were doing just fine.

And then my cell rang. I looked at the caller ID, hit Decline, and shoved the phone back into my pocket.

"Who was it?" Cheryl asked.

"It was Kylie, but I'm not accepting calls from damsels in distress this evening."

Cheryl laughed. "Are you serious? Was it really Kylie? After you told her not to call?"

"Looks like I'm not the only one who needs a shrink," I said.

Our waiter was just bringing me the check when Cheryl's phone rang. She took one look at the caller ID, and her expression changed. This was a serious call. She answered.

I could only hear her side of the conversation. She didn't say much, but the few words she did manage to get out sounded ominous.

"Oh no. Are they sure? Oh God, I am so sorry."

And finally, "Zach and I are at 92nd Street and Madison. Pick us up. We're going with you."

She hung up, and tears were streaming down her face. "That was Kylie," she said. "She just got a phone call from the captain of the Four Four in the Bronx."

"Jesus. What happened?"

"They found Spence's body in a vacant lot. He was shot through the head."

PART THREE

SOME DAYS ARE DIAMONDS.

SOME DAYS ARE STONES.

CHAPTER 41

"ANY DETAILS?" I asked.

"Bare bones," Cheryl said. "Anonymous tip to 911. First cop on the scene was able to ID Spence—his wallet was on the ground. No cash, but his emergency contact said 'Wife: NYPD Detective Kylie MacDonald.' That kicked the system into high gear. It's like 'officer down' once removed. That's all I know except that Kylie is on the way to identify the body."

"God, I hope she's not driving."

"She's not that crazy, and even if she tried, no one is crazy enough to let her."

We were on the corner of Nine Two and Madison, and I stepped off the curb to get a better look down the avenue. Flashing lights about a mile away. No sirens, but moving fast.

"Here they come," I said to Cheryl. "I don't know

when I'll be home, but I'll text you and keep you posted."

"*Text me?*" she said, her voice suddenly sharp. "Zach, where's your head? I'm going with you."

That threw me. "Cheryl, it's a crime scene. Since when does—"

"*Since when?* A police officer's husband was murdered. It's *my job* to evaluate Kylie to determine whether or not she's fit for duty, and having done this far too many times in the past, I can tell you my best guess: she's not."

"Sorry," I said. "We're all in shock. I wasn't thinking straight."

She didn't say a word, and I wondered if I'd just undone the last two hours of brilliant fence-mending with one dumb remark.

The convoy pulled up: two squad cars followed by a Ford van, then another two squad cars. The van stopped directly in front of us, and a uniform jumped out and slid the door open. I climbed into the back, and Cheryl sat in the center row next to Kylie. She'd been crying, and Cheryl put a comforting arm around her, although I wondered how much comfort was possible.

"It's my fault," Kylie said as soon as we started rolling. "I should never have kicked him out of the apartment."

"You didn't kick him out," Cheryl said. "You checked him into rehab."

Kylie shook her head. "It was a day program. I could have let him live at home."

"Do you really think that would have made a difference?" Cheryl said, her voice consoling and without a trace of judgment. "Addicts put their lives at risk every day—it's what they do. No one can stop them, and when it ends in tragedy, it's never anybody's fault but their own. I know you know that."

Kylie nodded her head and whispered "Thank you." Cheryl took a quick look over her shoulder and made eye contact with me just in case I still didn't understand why she was along for the ride.

The traffic was thin, and the ribbon of strobe lights quickly scattered everyone in our path as we sped through Spanish Harlem and over the Madison Avenue Bridge into the southern tip of our city's most ravaged borough.

Back in the seventies, the South Bronx was the epicenter of murder, rape, robbery, and arson in the U.S., and the cry *"The Bronx is burning"* was heard across America. Today, many of the burned-out buildings have been replaced, but with half the population living below the poverty line, the area is still a magnet for gangs, drug peddlers, and violent crime.

As we turned onto East 163rd Street, I thought about all the "safer places" in the city to cop drugs, and I wondered what drew a white-collar junkie to the dark, unwelcoming streets here in the shadow of Yankee Stadium.

And then Cheryl's words echoed in my brain. *"Addicts put their lives at risk every day—it's what they do."* Spence Harrington had done it once too often.

The van pulled to a stop, the door opened, and a tall man in an NYPD windbreaker introduced himself to Kylie. "Detective Peter Varhol," he said. "I'm sorry for your loss, Detective MacDonald."

He led the way to the crime scene. Kylie and I had seen it many times before: a fetid patch of ground in the bowels of the city, a drug buy gone bad, a body lying under a sheet. Some cops say they're immune to it, but for me it's always gut-wrenching. Only this time it was personal.

Cheryl and I stood back a respectful distance and let Kylie approach the body. A technician pulled back the sheet, and she fell to her knees. Within seconds she slumped over, and her body heaved with sobs.

Cheryl moved closer, knelt beside her, crossed herself, and then stood up abruptly. "Zach," she said, her head motioning toward the corpse.

I stepped forward and dropped to my knees next to Kylie. The man on the ground had a blood-caked hole in the middle of his forehead. His eyes were wide-open, a look of utter disbelief frozen on his face.

He was dead. Murdered in cold blood. But he wasn't Spence.

CHAPTER 42

"FIRST BODY I ever called wrong," Detective Varhol said to Kylie. "You must think I'm an idiot."

"It's not your fault," Kylie said. "The first responder saw my name in Spence's wallet. I got the call before you were even on the scene."

"I know, but the cop who ID'd the body is a rookie," Varhol said. "And the vic looks enough like the picture on your husband's driver's license that it's an easy mistake to make, but damn, once I got here, I should have taken a closer look."

It was a much bigger mea culpa than the situation called for. I was thinking what a stand-up guy Varhol was when he smoothly shifted gears. "You recognize him, don't you?" he said.

Kylie hadn't volunteered the victim's name, but

Varhol had good cop instincts, and he'd disarmed her just enough to catch her off guard.

Withholding information is one thing. Lying is another. Kylie owned up. "His first name is Marco. I don't know his last name. My husband is a TV producer, and Marco worked for the catering company that services Spence's productions."

Varhol waited for more, but that was all she was going to give up.

"Detective MacDonald," he said, "this was a drug deal gone south. If your husband is using, that's your problem. My problem is that I have a homicide to solve, and I need all the help I can get."

Kylie filled him in on what we found at Shelley's apartment.

"And this kid Seth," Varhol said. "Do you know his last name?"

"No."

"Any idea how I can track him down?"

"He works at Silvercup Studios. Why don't you swing by there first thing in the morning? They usually gear up by seven."

"The morning," Varhol repeated.

"Please," Kylie said.

Varhol looked at his watch. "It's ten thirty. I guess I could wait until morning."

Anyone listening to their conversation would have taken them for two cops talking logistics, but I knew enough to read the subtext.

Seth might have information that could lead to the killer, and Varhol wanted to interview him immediately. Kylie also wanted to talk to Seth, because he might lead her to Spence. But she wasn't connected to the case or the official investigation, so Varhol gave her until seven a.m. to do what she always does: bend the rules.

"Thanks," she said.

"And when you find your husband," he said, "give me a call. I have his wallet, and I'd like to know how it wound up in a dead man's pocket."

He walked off to talk with his crime scene tech, leaving me, Kylie, and Cheryl to talk in private.

"We have to find Seth and talk to him tonight," Kylie said.

"We can start by calling Shelley Trager," I said.

"No. He's gone through enough hell with Spence. Let's call Bob Reitzfeld. He can access the employee database, and he can keep a secret."

"Who's Bob Reitzfeld?" Cheryl asked.

"He was on the job thirty years," I said. "Great cop, but he couldn't handle retirement, so he got a job in security at Silvercup at fifteen bucks an hour. Now he's running the department. Kylie is right. Reitzfeld can help us."

Cheryl looked at Kylie. "Are you sure you're up to it?"

"I know why you're here, Dr. Robinson," Kylie said. "If that were Spence lying on the ground, you would take me out of the line of fire and chain me to a desk, and I wouldn't argue with you. But it's not Spence, so believe me when I tell you I'm okay—totally okay."

Cheryl nodded. "In that case, I don't want to slow you down." She looked at me. "Either of you."

"What are you going to do?" I said.

"Me?" she said, managing to look innocent and devilish at the same time. "This place is crawling with cops. I'm going to find the best-looking one and catch a ride into Manhattan."

"So, then I'll see you at home," I said.

She gave me half a shrug. "If you're lucky."

CHAPTER 43

I CALLED BOB Reitzfeld at home.

"Damn," he said when I told him about Marco. "I liked him, but the son of a bitch was a toe tag waiting to happen. I'm glad it's not Spence."

"Do you know this kid Seth?"

"Seth Penzig," he said. "Him I don't like."

"So far I haven't met anyone who does. Why doesn't the studio fire him?"

He laughed. "For a smart cop, Zach, you can ask some dumb questions. It's show business. If they got rid of all the assholes and the snow snorters, there'd be no show and no business. Hey, Spence destroyed two sets, but you can bet he'll be invited back as soon as he cleans up his act."

"First we have to find him, and to do that, we have

to find Seth. Can you help us track him down? We don't have a lot of time."

"I pulled up his home address while you were talking," he said. "Six three one Thirty-Ninth Avenue in Woodside. Fast enough for you?"

I thanked him and had the van drive me and Kylie to Queens. It was a working-class neighborhood a few miles from Silvercup. Seth's apartment was on the second floor, over a nail salon.

We rang the bell and were buzzed in, no questions asked.

"He didn't even ask who it is," Kylie said. "He must be expecting some sort of delivery."

Whatever Seth was expecting, it wasn't us. He opened the door, took one look, and tried to slam it shut. But Kylie pushed it in his face, and he teetered backward into his apartment.

"You got no cause," he said. "I didn't do anything wrong."

"The place reeks of marijuana," Kylie said, "which gives us plenty of cause, and which, according to part 3, title M, article 221 of the New York penal code, is not only wrong but highly illegal. And that bong on the table isn't going to help your case."

She took a step toward him, and Seth cupped his hands over his balls.

"But don't worry, I'm going to overlook the drug abuse," she said, "because your buddy Marco was shot tonight, and you've been upgraded from crack-head to murder suspect."

Whatever cockiness Seth had in reserve went out the window. He sat down on the edge of a coffee table that was scarred with roach burns and shook his head. "Marco was my friend. I didn't shoot him. I don't even have a gun."

"How about an alibi? Do you have one of those?" Kylie demanded. "Where did you and Marco go after he helped you hobble out of Shelley Trager's apartment this morning?"

"Starbucks. We were having coffee, and Spence called me. Told us to meet him in a hotel."

"Which one?"

"I don't know if it even has a name. It's one of those flophouses down on the Bowery where you can rent by the hour."

"That doesn't sound like Spence's style," Kylie said.

"That was the point. He didn't want to go where anyone might recognize him."

"What happened when you got to the hotel?"

"Spence had some blow, but it turned out to be crap—cut with baby-formula powder. Marco said he knew about this good shit he could get up in the Bronx. Colombian—95 percent pure. Spence wanted it bad. Said he'd buy if Marco would score it for him. Marco said, 'It's pricey. How much cash you got?'

"Spence was pretty wasted by then, so he just takes his wallet out of his pocket and says, 'Take it all, and don't come back empty-handed.' Marco says, 'This dude doesn't take plastic,' so he dumps out Spence's credit cards, puts the wallet in his pocket, and takes off. That's the last I ever saw him. I swear."

"And what about Spence?"

"Your husband is crazy, lady. After half an hour, he was climbing the walls. Couldn't wait for Marco to get back. Said he's going down to the meatpacking district. He's got VIP status in one of the clubs. Tells me to call him when Marco shows up."

"And then what?"

"I waited two hours. No Marco. I figured he scored the dope, and it's up his nose by now. And no Spence, because, hell, he's got an Amex Platinum card, so he's probably sucking down five-hundred-dollar bottles of Grey Goose. I bailed, took the subway to Queens, and stopped for a twelve-pack at the bodega around nine, so I got a witness who can tell you I wasn't anywhere near Marco."

"Don't move," Kylie said.

The two of us walked to a corner of Seth's half kitchen, where we could talk in private and still keep an eye on him.

"Dead end," she said. "I don't think he'll be much help to Varhol either, but why don't you call him and get him over here? Maybe Seth can come up with a name for the dealer Marco was meeting."

"What are you going to do?"

"I'm going to call Jan Hogle and have her monitor Spence's credit cards. Do you have any other ideas?"

"Just one. But you're not going to like it."

"Try me."

"Stop looking for Spence and start looking for the murderers and thieves that the City of New York is paying you to look for."

"Good call on the 'you're not going to like it' part," she said, "but you're right. It's my job. Besides, I have a better chance of tracking down a killer, a gang of medical-equipment thieves, and an eight-million-dollar necklace than I do of finding my husband."

CHAPTER 44

ANNIE RYDER COULD fall asleep on a rock. But not tonight. After lying in bed for over an hour, her brain was still doing laps like Dale Earnhardt Jr. at Talladega.

She wasn't worried about Jeremy. He wanted the necklace; she wanted the money—that would be easy. Annie wrestled with the hard part. *What next? Where do Teddy and I go? What do we do?*

She got out of bed, made some tea, and laced it with cognac. But the answers didn't come, and the questions refused to go away. She went to the living room and lifted Buddy from the sideboard.

"This is why I didn't scatter you all over Vegas," she said, carrying him into the bedroom. She set him down on the night table and pressed her hands against the sides of the bronze urn. "Sorry to disturb your eternal rest, but one of us has to worry about our son. You take the night shift so I can get some sleep."

A warm tingle let her know that Buddy was on the job. She kissed him good night, turned off the light, and fell asleep in minutes.

In the morning she gave Teddy a short list of things to do and a long list of things not to do.

"Why can't I go with you?" he asked as Annie changed the bandage on his wound.

"Let's see. Because you're cat-sitting, because you need your rest...and I'm trying to remember... there was a third reason. Oh yeah." She gave him a motherly whack on the back of his head. "Because you're wanted for armed robbery and the murder of Elena Travers."

"I can wear a disguise. Otherwise, who's going to protect you on the subway?"

"Don't worry. I am not about to risk carrying an eight-million-dollar necklace on the N train—with or without someone to protect me. I asked Tow Truck Bob to drive me to Manhattan, wait for me, and then drive me back."

"Tow Truck Bob?" Teddy said, frowning. "I don't know, Ma. You think that's such a good idea?"

"Relax, kiddo. Bob is one of those guys who never asks any questions. As far as he's concerned, he's giving me a ride into the city to pick something up.

That's all he knows, and believe me, that's all he wants to know. I trust him."

"I trust him too, but don't you think it's kind of crazy to go by tow truck? You'll stick out like a sore thumb."

Annie sighed. This was why Teddy needed her. Like Buddy always said, "The poor kid couldn't think his way out of a room with four doors if three of them were wide-open."

"No, sweetie," she said. "That's just his nickname. He retired from the towing business a few years ago."

"Gotcha," Teddy said. "What does he drive now?"

"A Jeep Cherokee."

Teddy's eyes lit up, and Annie knew what was coming next.

"From now on we should start calling him Jeep Cherokee Bob."

"Smart thinking, kiddo," she said, putting the finishing touch on his fresh bandage. "I'll tell him."

Annie sat back in her chair and closed her eyes. She still hadn't figured out where she and Teddy should run off to once they had the money, but there was one thing she was sure of: he wasn't smart enough to survive in New York on his own.

She hustled him along to the other apartment and went over his things-not-to-do list one last time.

"What time will you be back?" Teddy asked.

"I'm meeting Jeremy at noon. If it all goes the way

it's supposed to, the whole thing should take ten minutes. Then we'll hop on the BQE, and there's not a lot of traffic at this hour, so I should be home by one o'clock."

"Cool," Teddy said. "Could you bring me back some lunch?"

"Sure. What would you like?"

"Let's see. A pastrami sandwich, a cream soda…and I'm trying to remember…there was a third thing I wanted. Oh yeah." He tapped his forehead. "A hundred and seventy-five thousand dollars."

Annie laughed out loud. Sometimes the kid wasn't as dumb as she thought.

CHAPTER 45

WHEN I GOT to work the next morning, Kylie was at her computer. "Your girlfriend ratted me out to the boss," she said, not looking up at me.

"If what you're trying to say is that Dr. Robinson sent a report to Captain Cates about our late-night excursion to the Bronx, I know all about it," I said.

"Cheryl told you?" she said, finally deeming me worthy of eye contact.

"Only after the fact. She gave me a heads-up as we were on our way to work this morning."

"Why would you need a *heads-up?*"

"I don't know. Maybe just in case I got to the office and you were in a pissy mood. But I'm happy to see you're nothing but sunshine, lollipops, and rainbows."

She lifted one hand from the keyboard and gave me the finger.

"What's your problem?" I said. "Cheryl cleared you for duty. End of story."

"Not for Cates. She wants both of us in her office. Now."

"*Both* of us? This is between you and the captain. Why does she want me?"

"I don't know, Zach. Maybe Cheryl's opinion wasn't enough. Maybe you get a vote too. Do you think I'm fit for duty, Dr. Jordan?"

"Hell, if we're going to play good cop/bad cop, you're totally fit for baddest-ass cop ever. Otherwise, you're going to have to be on restricted duty."

She lifted the other hand so she could flip me the bird with both barrels.

"You're overreacting," I said. "And for the record, Mrs. Harrington, the boss didn't find out about Spence from Cheryl. That little card in his wallet that said 'I'm married to an NYPD detective' was the equivalent of sending up a Bat Signal. It lit up the radios across all five boroughs. It was the system that *ratted you out*, not Cheryl."

"Thanks. That makes me feel so much better." She stood up, mental body armor in place, ready to do battle with whatever the system had in store for her next. I followed her to Cates's office.

"I'm sorry to hear about Spence," Cates said as we walked through the door. "I know what it's like to be married to a man with a drug addiction."

That stopped Kylie cold. "I…I didn't know that," she said, her body language softening.

"Not many people do. It's ancient history. I'm only telling you because I wanted you to know that Delia Cates understands what you're going through—"

"Thank you," Kylie said.

"—but *Captain* Cates is about to come down on your ass like the hammer of Thor!" She pounded her desk to punctuate her point. "Last night you were called to a crime scene. As a witness—*not as a cop,* correct?"

"Yes, ma'am."

"After you learned that the victim was not your husband, did the lead detective on the case ask you for any help?"

"Detective Varhol asked if I recognized the victim. I gave him—"

Cates cut her off. "Did he ask you to *assist* him in his investigation?"

"No, ma'am."

"So if Varhol made it clear that this was not your rodeo, why do I have a civilian complaint from Seth Penzig saying that you and Jordan stormed your way into his apartment and told him he was a suspect in the murder of his friend?"

"*Stormed the apartment?* That's totally bogus. Zach and I had cause. You could smell the pot wafting out of Seth's place from a block away."

"Could you smell it from the Bronx? Because that's where you were when you told Detective Varhol that you had no idea where Penzig lived."

"We did a little digging after we left the Bronx."

"*Digging?* In what universe is it okay for you to shanghai an investigation and question a person of interest in another cop's homicide?"

"I was trying to find my husband."

"And Detective Varhol was trying to find Penzig, but you decided that your personal needs were more important than the mission of this department."

Some people find themselves in a deep hole and look for a way out. Not Kylie. She just grabs a bigger shovel. I jumped in before she could dig deeper.

"Captain," I said, "I'm just as much to blame."

"You're damn right you are," Cates snapped back. "Why do you think you're here?"

"It was a big mistake, and I apologize if you took any heat over it. There's no excuse for what the two of us did."

"And yet, I've heard nothing but excuses from your partner."

"She wasn't thinking straight. They told her that Spence was dead, and she snapped. It won't happen again."

Cates grunted. "Do you want to put in for family leave?" she asked Kylie.

"No, ma'am."

"Then if you want to look for your husband, do it on your own time, which, judging by your caseload, is going to be in short supply," Cates said. "But if you ever flash your department shield to solve your civilian problems again, you'll find yourself with more personal time than you ever dreamed of. Dismissed."

"You realize that you never even apologized to her," I said as soon as Kylie and I were back at our desks.

"It sounded to me like you were repentant enough for both of us."

"That's not how the concept works. You're supposed to own your—"

The text alert on Kylie's phone chirped, and she immediately tuned me out to look at the message. "Oh God," she said.

"What's going on?"

She didn't answer. She just handed me her phone. It was a text from Q.

Just got this pic from one of my girls. Q.

It was a picture of a stunning young black woman in a glittery low-cut top. Next to her was a bleary-eyed man with a drink in one hand and the other resting on the woman's bare shoulder. There were splashes of blue, purple, and hot pink behind them—the official pyrotechnics of every after-dark club everywhere. Below the picture was a text.

This the white boy you looking for? He say his name Spence.

CHAPTER 46

THE SILVER S550 Mercedes was parked outside the precinct. Q's driver, Rodrigo, opened the rear door, and Kylie and I got in.

Q, in a custom-tailored navy suit, white shirt, and blue and gold repp tie, looked more like a captain of industry than a purveyor of fine flesh and priceless information. "First things first," he said to Kylie. "Let me have your phone."

She handed it to him, and he deleted the picture he'd sent. "To quote the incomparable John Ridley," he said, "'Discretion—it never goes out of style.'"

"Where is Spence?" Kylie asked.

"Atlantic City. The Borgata. Room 1178."

"Yesterday he was in a flophouse on the Bowery. He's traded up. How did you find him?"

"My business is a lot like yours," Q said. "We both cater to the rich and powerful. If Spence had been holed up in a warehouse down by the Holland Tunnel, I'd never know. But five minutes after he rolled into the hotel, I got two texts: one from a valet, another from a bellman. I asked Tanya, the young lady in the photo, to get visual confirmation. For the record, she's not *with* him. She just worked him long enough to get the picture…in case you were wondering."

"For the record," Kylie said, "of course I was wondering. Thank you. It's very reassuring. Maybe I can have a T-shirt made: 'My Husband Isn't Cheating. He's Just on a Drug Bender.'"

"It appears that he's upped his game. I have it from a trusted source that the paperboy hooked him up with Aunt Hazel."

There's a vast lexicon of street terms the illegal drug trade uses to shroud their activity in mystery. New code names pop up every day, but the maiden aunts have been around for decades. Aunt Mary is marijuana, Aunt Nora is cocaine, but Aunt Hazel is the most deadly of them all: heroin.

"I'm sorry to be the messenger of such dire tidings," Q said, "but at least you know where he is—for now. If I were you, I'd get down there in a hurry."

"*A hurry?*" Kylie said. "Atlantic City is a six-hour round-trip."

"Not if you've got lights, sirens, and you push the needle to triple digits."

"The department tends to frown on cops who use the company car to resolve their marital issues," Kylie said. "I appreciate your help, but I can't leave the city for that big a chunk of time."

"How about if I have Rodrigo expedite things for you?"

"*Expedite?*" Kylie said. "Because nothing says 'loving wife' like having someone stuff your husband into the trunk of a Benz and hauling him a hundred miles up the Jersey Turnpike."

Q laughed. "I forgot how your cop brain works. I was just offering to get you there by helicopter. NYC to ACY in thirty-seven minutes."

"You own a—" Kylie twirled a finger in the air.

"Let's just say I have *access*. My employees are on call 24/7, so I can hardly rely on public transportation. Besides, it's an amenity my clientele are happy to pay for."

"Your clients have the five grand it costs to be airlifted to hooker heaven," Kylie said. "I can't afford that kind of happiness."

Q did his best to look offended. "Please—since when has our relationship ever been sullied with talk of money? The ride is a gift."

"If you take your mom up for a spin, it's a gift. If you take a cop, it's a bribe. Thanks, but no thanks."

"Damn it, Kylie, I do you favors; you do me favors. That's the basis of our relationship. I'm helping you track down a drug addict. Someday you'll pay me back. Straight-up quid pro quo. Why change the rules now?" He turned to me. "Zach, talk some sense into this girl."

"Only if you tell me what's going on," I said.

Q gave me a blank stare. "What are you talking about? Nothing's going on. I'm trying to help your partner out."

"You *did* help her. You found her husband. This is where you would normally walk away. But you're still *helping*. So I have to ask myself: why is Q so invested in getting Kylie to Atlantic City that he's willing to fly her there at his own expense? The only answer I can come up with is there's something in it for you. Would you like to share that with us?"

"Okay, full disclosure. I'm hosting a party at the Borgata this weekend. My best customers: seven oil dudes from Texas, all white, all married, and they love the ladies of color. Money is no object. All they care about is privacy—I don't even know their real names. Sunday morning they pay me in cash and fly home. It's a huge payday, and I'm afraid Spence could fuck it up."

"How?"

"Because he's a big-time TV producer *and* a cop's husband. If he's found dead in a bed, that hotel will turn into a media circus, and my camera-shy cowboys will pull the plug on the party before it starts. Can you help me out?"

"Maybe," I said. "Step out of the car so Kylie and I can talk."

I didn't have to ask twice.

"Do you want to take a personal day and drive down there now?" I said to Kylie as soon as we were alone.

"No. I'm done putting Spence's addiction ahead of my career. I'll punch out at six, rent a car, and be back by morning. You stay and cover for me."

"It would be a lot faster if you went by chopper."

"I've done a lot of stupid things, Zach, but I've never taken a bribe."

"It's not a bribe," I said. "Q is our best CI. He just gave us Raymond Davis and Teddy Ryder. Like he said, quid pro quo. We can't give him a get-out-of-jail-free card, but we can help him eliminate a minor business annoyance. We both fly down tonight. I help you drag Spence's sorry ass to a rehab, and if our phone rings, we're only thirty-seven minutes away. Win-win."

"Oh my God," she said. "I've created a monster. You're starting to think like me."

"It sounds like you and I are in violent agreement."

"Hell, yeah," she said, a broad grin spreading across her face.

It was the first time I'd seen her smile since she kicked Seth Penzig in the balls. Things were starting to look up.

CHAPTER 47

ANNIE RYDER KNEW better than to burden her son with too many facts. What she failed to tell Teddy was that Tow Truck Bob was also known as Lieutenant Robert Beatty, U.S. Marines—a lone-wolf sniper who had taken out high-profile targets in Lebanon, Somalia, and Nicaragua, plus in a few top secret locations known only to a handful of generals and their commander in chief, Jimmy Carter.

Jeremy might look like a candy-ass, but he'd already murdered Raymond Davis and barely missed killing Teddy. Annie wasn't taking any chances. Bob didn't know any of the details, but if Jeremy had thoughts about going after her, he'd have to get past 260 pounds of muscle, grit, and combat training.

Bob pulled the Jeep into the Edison ParkFast on

Essex Street, and the unlikely couple walked around the corner and one block west to 205 East Houston.

They'd already gone over the logistics. Annie went in first. As soon as she walked through the door, she inhaled the intoxicating aromas of corned beef, matzo ball soup, chopped liver, and artery-clogging pastrami that Buddy had said was worth risking his life for.

Katz's Deli was one of New York's most popular tourist attractions—a mecca for foodies of every stripe. For Annie it was the perfect drop spot. There was safety in numbers, and with the lunchtime crowd streaming in, she would be just another anonymous old lady to be ignored.

She went to the counter and ordered Teddy's lunch to go, along with knoblewurst on rye and a bottle of Dr. Brown's Cel-Ray soda for herself. She found a table in the rear and watched as Bob entered, bought a sandwich, and took a seat twenty feet away from her.

Jeremy showed up at noon on the dot. He bypassed the counter, scanned the room, spied Annie, and sat down at her table.

"Let's do this fast," he said, unslinging a canvas messenger bag from his shoulder and setting it on the floor. "The money is all here. You can check to see if it's real, but don't ask if you can take it into the ladies' room to count it."

Annie picked up the bag and unbuckled the front flap. The packets of hundred-dollar bills inside looked, felt, and smelled real. She closed the bag and hefted it up and down several times.

"What the hell are you doing?" Jeremy asked.

"I don't have to count it," she said. "A ten-thousand-dollar stack of hundreds weighs about the same as a Big Mac. This feels like you got my order right." She put the bag down on the floor.

Jeremy grinned. "At first I made you for one bat-shit old broad, but it turns out you're as smart as you are nasty."

"Well, aren't you the sweet talker," Annie said. "Maybe when this is all over, the two of us can be Facebook friends."

Jeremy took a jeweler's loupe out of his pocket. "I showed you mine. Your turn to show me yours."

Annie removed a small black LeSportsac makeup bag from her purse and slid it across the table. Jeremy opened a menu, slipped the bag between the pages, removed the necklace, and studied it with the loupe.

Had anyone bothered to look, he was just another farsighted customer squinting at the menu, trying to decide.

Annie took a deep breath. For the first time since Teddy called her on Tuesday night, she felt a sense of relief. She still didn't know what to do about Teddy, but the bag at her feet would buy her a lot of options. A hint of a satisfied smile crossed her face, and she took a sip of her soda to cover it up.

And then—*bang!*

Annie jumped. Jeremy had slammed the table with the base of his fist.

Heads turned. Jeremy didn't care. His teeth were gritted, his jaw was locked tight, and his eyes were aflame. "You conniving bitch," he said, spitting out every word. He stuffed the necklace back in the makeup bag and shoved it at her.

Annie tried to process what was going on. "I don't understand. What's the prob—"

Jeremy didn't stick around to explain. He scooped up the bag of hundred-dollar bills, pushed back his chair, and bolted for the door. Tow Truck Bob stood up and was about to go after him, but Annie held up her hand.

"Let's get out of here," she said, shoving the makeup bag into her purse.

Ten minutes later, they were crossing the Williamsburg Bridge.

"You okay?" Bob finally said.

Annie lowered her eyelids. It was the first question the strong, silent marine had asked since she'd recruited him, and based on what had just happened, it was a pretty stupid question at that. But Bob wasn't stupid. He was a kindhearted man doing his best to tiptoe around her feelings, and the last thing he deserved was one of her trademark wiseass answers.

"No, I'm not okay," she said, opening her eyes as the Jeep merged onto the ramp to the BQE. "Thanks for asking."

"It's none of my business," Bob said, "but what the hell happened?"

"I don't know. I'm still shell-shocked."

"Sorry," Bob said, "but that's the thing with these business deals. Sometimes they can just go south."

Con jobs could go south, Annie knew. Hell, if the mark caught on, a scam could explode in your face. It didn't happen to her and Buddy often, but when it did, they didn't ask why. They just packed up and ran like hell.

But this was a legitimate business deal. Okay, maybe not legitimate, but it was a straight-up agreement between her and Jeremy. It was about to go down when something spooked him. But what?

She clutched the Katz's Deli takeout bag that was sitting on her lap and closed her eyes again. On top of everything, she'd have to explain to Teddy why all she'd come home with was a pastrami sandwich and a cream soda. He'd ask why she didn't bring back the money.

She didn't have an answer. Maybe Buddy would know.

CHAPTER 48

JEREMY COULD BARELY swallow. His breathing was labored, and he hugged his chest, trying to ease the rib-crushing pain. He'd had anxiety attacks before, but this one was the mother of them all.

He sat up straight in the back of the cab, rested his palms on his knees, and took long, slow, deep breaths. Five minutes into the ride, the wave of panic passed.

You're okay, he told himself. *It's only a temporary setback. Relax and think about what to do next.*

The first option that popped into his head was to do exactly what he had told Leo he wouldn't do: take the hundred and seventy-five thousand dollars and run away with it.

He shook off the thought. After all he'd been through, he wasn't going to settle for chump change. He'd have to come up with a new plan, but he couldn't do it alone. "Shit," he said out loud. "I guess the relationship isn't quite over."

The taxi dropped him in front of the Flatiron Building, on Fifth Avenue at 23rd Street. It was a short walk to the Bassett brothers' minimansion on 21st, but he knew better than to show up unannounced.

There was a pocket seating area on the wide traffic island that separated Fifth from Broadway. Jeremy bought a bottle of water from a pushcart vendor, found an empty table, and sipped slowly. The water went down easy. He could swallow. He could breathe. *He could do this.*

He took out his cell and sent a text.

It did not go well. Can I come over?

The response came back immediately.

No!!! Brother here. talk later.

Jeremy fumed. *Later?* He drank the rest of the water and texted back.

Pick a place NOW or I'm banging on your front door.

It took two minutes for the answer to come back.

Trailer Park Lounge 271 West 23. Five minutes.

"Stupid rich asshole," Jeremy said to the text.

It took ten minutes to walk west to the Trailer Park Lounge. He'd never heard of it, but as soon as he walked through the door, he knew why it was the perfect spot to meet. It was the kind of intentionally tacky dive that Leo Bassett wouldn't be caught dead in.

Max Bassett, on the other hand, looked right at home. He was at a table in the rear, wearing jeans, a faded plaid shirt, and a ratty old baseball cap with a logo that simply said HAT. There were two bottles of beer in front of him.

"What do you mean *'It did not go well'*?" Max said, picking up one beer and pushing the other in Jeremy's direction. "I thought Leo gave you the cash. What did the old lady do? Hold you up for more?"

"No," Jeremy said. "She was drooling over the money. But the necklace she was peddling was a fake. So I pulled the plug and walked out on her."

Max's eyes widened in disbelief. "You…you had the necklace in your hand, and you gave it back?"

"You're damn right I did. Max, it wasn't worth a hundred and seventy-five grand, let alone eight million. I thought—"

"Since when do I pay you to think? You were given specific instructions: *'Buy the necklace from the old lady.'*"

"Max, I know enough about gems to be able to tell what real emeralds and diamonds look like. I took a good look at the necklace with a loupe. Annie Ryder was trying to sell me a fake—a total piece of shit."

"You know *nothing* about gems. What you were looking at was a perfectly crafted replica using cultured crystals instead of real stones. And it's far from a piece of shit. It may not be expensive, but it's still an original Max Bassett."

Jeremy tried to make sense of what Max had said, but the vise was starting to tighten around his chest again, and most of his brain was preoccupied with warding off the pain.

"I don't understand," he said. "Why would you dress Elena Travers up in a fake necklace?"

"Did you think I would trust you to steal the real one? If you ever got your hands on it, you'd be on a one-way flight to God knows where—first class."

"So *you* have the real necklace?"

"I never let it out of my sight. And as soon as the insurance company pays me for my loss, I will refashion it and make several wealthy women extremely happy. What I don't have is the imitation. Are you beginning to understand why I need it, Jeremy?"

Jeremy nodded. "Yeah, I get it. You're afraid the old lady will turn it in to the insurance company, and once they have it, they'll figure out that the original was never stolen."

"You really don't have a head for this, do you, Jeremy? The old lady *can't* turn it in to the insurance company. It would be like saying, 'Here's what my son stole.' And she can't find a buyer, because who would want to buy a *fake piece of shit?*"

"I can fix this," Jeremy said. "I know where she lives. I'll give her the hundred and seventy-five. She'll be happy to make the deal."

"Is that the money in the bag?" Max asked.

"Every penny."

"Let me see."

Jeremy slipped the bag from his shoulder and handed it to Max.

"You won't be needing this anymore," Max said. "I'll take care of the old lady."

"Don't be crazy. Give me the money. I'll be back with the necklace in two hours."

Max laughed. "Even Leo is not dumb enough to believe that. Good-bye, Jeremy."

"You want to get rid of me, fine. But you owe me. I put months into this job, and so far I haven't been paid anything."

"That's because so far you haven't earned anything," Max said. "You bungled the job from the get-go."

"Give me a break, Max. It's not my fault Elena wound up dead."

"Perhaps," Max said. "But it's definitely your fault that Leo is still alive."

CHAPTER 49

"THE ONLY REASON Leo is still alive is because he never made it to the limo," Jeremy said, his voice an angry whisper. "How can you blame that on me?"

"I'm not blaming that on you," Max said, resting a hand on his chin and gently stroking his beard. "But you've had plenty of other opportunities since then."

"Opportunities? What the hell are you talking about?"

"You spent all of last night shacked up with him at a hotel."

"And what was I supposed to do? Shoot him in bed and leave his body on the room-service cart?"

Max shrugged. "I'm not in charge of logistics,

Jeremy. You are. All I know is that we had an agreement. I promised you a shitload of money—far more than you're worth—and you would see to it that Leo was the unfortunate victim of a jewelry heist gone horribly wrong."

"And that's exactly what would have happened. Raymond Davis was a contemptible, cold-blooded scumbag. All it took to get him to agree to kill Leo was to promise him ten thousand more than I was giving Teddy. It was a solid plan."

"And yet," Max said, lifting his beer from the table and dabbing with a napkin at the wet ring it left behind, "Raymond not only failed to shoot Leo, he murdered Elena Travers and turned your *solid plan* into an international cause célèbre."

"Shit happens, Max."

"Apparently it happens to you more often than to most criminal masterminds. But I was willing to overlook it. Do you know why? Because I had faith that you could bounce back from your monumental blunder and get it right the second time around. I mean, after all, you still had Raymond Davis, and from what I understood, it wouldn't take much for you to convince him to try his luck with Leo a second time. But did you do that? Did you seek out Raymond and try to motivate your handpicked employee to finish the job?"

He slammed the beer bottle back down on the table. "No! Instead, you went to Raymond's apartment and you killed him. And now you want me to pay you for all your hard work?"

"Fine," Jeremy said. "So I didn't finish that part of the job. But I still want to be paid for stealing the necklace."

"Stealing it and losing it," Max said. "Twice. First you were outwitted by a half-wit, and then you had it in your hand, and you gave it back, leaving me in a position where I will have to negotiate with a woman who is as well versed in the art of the deal as a Wall Street banker. Bottom line: you failed at every turn, and Max Bassett doesn't reward failure. At the risk of repeating myself, good-bye, Jeremy."

Jeremy's shoulder slumped. "No. Please, Max, I know I messed it up, but don't dump me now. Give me one more chance to make it right."

Max folded his arms across his chest and sat back in his chair. His body language said it all. *I am impenetrable.*

Jeremy countered with body language of his own. He spread his arms wide and placed his palms on the table. *I am defenseless, vulnerable, and I trust you.* "I know what you need," he said in a near whisper. "Leo has been a thorn in your side your entire life. And now, with this Precio Mundo opportunity at your fingertips, the thorn has become a roadblock, a barricade."

Max's head moved. An involuntary nod. Jeremy had struck the right chord.

"I know him, Max," Jeremy said, leaning in. "I know him intimately, and he has sworn to me that he will never give in. Your brother will stand in the way of your dreams until the day he dies. Give me one more chance to make that day come fast. Today, if you want."

"How much do you want?" Max said.

"It's a one-time-only payment. Once I have the money, you'll never see or hear from me again."

"How much do you want, Jeremy?"

"A million dollars." Jeremy smiled. "I realize that you could shop around and get it done for less, but you've been grooming me for this job for months. Leo trusts me. Just say the word, and when you wake up tomorrow morning, the destiny of Bassett Brothers Jewelry will be in your hands, and yours alone."

"Do it," Max said. "I'll go to my club for dinner and play poker till eleven p.m. Leo will be home alone. If he's dead when I get there, I'll wire you the million. Otherwise, you're broke, unemployed, and wanted for murder."

"Don't worry," Jeremy said. "I won't let you down. Thank you."

"Of course you won't," Max said, a self-satisfied smirk crossing his lips.

Jeremy took a long, slow deep breath. The oxygen filled his lungs, and he realized how effortless it had been. He exhaled slowly. Another breath.

His chest pains were gone, his focus was back. Somewhere during Max's harangue the anxiety and the fear had turned to resolve. Max was not Leo. Max was a formidable opponent, and Jeremy was determined to crush him.

No, he thought, staring at the sardonic smile that mocked him from across the table. *More than crush him. Kill him.*

CHAPTER 50

I UNDERESTIMATED KYLIE. I figured she'd spend the entire day second-guessing her decision to put off rescuing Spence, but I was wrong. She was pleasant, productive, and we breezed through our shift.

First we met with Howard Sykes. "I had a long talk with Phil Landsberg, the CEO at Hudson," he said. "Needless to say, he's not jumping up and down at the thought of his hospital being the target of the next robbery, but he finally caved. I'd like to tell you that it was my four decades as an advertising genius that won him over, but it wasn't."

"So now you owe him," I said.

Sykes frowned. "Actually, Muriel owes him. I just have to break the news to her that she'll be the guest of honor at their next fund-raiser," he said. "I've done my part. What's next?"

"We do ours," Kylie said. "A mammogram machine that is 40 percent more effective at detecting breast cancer is newsworthy. We'll have our PIO reach out to the media to spread the word. Then we'll meet with ESU and the head of security at Hudson to work out the logistics. Do you want us to keep you in the loop as we go along?"

"Nobody likes a micromanager," Sykes said. "You don't have to report back to me till you've got those people locked up. But before I bow out, I have one message to pass on to the two of you from Phil Landsberg. He said, 'You can let those bastards into my hospital, but whatever you do, don't let them out.'"

By four p.m. the plan was in full swing. All we needed was for the gang to take the bait and move Hudson to the top of their hit list. At six we left the office.

"Did you tell Cheryl where we're going tonight?" Kylie asked as we slogged through rush hour traffic on the FDR.

"Not exactly."

"What's that supposed to mean?"

"I told her you and I would be working late, but she didn't ask me for the details, so I didn't volunteer. Plus she's going out to dinner and the theater with her mom, so she won't be home until eleven. If we're lucky, I'll be back by then."

Traffic opened up after 34th, and we got to the Downtown Manhattan Heliport by 6:35. Rodrigo was waiting for us in the VIP lounge.

"When we get to the hotel, go to the front desk and ask for your key," he said. "Just say 'Mrs. Harrington, room 1178.' Your name is in the computer."

"I don't have an ID with my married name," Kylie said.

"Don't worry. They won't ask," Rodrigo said. "It gets pretty noisy once we're in the air. Any more questions?"

"Just one," Kylie said. "I've had my IT people monitor Spence's credit cards, but so far we haven't gotten a hit. How did he check into the Borgata?"

"Corporate card. Silvercup Studios." Rodrigo was not the chatty type. "We good?" he asked, signaling an end to the conversation.

Kylie nodded, and he led us across the tarmac to a waiting Sikorsky S-76C. According to the brochure tucked in our seat pockets, the Borgata was the biggest hotel in Jersey, with a 161,000-square-foot casino, a 54,000-square-foot spa, and a 2,400-seat event center.

"Spence should be easy to find," Kylie said. "He'll be holed up in his room."

Thirty-seven minutes after liftoff we set down on the Steel Pier in Atlantic City. A car was waiting to drive us the two miles to the Borgata. Q had covered all the bases.

Walking into the main entrance of the hotel, my senses were bombarded by the over-the-top grandeur of the decor and the nerve-jangling flashing lights and clanging bells of the slot machines.

There were three clerks at the reception desk. "The one on the left," Rodrigo directed.

Kylie walked up to him, said a few words, and the clerk responded with a broad smile and a flat plastic room key.

"Smooth as silk," Rodrigo said as the three of us walked toward the elevator.

There was a Do Not Disturb sign hanging on Spence's door. Kylie looked at me and silently mouthed two words: *Thank you.* Then she took the key card, slid it into the lock, and pulled it out. A green light flashed, and she pushed the door open hard.

Spence, wearing nothing but boxer shorts and a single sock, was lying on the carpet, faceup, a trail of wet vomit trickling from the side of his mouth.

His drug kit had spilled onto the floor, and an empty syringe was only inches from his motionless body.

CHAPTER 51

THE NUMBER OF heroin overdose deaths among young white males has skyrocketed in recent years, and from the looks of him, Spence Harrington was well on his way to becoming the latest statistic.

His lips had a blue tinge, his pupils were black pinholes, and the ominous death rattle that came from the back of his throat was a sure sign that his respiratory system was shutting down permanently.

Kylie dropped to her knees and tried to breathe for him, but he was unresponsive. "Narcan!" she yelled. "My bag."

I grabbed her black leather handbag, turned it upside down, and everything poured out: money, makeup, tampons, keys, and then a small blue pouch with large white letters printed on it.

OVERDOSE PREVENTION RESCUE KIT
PREVENCION DE SOBREDOSIS EQUIPO DE RESCATE

In the war against drugs, Narcan—naloxone hydrochloride—is saving lives one junkie at a time. Normally it's issued to 911 responders, but Kylie had had the presence of mind to grab a kit at the station before we left.

I tilted Spence's head back while she loaded the syringe, inserted one end into Spence's nostril, and sprayed half the liquid up his nose. Then she switched to the other nostril, gave another short, vigorous push on the plunger, and shot the rest of the naloxone toward his brain receptors.

It worked instantly, and Spence bolted up, coughing, cursing, and fighting us off. There was no gratitude, just anger—the addict's natural reaction when you screw up his high.

"Rodrigo," Kylie said, "this stuff wears off in less than an hour. We've got to get him to a hospital."

"I'm already on it, boss," he said, cell phone to his ear. He swept his hand across the room. "This is nasty shit to leave for the chambermaid."

Kylie grabbed Spence's overnight bag from the closet and began picking up the drug paraphernalia.

I bent down to give her a hand.

"Don't!" she said.

I backed off. She was destroying evidence at a crime scene, and she didn't want me to help.

"But you can put my stuff back in my bag," she said.

There was a loud knock at the door.

"Housekeeping," a deep male voice said.

Rodrigo opened the door, and three stone-faced men in dark suits entered, one pushing a wheelchair. Without a word, two of them lifted Spence up off the floor, plopped him down in the chair, and seat-belted him in tight.

I retrieved Kylie's belongings while the extraction team helped her scoop up Spence's shoes, pants, and whatever might connect him to the makeshift drug den. Less than thirty seconds after they arrived, they ushered us out the door. Dark Suits One and Two led the way down the long corridor, followed by the man pushing the wheelchair, then Kylie, then me. Rodrigo brought up the rear.

Spence was ranting about his rights, but none of the suits cared enough to shut him up. A young couple passed us in the hallway and barely looked at us. I got the feeling that seeing a phalanx of people remove a crazy man from an Atlantic City hotel was not all that unusual.

The entire operation was perfectly choreographed: service elevator to an underground garage to an unmarked van for the two-mile drive to AtlantiCare Regional Medical Center. As soon as they handed Spence over to the ER docs, the rescue team from housekeeping disappeared, and Rodrigo escorted us to a VIP waiting room.

Forty-five minutes later, a bleary-eyed young resident walked in and said, "Harrington."

Kylie stood up. "How is he?"

"Lucky to be alive," the doc said, his tone clearly unsympathetic to those who clutter up his ER with self-inflicted wounds. "He has bilateral pneumonia. His lungs were compromised by the vomit he aspirated, so we're keeping him on an IV antibiotic drip for the next seventy-two hours."

"But he'll be okay," Kylie said, looking for reassurance.

The doctor shrugged. "This time around."

"Can I see him?"

"He said he'd rather not have any visitors."

Kylie flashed her shield. "I'm a cop. He's a junkie. Take me to his room."

CHAPTER 52

SPENCE WAS IN bed, staring at the ceiling, when Kylie and I entered. "Congratulations. You found me," he said, not turning his head to look at us. "What do you want?"

"I don't know," Kylie said, almost playfully. "For starters, I thought I'd save your life."

"Who asked you? I left New York to get away from you trying to save my life. Leave me alone, Kylie."

"Honey," she said, doing her best to stay composed, "I'm just trying to help you get through this."

He twisted his body so he could look at her. "*Help?* Is that what you call it when you kick my friend in the balls? Get it through your stubborn *I'm-a-rock-star-detective* brain, Kylie. You can't help me. I'm an addict. I tried rehab, and it didn't take."

"Bullshit!" she yelled, giving up the tolerant, empathetic wife charade that has never been her style. "You were clean and sober for eleven years. You can do it again."

"Don't you get it?" he yelled back, thumping his fist on the mattress. "I don't *want* to do it again. I'm a junkie, and I'm back in full-blown junkie mode. I need the high. I want the high. I don't want to do anything except get high, and all you want to do is preach the same program bullshit. It doesn't help, so unless you're here to arrest me, get out and stop trying to save me. If I want to kill myself, that's my business."

"You want to kill yourself, asshole?" Kylie said, spitting out the words in a low growl. She reached into her holster, pulled out her gun, and shoved it at him, butt first. "Go ahead. Blow your brains out right here and spare me the agony of another long ride in the back of a police van to identify your body."

Spence turned his head and looked away.

"Not ready yet?" Kylie said. "Call me when you are. I'll keep it loaded." She holstered her gun and stormed out the door.

"Don't go," Spence said.

"Too late," I said.

"I mean you, Zach," he said, rolling over and sitting up. "What the hell did she mean about identifying my body?"

"Your buddy Marco went up to the Bronx last night with a wallet full of money," I said. "Your wallet."

"So I lent a friend some money. Since when is that a crime?"

"You didn't *lend* him anything, Spence. You sent him on a drug run to a war zone and gave him enough cash to make him a target. It worked. Somebody put a bullet through his head. And since he had your ID in his pocket, your wife spent a couple of hours thinking it was you. She doesn't want to go through it again. And neither do I."

Spence didn't say a word.

"You're right about one thing," I said. "Kylie can't help you. I don't think you even want help. But just in case you ever feel like you do, hang on to this number."

I took a piece of paper out of my pocket.

He looked at me in disgust. "I already have your number, Zach. Don't hold your breath waiting for the phone to ring."

Kylie opened the door. "Cates called. We have to roll. Now!"

I handed him the number. "Good luck," I said, and left the room wondering if I'd ever see him alive again.

"I didn't tell Cates where we were," Kylie said as we double-timed our way down the hallway. "I just told her we're on our way to the scene."

"Let me guess," I said. "Another hospital robbery."

"If only," she said. "It's a double homicide, and it's got Cates climbing the walls."

"And she called *us* in on it?" I said. "She knows we're already stretched six ways to Sunday. Why would she dump two more bodies on us?"

"Probably because these two have our names written all over them."

"Who are they?" I asked.

"No positive ID, but they're lying on the kitchen floor of the Bassett brothers' loft building."

CHAPTER 53

"IF IT MAKES you feel any better," I said to Kylie once we were in the car on the way back to the chopper, "you saved his life."

"That's what cops do," she said. "But this is the first time I ever felt like I owed an apology to the guy whose life I saved."

"You don't owe Spence anything," I said. "There's nothing you can do that you haven't already done."

"How about you? I saw you give him your phone number."

"It wasn't my number. It was the twenty-four-hour hotline to NA right here in Atlantic City. There was a tear-off sheet on the bulletin board in the waiting room. I figured he's never going to call his counselor in New York, but on the outside chance that Marco's death is a wake-up call for him, maybe he'll reach out to a total stranger."

"Thanks." She turned and stared out the window to let me know the conversation was over.

We were almost at the helipad when my phone rang. "Oh crap," I said as soon as I checked caller ID.

"Sounds to me like it's either the boss or your girlfriend," Kylie said, "and since Cates just called, I'm guessing it's Cheryl."

It was. I had hoped to be back in New York before she knew I was gone, but like a lot of people in Atlantic City, I had gambled and lost.

"Hey," I said, answering the phone. "It's not even nine thirty. I thought you and your mother were at the theater."

"It was abysmal," she said. "We left at intermission. I thought you'd be home by now. Where are you?"

"Atlantic City."

"Atlantic—what's Red doing down there?"

"It's not police business. Kylie tracked down Spence, and she needed some help, so—"

"So you drove down there with her?"

"Actually, we took a chopper."

"Are you kidding me? The department paid for a helicopter just so Kylie could pick up her husband?"

"It's a private charter. A guy we know was trying to help Kylie out, and—look, it's a long story."

"And when, if ever, were you going to tell me about it?"

"Cheryl, I really can't get into this now."

"I'm sure you can't," she said. "Maybe you can find some time to get into it when you get home. When will that be?"

"I don't know. The Elena Travers case just heated up. We're on our way to the crime scene now."

"By helicopter," she said.

"Yes."

"So now you're on police business, but you're still using Kylie's private helicopter."

"We'll talk when I get home," I said.

"I can't wait," she said. "Have a nice flight." She hung up.

I smiled and kept talking. "Yeah, it looks like Spence is going to spend a few more nights in the hospital," I said into the dead air. "Okay, I'll tell her you send your best. Love you too."

The car came to a stop, and I put the phone in my pocket. "Cheryl sends her regards," I said.

I had no idea if Kylie bought my act, but she nodded a thank-you.

CHAPTER 54

IT WAS ALMOST ten thirty by the time Kylie and I got to West 21st Street, and once again the Bassett brothers' urban palace was awash in flashing police lights. A perimeter had been set up, and the usual contingent of uniforms had been posted to keep out the curious.

"That's weird," Kylie said, pointing at the lone figure standing outside the front door.

It was Chuck Dryden. It has long been a given that Chuck is a weird guy, but this was particularly out of character. Instead of being in the house, fussing over a body or ruminating over a piece of evidence, he was standing outside, vaping an e-cig. Even more unusual was his reaction when he saw us.

"Detectives," he called out. "I've been waiting for you."

"Sorry we're late," Kylie said. "Zach and I were out of the city, and—"

"No, no, no. I wasn't chastising you about the time," he said, pocketing the e-cig. "It's just that I've made some interesting findings, and I've been rather anxious to get the two of you in the loop."

"Chuck," I said, "we are so far out of the loop that we don't even know who the victims are."

"Even better," he said, clapping his hands together. "Let's go upstairs and take a look."

We took the elevator to the third floor, where Kylie and I had met with the Bassett brothers just a few nights ago. Leo's showpiece apartment now looked like a triage center where technicians wearing latex gloves and disposable shoe covers probed, dusted, and photographed every inch. The air smelled of wine and death.

We followed Chuck into the kitchen. There were two bodies stretched out on the slate-gray tile. The first was short, fat, and viciously mutilated. It was Leo Bassett.

"Twenty-two stab wounds," Dryden said. "Most of them defensive."

I surveyed the room. There was broken glass everywhere: wine bottles, ceramic bowls, a crystal decanter—all of which must have been knocked off the counter as Leo tried to fight off his assailant.

"He put up a good fight," I said.

"Not good enough. Here's the winner," Dryden said, pointing at the second body.

The man was about half Leo's age. The left side of his face was resting in a puddle of wine, and the front of his shirt had a similar red stain, only this one was emanating from the hole in the center of his chest.

"Do you recognize him?" Dryden asked.

I shook my head. "Should we?"

He produced an iPad and brought up a photo. It was the fuzzy surveillance screenshot we had captured from Elliott Moritz's security video the night Raymond Davis was murdered.

"It could be the same guy," I said.

"I ran it through facial recognition software. It is. His name is Jeremy Nevins. The weapon came from here."

There was a large wooden knife block sitting on the counter. Seven of the eight slots still had knives in them. One slot was empty.

Chuck held up an evidence bag. A bloody knife that matched the seven in the block was inside. "It wound up on the other side of the room when Nevins was shot, but his prints are all over it."

"Nevins killed Leo," Kylie said. "You could make our jobs a lot easier if you also happen to know who killed Nevins."

Dryden beamed. He was smitten with Kylie, but

he had limited social skills, so he relied on his forensic expertise to win her approval. He held up a second evidence bag. This one contained a .357 Magnum.

"It belongs to Max Bassett. He turned it over to the first officer on the scene. Said he was upstairs, heard the scuffle between Leo and Nevins, and raced down to see what was going on."

"He raced down with a loaded .357?" Kylie said.

Dryden shrugged. "I didn't ask. I'm not a detective."

"For a guy who's not a detective, you just helped us close out the Raymond Davis murder," she said. "No wonder you were so anxious to connect with us. Thank you, Chuck."

"My pleasure."

"Where can we find Max Bassett?" she asked.

"He's waiting for you in the den. Two officers are with him. But there's one more thing I need to share with you before you go."

"Share away," she said. "You're on a roll."

He held up a third evidence bag. Inside was a diamond and emerald necklace. He handed it to Kylie.

"Oh, Chuck," she said, playing to his male ego. "Thank you. It's just what I always wanted."

CHAPTER 55

"WHERE THE HELL did you find that?" I said.

"It was wrapped up in a chamois cloth in Mr. Nevins's backpack," Chuck said. "I've already verified the laser inscriptions. It's the necklace you've been looking for, but you don't seem particularly happy that I've recovered it."

"I'm sorry," I said. "It's just that three people have already died for that bag of green rocks and pressurized carbon. Elena Travers, Raymond Davis, and Leo Bassett. Every cop instinct in my body tells me that Teddy Ryder had the necklace—he was just too dumb to know how to unload it. But if you found it on Nevins, then Teddy's body is probably rotting in a dumpster somewhere."

"Along with his con artist mother," Kylie said.

One of the uniformed cops approached us. "Hate to interrupt you, Detectives, but Mr. Bassett says he needs a drink."

"Tell him to take a number," Kylie snapped. "Right about now, we all do."

The cop took a step back. "Sorry, ma'am, but he told me to tell you that his brother was murdered, he just killed a guy, and he'd like to get shit-faced, but he doesn't want to start until he's been interviewed by the detectives."

"How considerate," Kylie said. "Let's not keep him waiting."

The cop escorted us to what Dryden had referred to as Leo Bassett's den. There was nothing den-like about it. To me it looked more like the parlor of an eighteenth-century brothel, but then Leo and I didn't share the same design sensibilities. Brother Max, wearing camo cargo shorts and an Everlast T-shirt, looked equally out of sync with the decor.

He was standing next to a spindle-legged desk, a bottle of water in one hand. "Detectives," he said, frowning like a customer who had to wait too long for a salesclerk.

"We're sorry for your loss, Mr. Bassett," I said. "Please tell us what happened."

"It was about nine o'clock. I was in my studio on the fourth floor, working on a new piece, when I heard Leo's doorbell ring. Then I heard the elevator go up and stop on three. I didn't think much about it. Leo gets quite a few late-night visitors. After that I got lost in my work, so I'm not sure how much time went by before I heard the yelling."

"Who was yelling?"

"Leo. I told you when you were here the other night that my brother is a total diva. He's been throwing hissy fits and teary-eyed tantrums for sixty years. I'm immune to it."

"Could you make out what he was saying?" I said.

"Not at first, but then it got louder, and I heard the other guy scream 'a million dollars,' and my ears perked up. Leo has had more than his share of noisy breakups with boyfriends, which is none of my business, but this was about money—a lot of money—and if Leo is spending it, that *is* my business.

"I was deciding if I should go downstairs and find out what was happening when I heard glass break. Then Leo yelled, 'Max, help! He's got a knife!' After that, it was chaos. More glass shattering, and Leo screaming these horrible, ghastly shrieks and calling my name.

"I grabbed a gun and ran down one flight of stairs, but by the time I got to the kitchen, Leo was on the floor, the blood pouring out of him. Then this maniac came at me with the knife. I didn't hesitate. I'm an expert marksman, Detective. One shot, and it was over. I ran to my brother, but the knife must have severed one of his arteries. He was dead before I could even dial 911."

"Do you know the man who stabbed him?"

"I've met him a few times. His name is Jeremy Nevins."

"We showed you his picture yesterday," I said. "How come you didn't recognize him then?"

He stiffened. "Maybe because all you showed me was an out-of-focus black-and-white that looked like it was shot by a convenience-store camera sometime before the turn of the century. Of course I didn't recognize him from that picture. Hell, Leo had a schoolboy crush on the man, and *he* didn't even recognize him."

"Do you know what he and Leo were arguing about?"

"I told you that except for the phrase 'a million dollars,' I couldn't make out the dialogue."

"You know them both. What do you think they may have been arguing about?"

Bassett's eyes widened. "I didn't send for my lawyer because I want to help, and because I have nothing to hide. But if he were here, and you asked me to theorize what someone's motive was for killing my brother, he'd pull the plug on this interview in a heartbeat. Now, are there any more *questions?*" He spun the word so that it was clear he meant "stupid questions."

"Just one," Kylie said. "How did Nevins get involved in your company?"

"He wasn't *involved*. He showed up one night

about six months ago with Sonia Chen. She's the company's publicist. Nevins was her boyfriend."

"We'd like to talk to her. Do you have an address?" I asked.

"Sonia is upstairs in my apartment. She's drafting a statement."

"What kind of a statement?" I said.

"Leo loved the limelight, and over the years, he managed to become a bit of a *celebrity*," he said, making it sound more like an affliction than an achievement. "Frankly, I doubt if he'd even qualify for the D-list, but since I shy away from publicity, he became the face of the company, and he reveled in it. It's now fallen on me to make a statement to the press and to Leo's many fans that he's gone. I know that a lot of people will be heartbroken to hear of his death."

From the faint smile on Max Bassett's face I was sure that he wouldn't be one of them.

CHAPTER 56

LEO'S TRIPLEX ENDED on the third floor, and Max's began on the fourth, but the trip up the single flight of stairs was like a journey across the great cultural divide. If Leo's apartment looked like it was decorated by Marie Antoinette, Max's looked like Ernest Hemingway's man cave.

A young Asian woman was sitting on the floor, her back against a weathered leather armchair, a laptop propped on her knees. She stopped typing as soon as we walked in.

"Hi, I'm Sonia Chen," she said, standing up.

We introduced ourselves, and she forced a polite smile, but it didn't hide the fact that her eyes were red and puffy from crying.

"Max texted me and said you wanted to ask me some questions."

"We're sorry for your loss," I said. "We know you had a close relationship with both of the victims."

She nodded. "Leo's been my boss for three years. I adored him."

"And Jeremy Nevins?" Kylie said.

"I wouldn't exactly call it a relationship."

"Max said he was your boyfriend."

"'*Boyfriend*,'" Chen said, putting the word in air quotes. "You're a woman. You know what that means."

"I'm a homicide detective," Kylie said, "and we're not supposed to fill in the blanks from our own life experience. So why don't you tell us what your relationship was with Jeremy Nevins?"

"Consenting adults," Chen said as comfortably as if it had been a box to check on a government form alongside "single," "married," and "divorced."

"Could you elaborate?" Kylie said.

Chen smiled—a real smile this time, and I could only imagine that the question triggered memories of her time with the handsome young man lying dead one floor below. The smile turned to sobs, and she folded her arms across her chest to hold it all back.

"I'm sorry," she said, sitting down in the leather armchair. Kylie and I sat across from her on a matching sofa.

"Jeremy and I didn't have a relationship—certainly not in the classic sense. It was more of an arrangement. As a publicist I plan a lot of high-end events. Jeremy loved getting up close and personal with the rich and famous, so I'd bring him along as my plus one. In return, the two of us would get up close and personal together."

"So it was essentially physical."

"Yes, and I make no apologies for it, Detective. It's the age-old story of the overworked career woman. He got access. I got laid."

"Do you have any idea why he stabbed Leo Bassett?"

"Are you sure that's what happened? I find it impossible to believe that Jeremy would kill Leo. They were so wonderful together, and Leo was over the moon about Jeremy. He'd do anything for him."

"Wait a minute," Kylie said. "Leo was gay. So you're saying—"

"I'm saying what you think I'm saying. Jeremy Nevins was beyond incredible in bed. You spend one night with him, and you'd remember it for the rest of your life. It didn't matter if you were a thirty-two-year-old woman or a sixty-year-old man. Jeremy had a gift, and if you were lucky enough to be on the receiving end, it didn't matter what he wanted in return."

"You gave him entrée to people he wouldn't have met otherwise," I said. "What did Leo give him?"

"I don't know the details, but Leo loved the finer things in life, and Jeremy was happy to go along for the cash and prizes."

"One of those prizes was an eight-million-dollar necklace," I said.

"I heard. I don't even know how that's possible. Jeremy was with me when it was stolen."

Her cell phone rang.

"Excuse me. This is urgent," she said, taking the call. "Hi, Lavinia. I'm almost finished with the piece. I can email it to you in ten minutes. Talk soon."

She hung up. "Sorry. Business. Max wants me to get out the news of Leo's death."

"It sounded like you were talking to Lavinia Begbie," Kylie said.

"Yes. She's agreed to write the story if we give her a twelve-hour exclusive before we send out a release to everyone else."

"Shouldn't the news of Leo Bassett's death be on the front page instead of in the Style section?"

"Sweetie, in my world, the Style section *is* the front page, and Lavinia Begbie is the voice of the fashion industry. The fact that she agreed to devote an entire column to Max is living proof that every cloud has a silver lining."

"You said Max. Don't you mean she's going to devote her entire column to Leo?"

Chen shook her head. "Detective, you really don't understand our business, do you? Our company got a black eye when Elena was killed wearing our necklace. Of course Lavinia will talk about Leo, but having her write about Max Bassett's heroic actions to attempt to save his brother's life is exactly the kind of ink we need."

"Is that your job, Ms. Chen?" Kylie said. "To use Leo's murder as an opportunity to turn Max into a hero to help restore the company's image?"

"That's exactly my job," Chen said. "Now if you'll excuse me, I have a deadline to meet."

CHAPTER 57

I'M TIRED, I'M hungry, and I'm not sure Cheryl and I are still in a relationship," I said as soon as Kylie and I were back in the car. "Can we call it a night?"

"I'm just as tired and hungry, and if you want to talk about relationships on life support, my junkie husband trumps your pissed-off girlfriend," she said as we headed uptown on Sixth Avenue. "But no, we can't call it a night. Sonia Chen is talking to the press, and unless we can get the First Amendment repealed in the next few hours, everything that went down at Casa Bassett tonight is going to be public."

"Not everything," I said. "She'll probably leave out the parts where Max lied to us through his teeth and substitute some flowery bullshit about the noble great white hunter avenging his brother's death by conveniently killing the man who knew the answer to every question we had."

"Exactly. Which means that in a few hours it'll be on the front page of every paper and trending on the Internet. And since we can't stop Annie Ryder from getting the news, the second-best thing we can do is break it to her ourselves, so we can watch the expression on her face when she finds out."

I couldn't argue with her logic, and I grunted in agreement.

We hung a right on 34th Street and headed east toward the Queens Midtown Tunnel.

"You think Annie is still alive?" I asked.

"God, I hope so, because if we find her in a pool of blood, we'll be stuck at another crime scene till dawn."

Annie Ryder was very much alive and as charming as ever.

"Don't you two have anything better to do than harass law-abiding taxpayers in the middle of the night?" she said at her door. "I told you I haven't seen Teddy, and I have no idea where he is."

"Jeremy Nevins is dead," Kylie said, hitting her with our biggest gun first.

The old con woman was a pro. "Never heard of him," she said, doing her best not to react. But Kylie had been right. The news came as enough of a shock to Annie's system that a tiny corner of her right eye spasmed involuntarily. She rubbed it and yawned in an attempt to cover it up, but if this had been a poker game, she'd have lost her edge. She'd given up the tell.

"Sure you heard of him," Kylie said. "Nevins killed Raymond Davis, and he tried to kill Teddy."

"Then good riddance," Annie said. "Thank you for coming all this way to let me know. Good night."

"We've also recovered the necklace that Raymond and Teddy stole from Elena Travers," Kylie said.

The tic kicked in again, and her eye fluttered. "Teddy didn't steal anything. He's innocent."

"Then tell him to turn himself in. We'll cut him a deal."

"What kind of deal?"

"We'll charge Raymond with the murder and Jeremy as the one who orchestrated the robbery. If Teddy turns himself in now, we think we can get the DA to let him plead it down to involuntary manslaughter. He'll probably only get eight years. If we catch him first, the deal is off the table, and he's looking at life."

"You're barking up the wrong tree, girlie," Annie said. "I told you Teddy was right here with me that night. You might not believe me, but a jury will."

"Maybe yes, maybe no," Kylie said. "Juries want to buy a mother's testimony, but a smart prosecutor will make sure they know that in this case, Mom is a grifter, a professional liar. And if that's not enough, he'll make sure they see the traffic-cam footage from the night of the robbery. The two men who jacked Elena's limo were wearing masks on 54th Street, but one of them was stupid enough to pull his mask off when he got to 53rd. Now who do you think could be that dumb?"

"We're done here," Annie said, and shut the door.

"That was quite a picture you painted, Detective," I said to Kylie as we rode down in the elevator. "I particularly liked the part about the traffic cam. Very believable."

"I only wish it were true," Kylie said. "But people are obsessed about Big Brother watching them, and I'll bet Annie Ryder is more paranoid than most."

We spent the rest of the trip to Manhattan in blessed silence. Once again it was almost two a.m. by the time I got to my apartment, but this time I didn't have to wait to get upstairs to find out if Cheryl was there.

Angel, my doorman, handed me a note. "Dr. Robinson left this for you."

It was a single scrap of paper that had been torn from the bottom of a yellow pad. The rest of the page and the pad it came from was on Angel's desk. Cheryl had scribbled it out in a hurry as she was leaving the building.

Spending the night at my place. Be at Gerri's at 6:30 a.m.

I thanked Angel and took the elevator up to my empty apartment.

CHAPTER 58

I SHUCKED MY clothes, showered, fell into bed, and reread Cheryl's note.

It didn't take a detective to figure out what she meant by *"Spending the night at my place."* But *"Be at Gerri's at 6:30 a.m."* threw me. Did she mean *"I'll be at Gerri's, and I'd love to have you join me"*? Or was it *"You better be at Gerri's at 6:30 so I can read you the riot act"*?

I set my alarm for five so I could be at the diner early enough to get Gerri's worldview on my current situation.

She sat down at a booth with me, and I gave her the short version of what happened yesterday. "Any thoughts, Dr. Gomperts?" I said.

"Just one," she said. "Why do I even bother giving you advice? I warned you the other day about spending your nights with Kylie, but I don't think you remember a word I said."

"Of course I do. How could I forget one of your puppet shows where I'm starring as a packet of artificial sweetener?"

"I'll try one more time." She slid my water glass to the edge of the table. "This is Kylie," she said. "Her marriage is on a precipice."

She stared at me, a devilish look in her eyes as she slowly pushed the glass with one finger. "It's teetering, Zach. It's on the brink."

Just as the glass started to topple, I grabbed it. "You're crazy," I said.

"And you're hopeless. You can't let go of Kylie, and you always want to be there to catch her if she falls."

"Is there anything wrong with that?"

She stood up. "Good question. Why don't you ask the lady who just walked in the door?" she said, hurrying off to the kitchen.

It was Cheryl. She sat down across from me and got straight to the point. "What happened yesterday? And don't skimp on the details."

I told her everything, from Q's early-morning visit to our post-midnight house call on Annie Ryder. Skilled psychologist that she is, she listened without interruption.

"If you knew you and Kylie were flying to Atlantic

City, why did you lie and say you were working?" she said when I was finished.

"It was beyond stupid," I said. "I can't tell you how sorry I am."

"What really hurts is that you felt you had to lie. Did you think if you had told me the truth, I'd have tried to stop you?"

"Cheryl, I told you the truth Tuesday night when I ran out on dinner, but you were still pissed. And the next night at Paola's, you said you love being with me, but you're not sure you can handle living with me."

"Zach," she said, resting her hand on mine, "that's because a big part of living with you is about not living with you. When we were dating, and you got busy, I was at home in my own apartment. I missed you, but I could deal with it, because I understand the demands the job can put on a high-profile detective. But it's different when I'm at your apartment."

I shrugged. "Why?"

"Because when you don't come home, I'm not just lonely, I'm lonely in a place I'd rather not be. Everything I see reminds me of you, but you're not there. It's like living with a ghost."

"So you're moving out?"

"Not out of your life, but I'm seriously thinking about moving out of your apartment."

"When?"

"I don't know. I said I'd give it a month, and I'm a woman of my word. It's only been twenty-eight days, so let's try again tonight."

I closed my eyes and rubbed them with the heels of my hands. "I'm not going to be home tonight," I said.

She laughed. "Why?"

"Kylie and I are running a sting at Hudson Hospital, and we're going to spend the entire night on a stakeout. It's not the kind of thing I usually do, but I promised Cates and the mayor's husband. I'm really sorry."

"Don't apologize," Cheryl said. "It's what makes you such a great cop."

"Yeah," I said. "That's me. A great cop, but a lousy boyfriend."

CHAPTER 59

ANNIE COULD COME up with only one reason why a weasel like Jeremy would drop an eight-million-dollar necklace and run: it wasn't worth eight million.

There was one way to find out for sure. Ask Ginsberg.

"It's flawless," Ginsberg said after looking at the necklace through a loupe for less than twenty seconds. "Every stone is perfect."

Annie smiled for the first time since she left Katz's Deli. Ginsberg had spent sixty years in the wholesale jewelry business. "So it's real," she said.

"No, it's synthetic. Nature doesn't make perfect. Science does. These stones were grown in a lab. It takes a few months, so they look better than most of the dreck they use for costume jewelry. But real? No."

Annie's smile turned to despair, and Ginsberg wrapped his arms around her. For eight months out of the year they'd go to dinner, a movie, a Mets game, or just spend the night in his apartment on the third floor of her building. Just before Thanksgiving, he'd fly to Florida, and in the spring, they'd pick up where they left off.

"Sorry to give you the bad news, but you know what will make you feel better?" he said, giving her a wink. "A little afternoon delight."

At eighty-two, Ginsberg bragged that he had the libido of a sixty-year-old, and while the sex wasn't all that important to Annie, there were times when she needed the comfort of curling up against a warm man instead of a bronze urn.

This was one of those times.

An hour later, she broke the bad news to Teddy.

"So the necklace is junk," Teddy said.

"Not junk, but it's not worth enough money to stick our necks out trying to sell it."

"So, what are we going to do for money, Ma?"

Annie didn't know. "Don't worry, kiddo. I have an idea," she lied. "I just need some time to think it through."

She was still trying to come up with a plan when the two detectives showed up, told her Jeremy was dead, and offered Teddy a chance to plead the murder rap down. Eight years was a long time, but she'd never forgive herself if he got caught and had to spend the rest of his life behind bars. She decided to sleep on it.

The answer came to her in the middle of the night. It was so obvious she smacked her forehead in mock disgust for not seeing it sooner. She showered and made a pot of coffee, and at five fifteen she left the apartment, walked to the deli on 27th, and brought home a box of doughnuts and the morning papers.

Teddy was sitting at the kitchen table drinking coffee.

"What are you doing up?" she said.

"Damn cat woke me, and I'm more hungry than tired. What've you got?"

She tossed him the doughnuts and then opened the *Daily News* to a two-page spread on the Bassetts. "Your buddy Jeremy is dead," she said. "He stabbed one of those two jewelry brothers, and the other one shot him."

Teddy grinned. "Cool beans."

"Yeah, cool," she said. "I'll be right back."

She went to the bedroom and returned with the necklace. She set it on top of the news story about the Bassetts and took out her cell phone.

"What are you doing, Ma?"

"Taking a picture," she said, trying to get the right angle.

"Why? I thought you said the necklace was worthless."

"It's a fake, but it's far from worthless," she said, taking a photo and then deleting it. "Did you ever hear of Jack Ruby?"

Teddy took a few seconds and then smiled. "Yeah. He's the one who shot President Kennedy."

"Close. Ruby shot the guy who shot the president. He used a .38 that he bought for sixty-two dollars and fifty cents," she said. "I looked it up this morning on the Internet."

"So?"

"So what do you think the gun that killed Lee Harvey Oswald is worth today?"

Teddy shrugged. "I got no idea," he said through a mouthful of doughnut.

"Me either. But I can tell you that in 2008 the gun was sold to a collector for two million."

"That's crazy, Ma. Who would pay two million bucks for an old .38?"

"It's called murderabilia, kiddo, and there are a lot of nut jobs out there who will pay big money for anything connected to a major crime."

Teddy brightened. "So are you going to sell the necklace on eBay?"

"No," Annie said, clicking off a half dozen more pictures. "I already found a buyer."

CHAPTER 60

WITH ONLY THREE hours' sleep in the last twenty-four, my body was running on fumes, and whatever energy I might have had left was sapped by the time I finished my hapless breakfast with Cheryl. I went home, unplugged everything that beeped, buzzed, rang, or chirped, and slept nine hours straight.

By the time Kylie picked me up at six p.m., I was shaved, showered, caffeinated, and braced for the most boring part of every detective's job: waiting, watching, and wishing some bad guys would show up and make my existence meaningful.

"Spence called me this afternoon," Kylie said as she weaved in and out of Friday night traffic on the FDR.

"And?"

"There is no *and*, Zach. The very fact that he called me is a moral victory. You were there last night. He couldn't stand having me in the same room with him, let alone talk to me."

"And that was before you offered him your gun and encouraged him to blow his brains out on the spot."

"I did do that, didn't I?" she said, laughing. "That might have been a little reckless."

"Why did he call?"

"To thank me for saving his life."

"I hope you can see the irony in that," I said.

"Stop analyzing everything. The important thing is he opened the door to a possible dialogue. Speaking of which, how'd it go with Cheryl when you got home last night?"

"Fantastic. She welcomed me home like I was Richard the Lionheart returning from the Crusades."

"You're full of shit."

"Keep your mind on your driving, or you're going to miss your exit," I said.

She got off at Grand Street, and we headed west until we got to Hudson Hospital, an imposing steel and glass complex straddling the border between Chinatown and Little Italy.

We got in an elevator in the lobby and took it two floors down to the security operations room, where we met up with Jenny Betancourt, Wanda Torres, and Frank Cavallaro, the head of Hudson's security team.

They were sitting in front of a bank of monitors much more elaborate than the setup Gregg Hutchings had at Mercy Hospital.

"They made their first move this morning," Torres said.

"We have it queued up for you," Cavallaro said. "Watch this screen over here."

The camera covered a section of the third floor, which was in the final stages of being renovated. Per Howard Sykes's plan, the 3-D mammography machines were being "temporarily" stored there, where they were off-limits to staff and patients.

"Keep your eye on this guy in the green shirt," Torres said, pointing at a wide shot of a man who was spreading compound on drywall, getting it prepped for the painters. "He seems to have more than a passing interest in mammogram technology."

The man put down his tools, casually sauntered over toward the high-tech equipment, and took out his cell phone.

"He's not dialing out for pizza, is he?" Kylie said. "Can you get a close-up of his phone?"

"Are you kidding?" Torres said. "This thing can zoom tight enough to read the tattoo on a fly's ass and correct the spelling."

"Jesus, Wanda," her partner said. She looked at us

and shook her head. "Did I mention that she flunked out of finishing school?"

The tech at the console grinned, tightened the shot, and froze on the Sheetrock finisher's right hand. There was a tiny red square at the bottom of his cell phone screen.

"He's not dialing out for anything," Torres said. "He's videotaping and giving a running commentary."

Less than a minute later, he was finished. He tapped on the screen, waited, and then put the phone back in his pocket.

"He just sent them a video of the target," Betancourt said, "and you can figure that he also shot surveillance footage of every inch they have to cover to get in and out of the hospital."

"These guys are fast," Kylie said. "Twenty-four hours after we get the word out, and they've already managed to plant someone on-site."

"You'd think, but no," Cavallaro said. "The drywall crew started two weeks ago. That man's been here every day since then."

"They couldn't have known that far back that there'd be anything there worth stealing," I said. "Maybe they recruited him after we set up the sting. Do you know anything about him?"

Cavallaro nodded. "None of these hard hats get access to this building until we get a profile on them from the construction company, and we've fact-checked it. This guy's name is Dave Magby. Thirty years old, joined the army after high school, pulled two tours in Iraq, married, one kid, no criminal record."

"Another law-abiding citizen," Kylie said. "Just like Lynn Lyon."

"ESU just changed shifts," Betancourt said. "You've got a fresh team to keep you company all night. We'll see you guys in the morning."

They left, and Kylie and I sat down in front of the monitors.

"The good news is they took the bait," she said. "They'll be here. All we have to do is wait for them to show up."

CHAPTER 61

WE WAITED. At eleven o'clock Cheryl called to see how I was doing.

"I miss you," I said.

"I miss you too. How's the stakeout going?"

"Lousy. You ever throw a party and nobody comes?"

"Relax. The night is young. You still have another eight hours for them to show up."

They didn't. At six a.m. I got a text from Chuck Dryden letting us know that he had an updated report on the Leo Bassett murder. An hour later, Betancourt and Torres relieved us, and Kylie and I headed uptown to the crime lab.

Chuck's face lit up as soon as Kylie and I walked

through the door. I knew from experience that it had nothing to do with me.

"My apologies for intruding on your Saturday," he said, "but I know how important this case is to you."

"Is it Saturday already?" Kylie said. "Time flies when you're staring at a wall of monitors for twelve hours. What have you got for us, Chuck?"

He walked us over to a table that was covered with crime-scene photos.

"First, I can confirm that Jeremy Nevins stabbed Leo Bassett," he said, pointing to the knife-riddled corpse of the jewelry mogul. "The evidence is all there. Nevins's fingerprints on the murder weapon, the angle of the wounds, and the blood spatters from the victim leave no room for doubt."

"That's pretty much what you told us Thursday night," I said.

He held up a finger to correct me. "It's what I *surmised* Thursday night, Detective. At this point, I'm prepared to testify to it."

"Well, that definitely makes my Saturday. What else?"

"Mr. Nevins's death was caused by a single bullet fired from the .357 Magnum that Max Bassett turned over at the scene. Again, no question."

No question. Classic Cut And Dryden. "So you're batting two for two," I said.

"And finally, the necklace I found in Mr. Nevins's

290

backpack matched the one reported stolen from Elena Travers."

"Does it have Nevins's prints on it?" I said.

"Excellent question. I was about to get to that. Interestingly enough, it has no prints."

"None?"

He didn't respond. Chuck doesn't answer stupid questions by repeating something he's previously stated.

"Sorry," I said. "I know you said none, but shouldn't the necklace at least have Elena's prints on it?"

"Not if Nevins wiped the necklace clean, which seems like the kind of thing any criminal of average intelligence would do."

I disagreed. Why would Nevins wipe off his prints if he was trying to sell the necklace to Bassett? It didn't make sense, but it wasn't worth debating with Chuck.

A glimmer of an idea popped into my head, and I closed my eyes, trying to track my thoughts. Kylie and Dryden both knew me well enough not to say a word.

"Doc," I said slowly, my eyes still shut, "when you say the necklace was wiped clean, are you talking about the kind of clean you get when you take a diamond ring to a jeweler to be steamed and polished?"

"Oh no," Dryden said. "In that regard, the

necklace is filthy. Precious stones are a magnet for grease, which is why women are told not to put on their jewelry until after they've applied makeup and perfume. Several of the emeralds in this piece have lost their brilliance. They've been dulled by skin oils. But that fact notwithstanding, there are no prints."

My eyes snapped open. "Get me the crime scene photos of Elena Travers."

He shuffled through the pile on the table till he found several of the actress lying dead on a New York sidewalk, her white gown soaked in blood, deep gouges on her skin where the necklace had been ripped from her chest.

"Look at this," I said, tapping on one of the photos. I tapped two more. "And this, and this. Now how about you put that eight-million-dollar necklace back under your microscope."

"Oh my," Dryden said, catching on.

"Son of a bitch," Kylie said, right behind him. "Chuck, if Zach is right, we can nail Max Bassett."

"Oh my," Chuck repeated. "I know what you're looking for, and I can tell you the answer right now. You're not going to find it."

"No evidence at all?" I said.

"Not a shred," he said. "And I will testify to that as well."

"Thanks, but I don't know how well lack of evidence will hold up in court."

"Even so, Detective Jordan, my hat is off to you. Brilliant reasoning. I only wish I had figured it out myself. Bravo, sir."

His face lit up again. Only this time he was smiling at me.

CHAPTER 62

"SINATRA WAS RIGHT," Kylie said. "Saturday night is the loneliest night of the week."

"Then you're in luck," I said. "Another hour and twenty-seven minutes, and it will be Sunday morning."

We were back in the bowels of Hudson Hospital, scanning the monitors, looking for—no, make that hoping for—trouble. It was the second night of the stakeout. More important, it was the twenty-ninth night of my let's-try-living-together-for-thirty-days experiment with Cheryl, and once again we were spending the evening living apart.

"Guys, heads up." It was Frank Cavallaro. There was so much going on in the giant medical complex that we needed an insider to flag anything out of the ordinary. Frank teamed up with us while his second-in-command covered the day shift.

"Station fourteen, camera thirty-three," he said, pointing at the screen.

A sixteen-foot box truck had backed into the loading dock. It was pure white except for the words *Med Waste Evac* painted in red on the side.

"What's the issue?" I asked. "Don't you recognize them?"

"They're our regular biohazard removal service," Cavallaro said, "but it's only ten thirty. They're not supposed to show up till three a.m., when there's a minimal amount of patients roaming around. It skeeves people out to see a big container with the words *Infectious Waste* rolling down the halls."

I keyed my radio. "All units, this is Triage One. Code orange at station fourteen. Fourteen, he's not due till three a.m. Find out his story."

We turned the sound up on the monitor and watched as the guard at the loading dock, a decorated ESU sergeant, approached the driver's side of the truck, clipboard in hand.

"You fellas in a hurry to get home?" he said. "You're about four hours early."

"One of our trucks is out of commission," the driver said, "so they've got us covering two routes. And don't worry about us getting home early. Four hours from now we'll be working in Brooklyn."

"Wave them through, fourteen," I said.

The guard shrugged. "No skin off my nose," he said. "Go do what you've got to do." He walked back to his booth at the loading dock and picked up a newspaper.

The driver and three other men got out of the truck. They were all wearing hooded white Tyvek jumpsuits, chemical gloves, and gas masks. They dropped the hydraulic tailgate, opened the rear doors, climbed up inside, and wheeled out a large metal bin that also had *Med Waste Evac* signage on it.

"They're bogus," Cavallaro said. "First of all, they're overdressed. This is a hospital, not Chernobyl. Second, all they need is a couple of hundred-and-fifty-gallon plastic hampers. I wonder who they stole that shipping container from. It's big enough to hold four refrigerators...or a 3-D mammogram machine."

The four men moved quickly through the corridors, navigating their way past several elevator banks until they got to the one they knew would take them exactly where they wanted to go.

Because of privacy regulations, none of the surveillance cameras past the loading dock had audio capabilities, but we could visually track their progress every step of the way. Once they got to the third floor, the only thing between them and the mammogram machines was an oversize set of metal double doors with a single hasp and padlock holding them together.

"I could open that lock with a bobby pin," Cavallaro said. "It's only there to keep out the nosy staffers who want to see how the renovations are coming along."

The medical waste quartet didn't need a bobby pin. They had a bolt cutter. Within seconds they were inside the construction area, had wheeled up to one of the mammogram machines, and had opened the doors of their transport bin. The driver produced a walkie-talkie, removed his gas mask, and started talking.

"Who is he calling?" Kylie said. "Is it possible they have someone else in the—"

Every picture on the wall of monitors flickered, turned to gray-and-white electronic snow, and then blipped out.

"Shit," Cavallaro yelled. "How the hell did they do that?"

I grabbed my radio. "All units, code red. We've lost visual contact. We have four suspects in white jumpsuits. Lock it down. Repeat: lock down all exits."

I raced out of the security room, Kylie right behind me. Saturday night was no longer lonely.

CHAPTER 63

IN AN IDEAL world, we'd have tracked the theft on video just long enough to have conclusive proof of intention that would hold up in court. We hadn't quite gotten as much as we wanted, but as soon as they cut the power, all bets were off. The cat-and-mouse game was now a manhunt.

I had officers on the fourth, fifth, and sixth floors, and as Kylie and I raced up the stairs, I gave the order for them to converge on the third.

The first shots rang out just as we got to the lobby. Seconds later, I got the radio report.

"Shots fired, third floor. Suspects split up and are on the run. I'm in pursuit of one headed upstairs. The others went south."

The lobby was well covered. Kylie and I ran up

to the second floor just in time to see a man in a white jumpsuit racing down the hall. We drew our guns, and Kylie yelled, "Police! Freeze! Drop your weapon!"

He didn't stop, or freeze, but he did drop something. It wasn't his gun. Kylie and I both dove for cover as the black canister rolled toward us. It exploded in a blinding flash of light, and the ear-splitting blast was magnified by the acoustics of the hospital hallway.

Flash grenades aren't designed to cause permanent injury, but what they lack in destructive power they make up for in their ability to stun anyone who's on the receiving end. I couldn't see for at least five seconds, my legs were shaky when I tried to stand, and my ears were ringing. I helped Kylie to her feet, and by the time we both regained our bearings, our target was at the far end of the corridor.

We got there just in time to see him vault a nurses' station, grab a fire extinguisher off the wall, and race into a room.

We stopped and took positions on either side of the door. "You've got nowhere to go," Kylie yelled, breathing hard. "Come out with your hands up."

He responded by firing a shot. The bullet didn't hit anything, but he'd made his point. He wasn't giving up without a fight. The gunshot was followed by the sound of glass shattering. And then nothing.

Ten seconds into the silence, Kylie dropped low,

darted her head inside the room, and pulled back. "He went out the window."

"It's a two-story jump," I said as we entered.

"No, it's not," she said, looking down. "The roof to the emergency entrance is directly below us, which is why he made for this room."

He had smashed the window with the fire extinguisher, but he'd left jagged shards sticking up from the bottom, and the glass was bloodied.

"Looks like he cut himself up pretty good," Kylie said, picking up the extinguisher. "Maybe it will slow him down." She knocked out the glass stalagmites protruding from the sill, climbed out, and jumped.

I followed. It was only about eight feet to the ER canopy. It was a perfect vantage point to scan the area, and I spotted his standout white jumpsuit a block away, just as he ran down the stairs of the Grand Street subway station.

We dropped from our perch onto the top of an EMS truck parked below, scrambled down the hood of the ambulance, and ran toward the station.

Just as we got to the entrance, we heard the train pull in. We raced down the stairs and hurdled the turnstile. About a dozen people had gotten off the train, and we scanned them just in case he tried to double back and blend in with the people who were exiting.

We didn't see him, and by now everyone who

had been waiting for the train was on board. The platform was empty except for a crumpled heap of white Tyvek.

The conductor's voice bounced off the cavernous walls. "Watch the closing doors."

I body-blocked one just as it was about to shut, and the two of us squeezed onto the last car of the train.

A woman saw our guns and screamed. "Police," I yelled as we dug out our shields. "Everybody stay where you are."

It was a Saturday night crowd, so there were a lot of young people along with the usual melting pot of New Yorkers you find on any given subway ride. Nobody said a word.

"We have to find him before we get to the next station, or we'll lose him," Kylie said.

"He tossed the jumpsuit," I said, "but we don't even know if he got on the train."

"Yes, we do," Kylie said, pointing at the floor.

I bent down to get a closer look. It was small. No bigger than a dime. But it was fresh, and it was red.

Blood.

CHAPTER 64

WE SLID OPEN the door to the next car and made our way down the aisle until we found another small spatter. We kept walking toward the front of the train.

"Next stop, Broadway-Lafayette," the automated voice announced.

"We don't have time to search the whole train before it gets to the next station," I said.

"Then we'll make time," Kylie said, pushing the red button on the emergency intercom.

A female voice snapped on. "This is the conductor. What is your emergency?"

"This is Detective Kylie MacDonald, NYPD. I need you to stop the train now."

"Ma'am, we'll be at the next station in less than thirty seconds. Can this just wait till—"

Kylie exploded. "No! There's an armed fugitive on board. Stop the damn train now."

Within seconds, the train screeched to a stop.

Guns drawn and badges in plain sight, Kylie and I began to follow the trail of blood. We had just entered the next car when the conductor's voice boomed over the PA system.

"Ladies and gentlemen, we're sorry for the delay, but this train has been stopped due to a police investigation. Please remain calm, and we will update you shortly."

"Son of a bitch," Kylie said. "If he didn't know we were coming, he does now."

We opened the door to the fourth car. Nobody said a word, but a handful of awestruck New Yorkers pointed at an emergency window that had been pushed out.

I jumped up on the seat, climbed through the window, and lowered myself onto the catwalk that ran alongside the track. Kylie dropped down behind me.

This would have been the time to call for backup, but our precinct radios don't work underground. We were on our own.

The lighting was minimal, and we moved along the catwalk low and slow, knowing there was a man with a gun who could open fire on us from any dark corner in the tunnel.

I heard a noise behind me. I wheeled around and pointed my gun at a figure coming at me from the shadows. "NYPD!" I yelled. "On the ground. Now!"

"Don't shoot, don't shoot, it's just me. It's just me."

"Me" was a young Hispanic woman wearing a conductor's uniform.

"Get the hell back on that train," I ordered.

"The engineer just radioed me," she said, breathing hard. "Don't shoot. The guy...he's in front of the train. He's almost at the station. He's getting away."

Kylie and I ran along the catwalk. When we were past the first car, we jumped onto the track bed. A lone figure, about fifty yards in front of us, was hobbling toward the station. He grabbed the edge of the station platform, heaved his body up, teetered on the edge of the platform, and fell backward onto the tracks.

He tried to stand, but at this point we were on top of him.

"You win," he said, tossing his gun to the ground.

He was about thirty, with close-cropped blond hair and a pleasant white-bread face that was probably pretty good-looking when it wasn't contorted in pain. "What's your name?" I said.

"Rick Hawk," he said. "Can you do me a favor before you start asking too many questions? I'm bleeding out pretty bad here."

The left leg of his jeans was saturated in blood.

"You probably cut a vein," I said. "If it were an artery, you'd be dead by now."

"Can you get me to a hospital?"

"Sure thing, Mr. Hawk," I said. "We just have to see if there's one left in this city that will treat you."

CHAPTER 65

WHILE KYLIE AND I were escorting Rick Hawk back to Hudson Hospital, his partners in crime were being escorted out: the three men who had been on the biohazard truck with him and the woman who had disabled the security cameras.

"It was a fine night for New York's Finest," Frank Cavallaro said when we regrouped in his office. "No casualties, and best of all, when I wake up in the morning, I'll still be head of security at Hudson Hospital."

With one perp in need of a blood transfusion and the others being transported to Central Booking, Kylie and I decided to call it a night and interrogate them one at a time in the morning.

I got home shortly before midnight.

"Half a day?" Angel said as I walked through the door.

I grinned and resisted the temptation to ask him if my girlfriend was upstairs in the apartment.

She wasn't. And there was no note.

My clothes looked and felt like they'd been worn by a tunnel rat. I peeled them off, took a shower, put on a clean pair of boxers and a T-shirt, opened a cup of peach yogurt, plopped down on the sofa, and flipped on the TV.

It was twelve fifteen on Sunday morning—day thirty of my ill-fated experiment to cohabitate with the woman I loved. Tryouts were over, and I'd pretty much blown it. I was about to be cut from the team.

This is your life now, Zachary, I thought. *Sitting around the apartment in your underwear, clicking the remote, and spooning down fermented milk laced with bacteria and the fruit of your choice. Pathetic.*

I was just settling comfortably onto my pity pot when the front door opened.

"Hi."

It was Cheryl.

I sat upright. "Where the hell have you been?" I demanded. "I've been sitting around waiting for you all night."

I tried to keep a straight face, but it was impossible. The two of us cracked up. It wasn't going to change the facts, but at least it broke the ice.

"My mom had an extra ticket to see *Pagliacci,* and, having nothing better to do, I went," she said.

"Pagliacci is the new guy who plays for the Knicks, right?"

She laughed and sat down on the sofa next to me. "You're home early from an all-night stakeout. Did you catch the bad guys?"

"Five of them."

"Congratulations. So I guess you've been too busy to think about where the two of us go from here."

"Just the opposite. It's all I've been thinking about."

"And?"

"You want to give me your decision first?" I said.

"No. It's on you, Zach. Man up."

"I love you," I said. "And I don't want to lose you."

"I love you too," she said, resting her hand on my knee. "And I definitely don't want to get lost."

"I heard what you said Friday morning at the diner. I thought living together would bring us closer, but it turns out all it does is underscore how much time we spend not living together. You always seem so damn happy to see me when I walk through the door; I never thought about how you must feel when *you* walk through the door, and I'm not there."

"It feels lonely," she said. "I know I'm home, but it still feels like the apartment is empty."

"Okay. Here goes. Manning up," I said. "I realize that not living together works a lot better than living together. I'm willing to go back to the way it was."

Her eyes closed for a second, then she opened them and smiled. "Good call. I think we'll both be happier."

I did my best to smile back. "Plus, now I get my dresser drawers back," I said.

She wrapped her arms around me. "Not all of them. Just because I like waking up in my own bed doesn't mean I want to do it every morning."

CHAPTER 66

SOME COPS CAN crack a major case and ride high on their success for the rest of their careers. Having cracked a politically sensitive crime spree, I'd have been happy to have the euphoria last for a few days, but five hours after I hit the pillow, my trip on the glory train went completely off the rails.

My cell rang. It was Kylie.

"What?" I grumped into the phone.

"Cates just called. She wants us in her office in twenty minutes."

"Why?"

"She didn't elaborate. All she said was, 'Don't be late. Howard Sykes doesn't like to be kept waiting.'"

I jumped out of bed and started throwing on clothes.

"What's going on?" Cheryl asked, still half asleep.

"I'm not sure. All I know is that Howard Sykes is meeting me and Kylie in Cates's office."

"He probably wants to give you the key to the city after what you did last night."

I looked at my watch. I was pretty sure the city didn't start handing out keys at 6:26 in the morning.

I grabbed a cab to the One Nine. Kylie was waiting for me outside. We bolted up the stairs and were in Cates's office by 6:44. Sykes was already there.

Cates skipped the usual foreplay. "Did you interview Rick Hawk last night?" she asked.

"The man was in no condition to talk," I said. "He was a couple of pints low on blood."

"Did you run his name through the system?"

"Our priority was getting him on life support," Kylie said. "The task force collared four other perps, so we turned the whole lot of them over to Central Booking to sort out. Why? Did Hawk have any priors?"

Cates nodded toward Howard Sykes. It was his show now.

"He had one big prior," Sykes said. "Three years ago, Staff Sergeant Richard Hawk saved the lives of hundreds of soldiers, coalition partners, and civilians by holding off a half dozen Afghan suicide bombers who breached a NATO base. He was awarded the Silver Star."

Sykes handed us a photo of a four-star general pinning the award on Hawk's chest. "Hawk left the military two years ago," he said. "Since then he's been a champion for veterans' rights. Bottom line: the man you arrested last night is a national hero."

My stomach dropped. Kylie, however, tackled the news head-on.

"With all due respect, sir," she said, "national heroes don't steal millions of dollars' worth of medical equipment."

"Understood. But you're thinking like a cop."

"I thought that was my job, sir."

"It is, but it's my job to think about the public backlash that's going to erupt when word gets out that my wife's elite task force locked up America's poster boy."

"Sir, I am patriotic to the core," Kylie snapped, "but a Silver Star isn't a get-out-of-jail-free card. What are we supposed to do, unarrest him?"

"Rein it in, Detective," Cates ordered. "Last night we had a police problem. You solved it. Now it's about to become a political shit storm, and if you think that's not your problem too, then you're in the wrong unit. This team was founded to serve at the mayor's pleasure. When she has a problem, we all have one."

"Yes, ma'am," Kylie said. And then, in a rare moment for her, she apologized. "Howard, I'm sorry. What can we do to help?"

He shook his head. "I don't know. I'm an ad guy. Muriel has only been mayor for three months. Before that, she was a U.S. attorney. We both swam with sharks, but they were toothless compared to the ones we're up against now. Especially Woloch."

I winced when I heard the name. "Dennis Woloch?" I said.

Sykes nodded.

Woloch is every ADA's nightmare. He's the most formidable defense attorney in the city—a cross between Clarence Darrow and Lord Voldemort. His remarkable ability to mesmerize twelve people in a jury box is so legendary that the press dubbed him the Warlock—a name that only enhances his mystique.

"He's been retained by the Hudson Hospital Five," Cates said. "He called the DA this morning. He wants the city to drop the case."

Kylie exploded. "*Drop the case?* Captain, we caught them stealing the equipment. They *shot* at us."

"It turns out they used nonlethal weapons and rubber bullets," Cates said.

"Nothing is 100 percent *non*lethal."

"The Warlock will claim that these were trained marksmen. They only used the guns to deter the police."

"What about the ten hospitals they robbed?"

"He informed the DA that he plans to use the Robin Hood defense."

"Correct me if I'm wrong," Kylie said, her tone barely on the right side of snarky, "but didn't Robin Hood steal from the rich and give to the poor?"

"Yes, MacDonald. I read the book, saw the movie," Cates said. "But according to Woloch, Congress has turned a deaf ear on the sergeant's campaign for better health-care benefits for veterans, so Hawk and his band of Merry Men have decided to fund it on their own. They're not selling the stolen equipment on the black market. It's all going into an underground health clinic they're building for veterans. A jury will eat it up."

"A jury?" Sykes said. "The whole purpose of bringing Red into this was to keep everything out of the press. If this goes public, it will be a front-page nightmare of global proportions and a political disaster for Muriel."

"I have a possible solution," I said.

Sykes exhaled. "Tell me. Please."

"You're not going to like it," I said.

"It doesn't matter if I like it," Sykes said, "as long as my wife likes it."

"She'll probably hate it," I said. "It's got no political artistry to it. It's pretty much straightforward, get-the-job-done cop logic."

"I don't give a rat's ass about political artistry,"

Sykes said. "All I want to do is keep Woloch the Warlock from positioning Sergeant Hawk as a modern-day Robin Hood. Because if he does, my wife will come off looking like the goddamn Sheriff of Nottingham."

CHAPTER 67

"THE MAN IS in over his head," Cates said as soon as Howard Sykes left her office. "I don't care what he did in advertising. He's got a lot to learn about damage control."

"At least he was smart enough to give us the green light on Zach's idea," Kylie said.

"Good luck making it work," Cates said. "Ivy League smarts are no match for a street fighter like Woloch. He's got the mayor up against the hot pipes, and he's going to ask her for the moon. The son of a bitch is cunning."

"Speaking of cunning," I said, "Max Bassett has been lying to us big-time."

"About what? He copped to shooting Jeremy Nevins."

"Why wouldn't he?" I said. "A grand jury won't indict him for shooting a home invader who killed his brother."

"Then what is he lying about?"

"He ID'd the necklace that Chuck Dryden found in Jeremy Nevins's backpack as the one that was taken the night of the robbery."

"And the insurance company confirmed it," Cates said.

"Not exactly. All they did was confirm it's the one they insured. Once they got it back, they were off the hook for eight mil, so why bother doing forensics to see if it was the same one that was stolen?"

"The *same* one? You're telling me there was more than one necklace?"

"We think so."

"Based on what?"

"Based on the fact that when your brother is lying in a pool of blood, and you just shot the man who killed him, your story on how it all went down can't be so perfect that it sounds like you've rehearsed it for hours. We knew Max was hiding something, but we didn't know what, so we had Chuck run a DNA test on the necklace. The crime scene photos showed that Elena's neck and chest had been lacerated during the robbery, but the necklace that came out of Nevins's backpack didn't have a single trace of her hair, her skin, or her blood."

Cates shrugged. "So Nevins had it steam cleaned,

or whatever jewelers do to get the gunk off and the shine back."

"It wasn't clean. Dryden said the necklace was ripe with a buildup of grease and skin oils, but none of the DNA belonged to Elena."

"Because she never had it around her neck," Cates said, connecting the dots.

"We think the Bassetts gave Elena a fake, then had it stolen so they could collect the insurance on the real one," Kylie said. "So we contacted the insurance investigator. Turns out the Bassetts filed three claims for theft in the past twenty-two years, each with a different insurance company. Each claim was paid in full, a total of nineteen million. This robbery was probably supposed to go down just like the others, but it all went to shit when Elena got killed."

I picked up the story. "After that, they all turned against each other. Nevins shot Davis. Teddy Ryder took off with the bogus necklace, which he probably thought was real. Then Nevins kills Leo. And finally Max conveniently overhears them fighting, kills Nevins, and plants the real necklace on him. He won't collect the insurance, but he doesn't care, because it looks like the case is all neatly tied up, so the heat's off."

"And with his brother dead," Kylie said, "Max would now be the sole owner of the company, which is probably an even bigger payout than eight million."

"Can you prove any of this?" Cates said.

"The only way we can prove anything would be to find the fake that Elena Travers was wearing."

"Then find it, because the DA will laugh you out of his office if you ask him to hang a case on a *lack* of DNA. Do you even know where to look?"

"We'll start with Annie Ryder," Kylie said. "If her son, Teddy, has it, she may be willing to turn it over if we cut him a deal."

"Talk to her and see what she wants," Cates said.

"If we can find her," I said. "The way the bodies have been piling up, we're hoping she's still alive."

CHAPTER 68

MAX BASSETT PULLED the Land Rover off the Taconic at the Shrub Oak exit and was happy to catch the red light at the bottom of the ramp. It gave him time to take another quick look at the *New York Post* sitting on the passenger seat.

He grinned. His picture was on the front page. He read the headline for the tenth time.

BIG GAME HUNTER BAGS ELENA JEWEL THIEF

He flipped to page three and reread the first sentence of the story.

Maxwell Bassett, the big-game-hunting, Hemingway-esque celebrity jeweler, added "hero" to his list of accomplishments when he shot and killed Jeremy Nevins, the man behind the murders of actress Elena Travers and Bassett's brother, Leopold.

The car behind him honked, and Max turned west onto Route 6. "I'm a hero, Leo," he said. "Too bad you're not around to throw one of your soirees in my honor."

The fifty-minute drive from Manhattan had been a breeze, but the last leg required his full attention. He tossed the newspaper to the floor of the car so he could focus. It was early spring, and while Mohegan Lake had thawed, the three-mile stretch of winding unpaved road that led to his twelve-million-dollar waterfront home was still patched with the ravages of a brutal winter.

Ten minutes later, he eased the Land Rover into the garage and went directly to the boathouse. His Skeeter FX-21 had been idle since October, but one phone call to his longtime caretaker, Tom Messner, and the sleek twenty-one-foot bass boat was ready for the season. He opened the cooler Tom had stowed on board. Inside were the roast beef sandwiches, thermos of coffee, and cigars he'd requested, along with something the eighth-grade-educated Messner hardly ever left: a handwritten note.

Dear Mr. Bassett. Sorry to here about your bother Leo. From, Tom.

"My *bother?*" Max said, laughing out loud. "Good news, Tom. My bother Leo won't be bothering me anymore."

Max turned over the Skeeter and piloted it slowly toward the center of the lake. He reflected on what had happened since he'd last been on the boat.

It started six months ago at one of Leo's overpriced vanity parties. As soon as Sonia arrived with Jeremy Nevins in tow, Max recognized the type: a pretty-faced sleazebag who would fuck anyone who could get him close to the rich and powerful. Max said a cold hello and watched as Jeremy's eyes darted hungrily to Max's rose gold and diamond Audemars Piguet watch. Pretty *and* greedy, Max noted.

Leo, of course, couldn't stop drooling over the boy. That night, the brothers had their usual screaming match over franchising the Bassett name. It ended with Leo storming out, shrieking, "Over my dead body."

So be it, Max decided. The next day he invited Jeremy to lunch.

"Let me cut to the chase," Max said as soon as the drinks had been served. "My brother has a crush on you. I'd like you to ask him out."

"Why doesn't he ask me himself?" the young cocksman said, sipping a Kir Royale.

"He's not stupid. You're thirty years younger and totally out of his league."

"True. Then why would I go out with him if *you* ask me?"

"Because," Max said, removing the eighty-thousand-dollar watch from his wrist and sliding it across the table, "I think you appreciate the finer things in life, and you'll do what it takes to get them."

Maxwell Bassett had stalked elephants in Africa, rhinos in Namibia, and crocs along the Nile, so baiting the trap for a rat was easy. Jeremy's hand trembled as he picked up the watch.

After that it was a simple game of raising the stakes. It all went flawlessly until Leo had a hissy fit and bailed out of the limo, and Jeremy's bungling minions shot the wrong person. But Max adapted, and on Thursday night, it all fell into place in Leo's kitchen. There was only one last loose end: find the cultured crystal necklace he had crafted before the cops did.

And then, out of the blue, it found him. An email had arrived last night with a picture of the fake, the words For Sale, and a phone number.

He called. The seller was none other than Annie Ryder. Negotiating with her dim-witted son would have been easy: agree to any price, and as soon as Max had the necklace in his hands, he'd pay Teddy off with a single bullet. But Jeremy had clued him in on the old con woman. She was too smart to believe that Max would roll over without bargaining. He'd have to haggle, make her think she was working for the money, and finally let her win.

All he needed was a little patience. And a second bullet.

He killed the engine midlake and the boat drifted to a stop. The NorCross HawkEye depth finder on the dash told him it was fifty-nine feet to the bottom. *Deep enough.* Teddy and Annie Ryder would be at the house at two p.m. By nightfall, they'd be at the bottom of Mohegan Lake, their feet weighted and their stomachs slit to keep the gases from letting them float to the surface.

A few days after that, the cops would release Leo's body, and Max would pose solemn-faced and grief-stricken for the press at his funeral. After that he'd sign the contract with Precio Mundo, and his first design would be a tribute to his dear departed brother.

He lit one of the cigars Tom had left, sat back, and soaked up the April sunshine. The hunt was almost over.

CHAPTER 69

IN AN ALTERNATE universe, Annie Ryder decided, she and Max Bassett would have made a great team. He was a master at forging high-end jewelry, and she…hell, she was a legend.

They could have made millions, but she'd have dropped him like a bad check the minute the shooting started. She could deal with the big-game-hunter shit. It was a dick thing. But killing Elena Travers—that was a deal breaker. Bassett didn't pull the trigger, but he'd hired Raymond to do his dirty work, and that left Teddy facing an accessory-to-murder rap.

The Partner That Might Have Been was now her sworn enemy, and Annie Ryder was on her way to settle the score.

"This guy's driveway is like a hockey rink," Teddy

said as he navigated the beat-up Chevy van down a stretch of icy road leading to Bassett's house.

"Just drive slow," Annie said as she caught sight of a security camera on a tree. "And smile: we're on TV."

Teddy, simple boy that he was, slowed down and smiled.

"Remember: no talking," Annie reminded Teddy after he'd parked the van and they were walking toward the house.

Teddy drew an imaginary zipper across his lips, and Annie rang the bell. Max Bassett opened the door and patted Teddy down.

"He's clean," Max said, turning to Annie. "How about you?"

"I don't believe in guns," she said, "and unless you have a female security officer, you're not laying a finger on me."

Max didn't care if she had an arsenal under her red and black Rutgers sweatshirt. She'd be dead before she could get off a shot.

"We can talk in my den," Max said, leading them down a hallway to a thick slab of Makassar ebony that he'd cut himself in an Indonesian jungle. He tapped a code into a keypad and the ebony door swung open.

They entered, and Annie heard the electronic click as the door shut. Architecturally, she thought, the room was magnificent. A stone fireplace soared to the roof, intersecting a hand-hewn wooden balcony that was bathed in soft light. But the entire space was awash in death. A snarling white tiger frozen midleap took center stage, surrounded by dozens of other stuffed carcasses, horns, skins, and mounted heads—a lifetime of trophies collected by a man whose passion was to kill other living creatures.

She and Teddy settled onto a zebra-skin sofa while Max took a seat behind an ivory-trimmed leather desk. "How much do you want?" he said.

"The necklace was insured for eight million," Annie said.

"That one was recovered. By now you must have realized that the one you have is a relatively worthless fake."

"Don't sell yourself short," Annie said, smiling. "It's an original Max Bassett, so it's far from worthless."

"You flatter me, madam, which I'm sure is your intent. However, even with my name attached, it would only be worth a hundred thousand, tops."

"And why would I take a hundred grand when the insurance company is offering a reward of a quarter of a million?"

Max's jaw tightened. "I hate to break it to you, but the reward has been off the table ever since the necklace was recovered."

"And I hate to break it to *you*, but the necklace they recovered was the one you planted on Jeremy after you killed him. The reward is for the one that was ripped off Elena's neck. The stones may be fake, but put it under a microscope, and you'll find some very real traces of Elena Travers's blood, skin, and DNA. Surely that's worth more than a hundred thousand dollars to you—especially now that you're about to enter into holy matrimony with the big boys at Precio Mundo."

Max forced a smile. "You do your homework."

"That's what career criminals do, Mr. Bassett. You know what your problem is? You have an evil soul and a black heart. What you lack is a criminal mind. You paid Raymond to kill Elena, and because of your stupid thinking, my son is wanted as an accessory to murder. So don't expect to get off cheap."

Max bolted from his chair. "I have three million dollars in my safe. You produce the necklace, and I'll give you the cash, but let's get one thing clear. I did not pay Davis to kill Elena. What happened was an accident. Leo and I were working an insurance scam, and it went bad."

"And that, sir, is why I never play with guns," Annie said. "When my scams go sour, nobody dies."

"Ma." It was Teddy. "Let's go. We got enough."

Annie smacked the back of his head. "What did I tell you about talking?"

"Don't do it. But I didn't say anything bad. I just said let's go."

No, Max thought. *You said, "Let's go. We got enough,"
and Mama Bear got upset.*

"Three million—cash," Annie said. "Pack it up.
Teddy and I will get the necklace."

You do that, Max thought. *You bring me the necklace,
and we'll see who looks stupid when I put a bullet through
your—*

And in that instant, Max Bassett realized he'd
made the biggest mistake of his life. He'd been a
hunter since he was old enough to hold a bow and
arrow. But long before he learned to shoot, his father had taught him how a hunter thinks.

*It's not about who's faster or stronger. It's about who's
smarter. Hunting is a test of wits, Max. They're not dumb
animals. They're cunning. So never, ever underestimate the
intelligence of your prey.*

Annie Ryder was extremely cunning. She was far
too smart to give him the necklace and expect to
walk away with the money. She hadn't come for the
money. She had come for the confession that she
had just goaded out of him.

And her son, as dumb as he was, knew they had
gotten what they had come for. Only instead of
putting on a high-stakes poker face the way his
mother could, Teddy had blurted out, *"Let's go. We
got enough."*

The old woman and her son weren't the prey.
They were the bait. And Max wasn't the hunter. He
was the hunted.

CHAPTER 70

"WE GOT HIM," Kylie said as soon as Max Bassett admitted that Elena's murder was an insurance scam gone bad.

"We've only got him on tape," I said. "I'll feel better when we have him in cuffs."

Kylie and I were in the back of Teddy Ryder's van, listening to the dialogue inside Bassett's lake house. A few hours earlier, we had made a deal with the devil. In this case, Satan looked like a sweet old lady who had just stepped out of a Norman Rockwell painting, but she had the negotiating skills of a Mafia underboss.

Annie knew we didn't have enough hard evidence to prosecute Bassett, so she had offered to help us take him down. All she wanted was immunity for her son. She may as well have asked that the city throw him a ticker-tape parade. Senior ADA Mick Wilson was not in the habit of dropping accessory-to-murder charges, but in this case, he didn't blink.

Locking up a patsy like Teddy Ryder would barely register as a blip on the media Richter scale, but indicting a high-profile New Yorker like Max Bassett would reverb around the world. Mick was happy to trade the little fish for the big one, and I'm sure that as soon as he gave us the green light, he started daydreaming about who would play him in the movie.

All Kylie and I had to do was arrest Bassett on a charge that would stick. And we only had three hours to pull the entire operation together. Annie had already agreed to a two p.m. meeting with Bassett, and asking him for more time would push the needle on his trust meter into the red.

Our first challenge was finding a command vehicle. The department has a lot of tricked-out vans for stakeouts and surveillance, but since this one had to look like it belonged to Teddy, we pulled a 1996 four-wheel-drive Chevy Astro out of the impound lot and had the techs slap together a sound system. We had no video, but on the plus side, we did have heat and brakes.

Body wires have gotten smaller over time, but they're still easy to detect if the informant gets frisked. So wiring Teddy was out. But Annie assured us that Bassett wouldn't touch her. "He'll never suspect that I cut a deal with the cops," she told us. "Hell, I can't believe it myself."

The ground rules were simple. Go in, get a confession, and get out.

"You'll need a safe word," Kylie said. "If anything goes wrong, just say it once, and we'll come running."

"How about *help?*" Teddy said.

"Smart thinking, kiddo," Annie told her son. As soon as he was out of earshot, she changed the safe word to *hot chocolate*.

The four of us piled into the junker, and by one thirty we were in a parking lot behind an Audi dealership on Main Street in Mohegan Lake, waiting to rendezvous with our backup, an ESU entry team from the Bronx.

At 1:50, the team leader radioed us with the bad news. "We hit a deer on the Taconic. Two of our guys are on the way to the ER, and the truck is out of service until the motor pool picks Bambi out of the fan housing. I radioed dispatch, and they can have another unit in place by sixteen hundred hours."

Annie shook her head. "No. We've got to go now."

"We can't," I said. "The man's got enough firepower to defend the Alamo. We're waiting for backup."

"Then you can wait for them without me. If I

call a mark ten minutes before showtime and try to put him on hold for two hours, he's going to know something's going down. Just get me there on time, let me do what I have to do, and once I'm out, you can wait as long as you want before you storm the castle."

"Annie…"

"I'm serious, Detective. I talked to the man on the phone last night. He's squirrelly enough as it is. Either we go now or the deal is off."

She was bluffing. She'd do anything to keep her kid out of jail. But I couldn't take the chance. I looked at Kylie. It was easy to figure where her head was at.

"Let's roll," she said, and Teddy pulled the van out of the parking lot for the final three-mile drive to Bassett's house.

Less than twenty minutes later, Annie had delivered. She'd wormed a confession out of Bassett. Now all we had to do was wait for our two informants to get out of the house.

And then Teddy, who had been told not to talk, talked. "We got enough," he said.

"Did Teddy just tell Bassett that they got the confession they came for?" Kylie said.

"It sounded that way to me," I said. "But we know what he means. The question is, will Bassett pick up on it?"

We waited for Annie to ask Bassett if he could

make her a cup of hot chocolate, but she didn't. And then she said, "Teddy and I will get the necklace."

"They're coming out," Kylie said. "You ready?"

"We're not waiting for backup, are we?" I said.

"Too risky. If she doesn't come back right away, he'll know we're out here, and we'll lose the element of surprise. As soon as she and Teddy are safe, you cover the back, I'll go in the front, and we'll take him down."

We heard footsteps over the wire as Annie and Teddy walked through the house. As soon as the front door opened, the signal started to break up.

"Fabric rubbing against the mic," Kylie said. "It's freezing out there. She's probably hugging her arms to her chest."

The static continued, and then the signal dropped. "Lost her," I said.

"It doesn't matter," Kylie said. "She and Teddy are on their way back to the van, and Bassett is probably sitting in his living room with a loaded elephant gun, waiting to get his hands on the—"

The impact was bone-jarring. It felt like the van had been hit by a train. We found out later it was a Land Rover, which is almost as lethal.

The side panel caved in, and the van slid across the frozen ground. Neither Kylie nor I had been braced for the collision, and we both wound up on the hard metal floor.

Before I could get my bearings, I heard an engine roaring, bearing down on us hard. The second crash was a bigger jolt than the first. The van flipped over, teetered, and then rolled downhill, flipping over one more time, and another, and another, until something big—a tree, probably—broke our descent.

If it hadn't been for a wall-mounted safety bar, I'd have been thrown around like a rag doll in a washing machine. Even so, my left shoulder and my right knee took a pummeling.

Kylie wasn't as lucky. She was holding on to the back of the driver's seat, a glazed look in her eyes, blood streaming down her face.

"We should have waited for backup," she said.

CHAPTER 71

AS SOON AS Max realized that the Ryders were there for his confession and not for the money, he reached behind his back for his gun, held it inches from Annie's head, and put his index finger to his lips.

Slow-witted as he was, Teddy got the message. He froze.

Max carefully lifted the bottom of Annie's sweatshirt. *No wonder the old crone didn't want to be patted down. She was wired.*

He turned the gun on Teddy and whispered in Annie's ear, "How many cops in the van?"

She held up two fingers.

Maxwell Bassett was a doomsday prepper—a lifelong survivalist. For decades he'd been prepared for that apocalyptic day when he would have to run from life as he knew it. In all his Armageddon scenarios, he pictured a foreign invasion, a catastrophic natural disaster, or a total societal collapse. Never in his wildest fantasies could he have imagined that he'd be taken down by a conniving old hag and her idiot son.

It didn't matter. He was ready. With the gun trained on them, he went to a closet and pulled out a timeworn, well-traveled Rufiji Safari bag. It was filled with everything he'd need to escape to the fortress he'd built thirty years ago in the middle of the British Columbian wilderness.

He'd have liked to put a bullet through Teddy's empty skull, but the need for silence trumped the desire for payback.

"Now you just sit here and be a good boy," he whispered in Teddy's ear. "If you're not, you know what's going to happen to your mother, don't you?"

Teddy nodded, and then sat stone-faced as Bassett led Annie out of the room and closed the door behind them.

As soon as they were outside, Bassett manipulated the old lady's microphone just enough to convince the two cops that she was on her way to the van. Then he yanked it out of the transmitter and tossed it in the snow.

"Get in," he said, opening the driver's-side door of the LR4 and shoving her over to the passenger seat.

"Buckle up," he said, starting the car. It was a noisy beast, but the odds were that the cops would have their headsets pressed to their ears, trying to pick up a signal from their informant. They'd never know what hit them. The 340-horse supercharged V-6 engine roared to life.

The aging van was sitting a hundred feet away, its side panel a perfect target for the Rover.

Annie held her hands up to shield herself.

"What are you afraid of, Grandma?" Bassett said. "You're the hammer, not the nail."

"What do you think I'm afraid of, asshole? You T-bone that van, and we're both going to get a face full of air bag."

"How dumb do you think I am?" Bassett said, turning the Rover so that it was facing away from the Chevy.

Then he threw it into reverse and hit the gas, and the two-and-a-half-ton all-terrain vehicle lurched backward, barreled down the driveway, and plowed into the sweet spot of the soccer-mom sedan.

The side caved in, the van skittered across the ice, and even at thirty miles an hour, the Rover's air bags didn't deploy.

"One more should do it," Bassett said as he jammed the car into low and pulled forward so he could get up another head of steam. Once again he shifted into reverse, stepped on the accelerator, and plowed backward into the wounded cop car.

This time the Rover's powerful six-foot rear end did the job. The van rolled onto its roof, flipped onto its side, and wavered at the top of an embankment. Then gravity took over, and Bassett listened to the music of tearing metal and breaking glass as the van careened down the hill.

He didn't take the time to examine his handiwork. Even if the cops inside weren't dead, they were in no condition to follow him.

He was 3,152 miles from the sanctuary where he'd spend the next few years hunting, fishing, and reengineering his life.

He looked over at the old lady in the passenger seat next to him. She wasn't going for the entire ride. He was sure he'd find a permanent home for her in less than fifty miles.

CHAPTER 72

KYLIE'S BLOND HAIR was streaked with red, and there was a four-inch gash across her scalp. "Son of a bitch blindsided us," she said, wiping the blood from her face with her shirtsleeve. "Don't let him get away. Call it in. Fast."

I was about to reach for my radio when I heard someone at the back door. The van was on its side, so whoever was trying to get in had to pull the right rear door straight up. Daylight flooded in, and Kylie and I drew our guns and yelled "Freeze" in unison.

"Don't shoot, don't shoot, it's me." It was Teddy. "Are you guys okay? Because Bassett's getting away. You gotta catch him." His hands were flying in all directions as he jabbered wildly.

"Hold your hands in the air where I can see them," I said. "Where's your mother?"

He flung his arms high, annoyed that we suddenly didn't trust him. "Bassett pulled a gun on us and took her hostage. Then he got in his car and smashed into your van. Twice. Knocked you right down a hill," he said, stating the obvious.

"Do you know where they're going?"

"How the hell would *I* know where they're going? He found the wire, and now he's mad at Ma. The guy is crazy. You said you had backup. Where are all the other cops?"

He was frantic, bordering on hysterical, tears streaming down his cheeks. I put my gun away. "All right, calm down. We're doing all we can," I said. "You can help us. What kind of car was he driving?"

"A Land Rover. Silver. But don't shoot at him. He's got Ma in the car."

I got on the radio and called in a ten thirteen— officer needs assistance. And in our case, we needed lots of it.

I gave the dispatcher a quick rundown of the situation, along with a description of the fugitive, the car, and the hostage. It all went smoothly till I gave him my location.

"And you want NYPD to respond to an incident up in the sticks?" he said.

"An incident?" I screamed. "A maniac just tried to kill two NYPD detectives. Jurisdiction be damned.

I don't care who you send. There's a killer on the loose, and he's got a hostage. I want local backup, state troopers, air support—anyone and everyone who can help us cut off his escape route and close in on him."

Teddy stared at me from the back door, his hands still over his head. "They coming?" he said.

"Your guess is as good as mine. Now put your hands down and help us out of this van."

Teddy held the door up high, and we crawled out. After we'd spent so many hours in the van, the cold air felt good. I stood up and put as much weight as I could on my right knee. It was sore, but it held me up.

Kylie sat on a log, picked up a handful of snow, and pressed it to the gash on her skull.

My radio crackled, and I took a call from dispatch. It was a different voice this time—older, calmer. "We're on it, Detective," this one said. "The staties are sending up a bird, and the county sheriff is setting up roadblocks at the entrances to the Taconic for fifteen miles on either side."

"That's not going to help," I said. "This guy is on the one road out of here, and it's slow going. The best way to stop him is to cut him off now. How soon can you get a unit to where Lakeshore Drive intersects with Mohegan Avenue?"

A long pause, and then, "I can divert some of the county cops and probably have them in place in twelve minutes."

"He'll be in the wind by then, and he's not going to be getting on the Taconic," I said. "He knows every back road, off road, and rabbit trail for miles. Tell state we need that bird in the air now, or we'll lose him."

I put my radio down and shattered the serenity of the woodlands with a loud string of four-letter words.

"What's going on?" Teddy asked.

I was in no mood for Teddy's constant questions. "We're trying to get some goddamn backup over to the other side of the lake before Bassett gets there," I said, "but in the entire state of New York, not one cop is close enough. That's what's going on."

"So why don't you two guys go? I promise, I won't try to escape. I'll wait for you right here."

"We can't go, Teddy," I said. "As you may have noticed, we don't have a car."

"Right." He thought about it for a few seconds. "I have an idea," he said.

"What?" I snapped, my patience out the window.

"If you want to get to the far side of the lake," Teddy said, "why don't you just take Mr. Bassett's boat?"

CHAPTER 73

"HOW WERE WE supposed to know he had a boat?" Kylie grunted as we clambered up the steep embankment. "We were working blind inside that van."

"Right," I said. "Millionaire outdoorsman. House on a lake. It's not like we're trained detectives."

Teddy helped pull us up over the ridge and onto the driveway. "It's over there," he said, pointing to a covered boathouse attached to the garage.

We were both operating on high-octane adrenaline, and we sprinted to the dock, where a sleek red Skeeter bass boat was waiting, keys still in the ignition. We jumped in. Kylie cranked up the engine and leaned on the throttle.

"Bassett's got a good head start," she yelled, "but he's got to navigate three miles of bad road."

Skimming across the lake at seventy miles an hour, we closed in on the northern tip fast, and Kylie, who pilots watercraft as recklessly as she drives, waited until the last possible second to kill the engine. The Skeeter coasted into a patch of frozen wild ricegrass and came to rest against a guardrail that separated the lake from Mohegan Avenue.

"We're in luck," she yelled as she hopped the rail and ran toward a dark green Ford pickup that was parked on the shoulder. The gold lettering across the side said *New York State Environmental Conservation Police.*

EnCon cops, who started out over a century ago as game and fish protectors, still focus on environmental crime, but the modern day ECO is armed and empowered to enforce all the laws of the state.

The cop who got out of the truck was beanpole high and thin, with a longer than average neck, a smaller than average chin, and the standard wraparound Oakley shades.

Kylie and I flashed our shields and identified ourselves.

"John Woodruff," he said. "What's NYPD looking for up here in the sticks?"

"Did you see a silver Land Rover come out of Lakeshore Drive?" I asked.

"That'd be Mr. Bassett," the cop said. "He rolled

by maybe five minutes ago. He had a passenger in the front seat. What's going on?"

"The passenger is a hostage, and Bassett is wanted for murder," I said.

"There's a couple of countries in Africa that would like to prosecute him for killing endangered species," Woodruff said, "but I'm guessing you're talking about murdering another person."

"Several," I said. "We're going to need to take your truck."

"It's all yours, Detective, but unless you know what you're doing, you're not going to catch him."

"Why's that?" Kylie said, climbing into the front seat of the pickup. "Because we're city cops?"

"No, ma'am," Woodruff said. "I know some damn smart city cops. But it's hard to catch someone if he ain't running."

"What is that supposed to mean?" Kylie said.

"Bassett's crazy, but he ain't stupid. He's got hidey-holes from here to Saskatchewan. He'll hunker down in one, bide his time till he can jack a car from some drunk fisherman, then move from one bunker to the next until he finally gets to the big prepper palace he's built in the middle of God knows where."

"He can't hide," Kylie said. "We've got air support, we'll call in K-9—"

"Choppers? Dogs? Lady, now you sound like a city cop—and not one of the smart ones."

"What do you suggest?" I said.

"Me?" he said, taking off his shades. His eyes were a deep blue, calming and commanding at the same time. Hands down, they were his best feature. "Stop wasting time and hunt him down before he can settle in. And since you don't know where to hunt, I'd suggest you take along some good ole boy who's lived here the past thirty-four years, is a trained law enforcement officer, and can shoot the winky off a chipmunk at a hundred yards."

"Get in," Kylie said, nodding her head toward the passenger seat.

Woodruff opened the driver's side door. "All due respect, ma'am, how about you slide over?"

She did, and the two city cops and the good ole boy headed toward the woods to track down the millionaire version of Rambo.

CHAPTER 74

WOODRUFF DROVE WITH one hand and dialed his cell phone with the other.

"Andy," he said, "I got two NYPD detectives in the truck, and they're looking for the butcher." Pause. "No—murder and kidnapping. He's got a female hostage in his Rover. He rolled by me on Mohegan six minutes ago. If he can make it to the caves on California Hill, we'll never dig him out. Get on the radio and shut down Peekskill Hollow at Tompkins Corners."

Another pause. "No. Put it on the air. Loud and proud. He's got a scanner, and we want him to know he's cut off—force him to go to ground sooner rather than later. If there's anything you don't want him to hear, use your cell."

He hung up.

"The butcher?" Kylie said.

"What else would you call a man who paid thirty thousand dollars to slaughter a giraffe who had been nursing her calf, then posed for a trophy photo standing over her with a .458 Winchester Magnum?"

"Do you hunt?" she asked.

"Since I was a kid. I shoot what the law allows, and I eat what I kill. But people like Bassett are thrill seekers. The rarer the breed, the more protected the species, the greater his bloodlust." He shook his head in disgust. "Do you fish?" he said.

Kylie looked at him like he'd asked if she crocheted. "No."

"Trout season just opened. You ever want to unwind from the stress of the big city, come up here, and I'll take you out on the lake," he said. "Both of you," he added quickly, lest anyone think he was hitting on a fellow police officer in the middle of a manhunt.

The radio was tuned to the universal police frequency, and we picked up bits and pieces of the dragnet as it came together. The chopper was airborne, the Taconic was covered, and the roadblock at Tompkins Corners was in place. Woodruff drove with purpose, making turns without hesitation.

"You know where he's going, don't you?" I said.

"I've got a pretty good idea. I'm a fourth-generation ECO, Detective. My great-grandfather was murdered by a poacher in 1919. I've had my sights on the butcher for years. I know his habits and his habitats. Bringing him down would be an honor and a privilege."

We drove along a two-lane that cut through a thick forest caught up in the confusion of seasonal change. Broad patches of snow-covered ground proclaimed that winter was not ready to move on, while tiny green buds and dots of purple and white crocuses declared otherwise.

Woodruff slowed the truck down to thirty. Three times he brought it to a full stop, got out, surveyed the area, and moved on. At the fourth stop, he walked to the shoulder, picked something up off the ground, and came back.

"There's an old logging trail through here," he said. "We keep it dozed as a firebreak, and campers or hunters who know about it will use it to go a couple of miles off-road. There are fresh tire tracks, and I found this."

There was a small ball of red cotton in his hand.

"It looks like fabric pilling, and it's the same color as the sweatshirt the hostage is wearing," Kylie said. "She could have picked it off and flicked it out the window."

"I'm going to go in and find out," Woodruff said.

"We're going with you," Kylie said.

"I'm wearing body armor," he said.

"What do you think this is?" she said, slapping the vest on her chest.

"Kevlar. It holds up pretty good against a low- or medium-velocity pistol round, but Bassett is going to be carrying a high-velocity rifle. I'm wearing ceramic. I can take the hit. You can't."

"And if he aims for the head, none of us can take the hit," Kylie said. "This is our show, and we're not going to sit by the side of the road and watch it play out without us. Now let's move out and take this bastard down."

"Yes, ma'am," Woodruff said, an expression of newfound appreciation in his eyes. The look only lasted a split second, but I recognized it. I'd seen it from other men in the past when they realized that Detective Kylie MacDonald is as ballsy as she is beautiful.

I had the feeling that the subject of a fishing trip was going to come up again. And this time, my name wouldn't be on the guest list.

CHAPTER 75

"WE'RE GOING TO need some firepower," Woodruff said, grabbing a Smith & Wesson .308 semiautomatic rifle and a Mossberg 500 tactical shotgun from the gun rack. "Which one of you is the better shot?"

I pointed at Kylie, and she took the Mossberg.

"A lot of hunters set up trail cams," Woodruff said. "The one in that tree is probably his. If the motion detector picks you up, it'll send an instant picture to his cell phone. It's got a range of about seventy-five feet, so keep your distance."

Even with him pointing straight at it, I could barely make out the camouflaged box that blended in with the bark. "How about you point them out along the way?" I said.

He grinned, took the lead, and headed into the woods. Kylie and I flanked out to either side and kept ten feet behind. It had been thirty minutes since Bassett had plowed into our van, and by now my right knee had swollen to the point where it strained against my pant leg, and I was favoring it by limping.

Woodruff spotted two more trail cams, and we gave each one a wide berth. We were about a half mile in when we heard the shot.

The three of us hit the dirt and waited. Nothing. Just the single gun report.

"It was a pistol," Woodruff said. "Maybe a quarter mile away."

An engine roared to life. "Shit. He's got a trail bike."

We listened as the bike drove off and faded into the distance.

"He shot the hostage," Woodruff said. "She made sense when he had the car, but once he swapped it for two wheels, she was excess baggage."

We stood up and ran toward where the shot came from, Woodruff and Kylie in the lead, me hobbling behind.

We came to a clearing, and there was the Rover parked at the far end. Right next to it, facedown in the dirt, was Annie Ryder. As I got closer, I could see the pool of blood around her head.

Just as Kylie knelt beside the body, an automatic

weapon coughed a hail of bullets into the tree over our heads.

"That was a warning shot," the voice behind us bellowed. "The next one won't be." I didn't have to turn around. It was Bassett.

"Now drop your weapons," he commanded. "One at a time. Ladies first."

Kylie set down the shotgun, took the Glock from her holster, and lowered it to the ground.

"All your guns, Detective," Bassett yelled.

She added her ankle piece to the pile. Woodruff and I went through the same drill.

"On your feet, Grandma," Bassett ordered, and Annie Ryder came back from the dead.

She stood up, brushed herself off, and wiped the blood from her hair and face. A gutted rabbit carcass was still on the ground where her head had been.

"Give the old lady your cuffs, officers," Bassett said.

We each produced a pair of handcuffs and gave them to Annie.

"Now the three of you hold hands and make a circle around that tree."

We joined hands and hugged the trunk.

"Cuff 'em," he yelled.

Annie came up behind me, put the bracelet around my left wrist, and ratcheted it shut. "Sorry," she said.

"Shut the fuck up," Bassett shouted.

Annie turned. "I was apologizing for your bad behavior, asshole."

The AR15 in Bassett's hands opened up, and a barrage of bullets splintered the tree not more than six inches above my head.

"I'm not anxious to kill three cops and have half the uniforms in the state of New York looking for me," he bellowed, "but I will if I have to."

"He means it, Annie," I said. "Just cuff us."

She snapped the other half of my cuffs onto Kylie's right wrist, then hooked Kylie's left wrist to Woodruff.

Annie moved behind Woodruff and me, then fumbled with the last set of cuffs.

"Faster," Bassett yelled.

"My hands are freezing," Annie yelled back. "If you don't like my work, find someone else."

She finally managed to link my wrist to Woodruff's.

"Move away," Bassett told her, and she slowly backed off.

He lowered his weapon, sidestepped over to the tree, and yanked hard on each set of handcuffs. They held tight.

"Good job, Granny," he said, turning to her. "I meant what I said about not wanting to kill them. You, on the other hand, are totally expendable. No cop is going to give a shit if you're alive or dead, and they're certainly not going to rise up in force to avenge your death."

"Please don't," she said, raising her hands in the air and holding them behind her head.

"Don't? Oh, but I must. But not with this," he said, setting the AR15 down. "I'm going to use Detective MacDonald's gun."

He picked up Kylie's Glock from the pile. "Nice piece," he said, examining it with the eye of a professional.

Max Bassett knew a lot about guns, but he didn't know enough about people. He certainly didn't know anything about the seventy-year-old woman standing thirty feet away with her hands held high in the air.

Annie Fender was only fifteen when a carnival came to Enid, Oklahoma. When it left, she left with it, having fallen madly in love with a German trapeze artist.

For the next five years, young Annie's life was filled with fire-eaters and fortune-tellers, knife throwers and blade box queens, pitchmen and pickpockets.

And then she met Buddy Ryder. Within days, she dumped her high-flying boyfriend to spend the next forty-seven glorious years with the smooth-talking confidence man.

Max Bassett knew nothing of Annie's backstory. Had he known, he might not have been quite so cavalier when he leveled the Glock at her chest and said, "Any last words?"

"Just three," she said defiantly.

"Then spit them out, bitch, because nothing would give me greater pleasure than to be the one who snuffs out your wretched exist—"

What happened next went down so fast that it was over before I could process it. Annie's right arm came hurtling down with all the force and precision of a former big-league pitcher at an old-timers' day game. The three-and-a-half-inch gut hook skinning knife, which had only seconds earlier been tucked in a sheath at John Woodruff's right hip, came whirring through the air, and the blade sank deep into Max Bassett's chest. A red splotch blossomed over his blue denim shirt, and he dropped to the ground like a stone.

Annie walked slowly to the body, looked down, and said the words that Maxwell Bassett would never hear.

"I hate guns."

PART FOUR

THE NEW NORMAL

CHAPTER 76

MONDAY. A WEEK ago people were mourning the death of Elena Travers. Today they were celebrating the life of the woman who avenged her murder.

Annie Ryder—tough-talking, fast-thinking, knife-wielding Annie Ryder—had gone from obscurity to notoriety with a single fling of her practiced right arm.

The saga of the trap we set for Max Bassett was on the front page of every city paper and at the top of the hour on every TV news program. It was the kind of story that left everyone smiling.

Everyone except our boss, who was fuming. "Annie Ryder is a penny-ante crook, a blackmailer, and a con artist," Cates said, "but they're making her out to be a hero."

"Technically, she is," I reminded her.

"Bullshit. Her son stole the necklace, was an accessory to murder, and the DA's office decided to cut a deal with the devil."

It seemed like a bad time to remind Cates that less than forty-eight hours ago, she was the one who had urged us to recruit Annie to trap Max Bassett.

"If it's any consolation," Kylie said, "the DA is thrilled that the devil came through. Mick Wilson would have given up a thousand Teddys to bring down a high-profile murderer like Bassett."

"It's a win-win-win, boss," I said. "Mama Bear bought her son immunity, the DA will milk this for all the votes he can muster, and Red gets credit for solving the murders of Elena Travers, Jeremy Nevins, and Raymond Davis."

"I know. I saw your pictures in the papers," she said. "I'm glad the photographers didn't get there while you were still handcuffed to a tree with a game warden."

"You can thank Annie for that," Kylie said, a smirk spread across her face. "She unlocked the cuffs."

"Next subject," Cates said, not cracking a smile. "Howard Sykes called. He and the mayor are coming here at six o'clock to hear how you're going to solve her problem with the Warlock and his Robin Hood defense."

"The plan was for us to meet her at city hall at noon," Kylie said.

"The mayor bagged that idea when she heard who you're bringing to the party. She doesn't want the press corps to know that they're even talking to each other."

"Six o'clock?" Kylie said. "I was planning to leave early and drive down to Atlantic City to bring my husband home."

"No problem. Zach and I can handle it," Cates said. "I'm glad to hear he's doing better." The phone rang and she grabbed it, grateful for the interruption.

"Send her to my office," she said to the caller. Then she hung up and turned to us. "Speak of the devil."

"Mayor Sykes is here?" Kylie asked.

"I didn't say the mayor," Cates said, smiling for the first time that morning. "I said the devil."

A minute later, Annie Ryder walked in. She looked twenty years younger. The gray hair had been colored, her makeup was flawless, and her dress and coat were a far cry from the grimy pants and Rutgers sweatshirt she had on the last time we saw her. I introduced her to Cates.

"Annie, you look fantastic," Kylie said.

"I know. Lavinia Begbie had her people give me a makeover. I'm going to be a guest on her cable show tonight. Also, now that we're doing a book together, she doesn't want me to look like a bag lady."

"You're writing a book?"

"*Jewelers to the Stars*. Lavinia is writing it. I'm

supplying the juicy details. I didn't mean to interrupt your meeting. I just came to thank you and to say good-bye."

"Where are you going?"

"Vegas. Me, Teddy, and my late husband. Buddy always wanted to move there. We could never afford it, but Bassett's insurance company agreed to pay me the two hundred and fifty thousand reward money for recovering the stolen necklace."

"I guess they had to," Cates said, "but they must have been pretty upset to cough up that much for a fake."

"Hell, no," Annie said. "Now that they can prove the Bassetts set up this scam, they're going to help the other insurance companies reopen the prior claims and sue the estate for nineteen million. I'm their star witness, so I'll be getting a piece of the action."

That was more good news than Cates could handle. "Sounds like you're going to have a grand time in Vegas," she said, coming around her desk and ushering Annie to the door.

"I'd have a much grander time if I could become a blackjack dealer," Annie said, "but they have a thing about people with a criminal record. That really pisses me off."

"Then why go?" Cates said.

"Nice weather," the old con artist said with a wink. "And suckers with money."

CHAPTER 77

IRWIN DIAMOND WAS a legend in New York politics. For forty years he had cut through red tape, party lines, and political bullshit to get things done. The press referred to him as the Fixer, the Deputy Mayor in Charge of Damage Control, and the Jewish Godfather.

At the moment, the legend was sitting in the precinct's roll-call room, arms folded across his chest, head resting against the back of the chair, eyes closed.

Cates and I exchanged a knowing smile. Irwin, who was a master of the five-minute power nap, was charging his battery for his head-to-head with the mayor.

The alarm on his cell phone beeped, his eyes popped open, and his entire body sprang to life. He was geared up and ready for action. He looked at the clock on the wall. It was 6:17.

"The mayor is not usually this late," Cates said, half apologizing for something that was out of her control.

"She'll be here in three minutes," he said.

"And you know that how?" Cates demanded. Not many people could openly challenge Irwin Diamond's pronouncements, but over the years, the fortysomething African American cop and the septuagenarian investment banker–political adviser had spent enough time in the same foxhole to become close allies.

"Because she's afraid if she keeps me waiting a half hour, I'll walk, but she's pissed at me for backing Spellman in the election, so she's sending me a message. She's in, I'm out."

"Ha!" Cates said. "You may have retired when Sykes took office, but you will never be *out*."

"Thank you, Delia. Don't get me wrong. Muriel Sykes was a damn good U.S. attorney, but she knows bupkis about politics. She's only been mayor for a hundred days, and it shows. She'd have been smarter to get here *before* I did. It might not have thrown me off my game, but it would have let me know she doesn't think like a rookie."

"On the other hand," Cates said, "if she had your political savvy, you wouldn't be here helping her out of a jam."

I sat there quietly soaking up their camaraderie.

At exactly 6:20, Mayor Sykes entered the conference room, her dutiful husband at her side, a large chip on each shoulder. She sat at the far end of the table.

"Madam Mayor," Irwin said politely.

"Mr. Diamond," she said. "Detective Jordan thinks you can help. I'm all ears."

"Let me see if I can sum up your unfortunate dilemma," he said.

She hardly needed a summary, but the old political warhorse wanted to send a message of his own. *You need me more than I need you.*

"Some bad guys stole a lot of expensive medical equipment from your most prestigious hospitals. Very embarrassing. So your hubby recruited your elite police force to quietly catch the bad guys, who turned out to be good guys, which was even more embarrassing. As an officer of the court, you want justice, but as the fledgling mayor of our fair city, you are afraid that you'll look like a complete ass in the court of public opinion. As they say in political parlance, you, Madam Mayor, are in deep shit."

Irwin gave her his best payback's-a-bitch smile. "Have I got it right so far?" he said.

"Cut to the chase, Mr. Diamond," she said. "How do I prosecute?"

"You don't. Not unless you want to be a very unpopular one-term mayor."

"That's your answer? Do nothing?"

"Did I say do nothing? No. I said don't lock up a bunch of do-gooder war heroes for trying to help their less fortunate comrades. Instead, I suggest you give them what they want."

"Which is what?"

"They want a state-of-the-art, fully funded ambulatory health-care facility for the men and women who put their lives on the line for this country. And you, Madam Mayor, should lead the charge to see that they get it."

"How am I supposed to—"

"For starters," Irwin interrupted, "the city should generously give them the land. Trust me: you have plenty just sitting around doing nothing. Then you should call the heads of all the hospitals that were robbed and ask them to donate all the equipment that was stolen and to kick in a few million apiece to put up some bricks and mortar."

"They'd hang up on me," Sykes said.

"They didn't hang up on me," Irwin said. "I've called seven since yesterday, and here's what they've pledged so far." He handed her a sheet of paper.

"Twelve million dollars?" Howard said, looking at the list over her shoulder.

"Howard, you of all people should know what these institutions spend each year on advertising. A couple of million is chump change to these guys. And if you position this as a joint venture between the city and the private sector for the benefit of veterans, I guarantee you that every hospital— whether they were robbed or not—will want to be on the list of donors."

"Very creative thinking, Mr. Diamond," the mayor said, "but these people broke the law."

"I spoke to the district attorney, who also doesn't want to be the bad cop in this scenario. He's willing to offer them a long-term community-service commitment. I'm sure they'd rather work at the new medical facility than pull jail time. What do you think, Madam Mayor? Would you like to be the one who helps these heroes get what they fought for?"

For the first time since I'd met him, Howard Sykes went on record before his wife had a chance to react. "I think it's brilliant," he said. "Muriel is only three months into her first term, but you've given us a boatload of bullet points and photo ops for her re-election campaign."

He turned to his wife. She sat quietly for a solid twenty seconds, then slowly got out of her chair and walked around the table. "Howard is right, Mr. Diamond. You've taken a worst-case scenario and turned it into a golden opportunity. Thank you." She extended her hand to her former opponent.

Irwin stood up and wrapped both of his hands around hers. "A pleasure to be of service, Madam Mayor."

"Muriel," she said.

"Irwin," he responded.

"Well then, Irwin, how would you feel about staying on and helping us nail down the details? We could discuss it over dinner tomorrow night. My house."

"I'll be there, Muriel," the Fixer said with a warm smile. "I believe I know the address."

CHAPTER 78

AT THREE O'CLOCK, Kylie left the precinct and walked to the Hertz office on East 64th Street. *One more chance,* she thought as she got behind the wheel of the Chevy Malibu. *Just give him one more chance.*

How many times had she said those words? And the answer was always the same.

"I can't, Kylie," her mother had said. "I love your father, but I'm out of chances."

She was ten when her parents got divorced. She couldn't understand her mother's logic. If you loved someone, really loved them, how could you not give them one more chance to make the marriage work?

Twenty-five years later, faced with the same life choice as her mother, she was able to make some sense of it.

She loved the man she married ten years ago, but that was not the man whose heart was filled with vitriol when he attacked her from his hospital bed. Spence's drug addiction had taken its toll on them both. How had she become the woman who handed her husband a loaded gun when he threatened to kill himself?

They'd talked since then, and with each phone call he was starting to sound more like the old Spence. He was talking the talk, and she was hoping he could pick up the pieces and get back to walking the walk.

She hadn't told him she was coming. He might say no, and Kylie hated taking no for an answer. It was time for her to clean up her side of the street, and as unaccustomed as she was to apologizing for her actions, there was one thing she knew for sure: you don't phone in your amends.

She would meet him halfway. He could move back home. She'd be there for him when he needed her, but she wouldn't try to micromanage his recovery. He had to want it as much as she did.

It was six p.m. when she got to AtlantiCare Regional. She freshened up in the ladies' room, and then, hair, makeup, and ego in place, she went to his room.

"Can I help you?" the woman in Spence's bed asked.

"I'm sorry. I thought this was my husband's room."

"This is 202," the woman said.

"Oh," Kylie said. "My mistake."

There was no mistake: 202 was Spence's room. She went to the nurses' station.

"I'm looking for Spence Harrington," she said. "Can you tell me what room he's in?"

"Harrington?" the nurse said, checking her computer screen. "He was discharged this morning."

"Are you sure?"

The nurse gave her a look: she was sure. "But don't take my word for it," she said. "Give him a call."

Spence had a burner phone. Kylie dialed the number. He answered on the first ring. "Hey, how's it going?"

"Things are crazy at work," Kylie said. "We have a meeting scheduled with the mayor. She should be here any minute. What are you doing?"

"Nothing much. You know hospitals."

"How about if I drive down and say hello tomorrow or Wednesday?" Kylie said.

"That's probably not the best idea," Spence said. "Zach gave me this NA hotline number, and I called it yesterday. There's a real good recovery center right here in Atlantic City. They have an opening, and someone is going to pick me up in the morning and check me in."

"That's great, Spence. I can visit you there."

"Not right away. They're pretty strict. Even

tougher than the rehab in Oregon. No visitors. No phones."

"How long will you be out of touch?"

"Not long. Four weeks, tops."

"And then what?"

"Hey, babe," he said, laughing. "Not a fair question. I'm supposed to be doing this one-day-at-a-time shit."

"Spence..."

"What?"

"I'm sorry."

"About what?"

"About everything. Especially Thursday night when I tried to give you my gun."

He laughed again. "Don't try that next time you arrest some asshole. He might take it and shoot you. Hey, the guy with the food cart is here with my dinner. I should go."

"Mayor Sykes just got here. I've got to go too."

"Kylie..."

"What?"

"I'm sorry too."

"About what?"

One more laugh—not because it was funny, but because it eased the pain. "I'll make a list and send it to you," he said. "I better go before my dinner clots."

"I love you, Spence."

"I love you too, Kylie. I always have. I always will." He hung up.

She believed him. Not the blatant lies about being in the hospital, or the food cart arriving, or checking into a recovery center. But she believed with all her heart that he loved her.

And she knew in her heart that she would always love him.

But they were both out of chances.

CHAPTER 79

THERE HAD BEEN an Evite in my email inbox that morning, and I'd printed it and carried it with me all day. The picture was a bottle of Chianti and two glasses on a red-and-white-checkered table-cloth. The copy was pure Cheryl.

You are cordially invited to
Cheryl's Lasagna Dinner: Take 2
My place. 7:30 p.m. Don't screw it up.

I arrived at her apartment ten minutes early. She put her arms around me and kissed me sweetly in the open doorway, lingering on my lips. She tasted like heaven.

"I come bearing gifts," I said, handing her a bouquet of flowers and a bottle of wine several notches up from the Chianti on the Evite.

"It would be gracious of me to say 'Oh really, you shouldn't have,'" she said, closing the apartment door and clicking the lock. "But who am I kidding? Of course you should have."

"There's more," I said, taking a plastic CVS bag from my pocket. "A housewarming gift."

She opened the bag. Inside was a package of men's underwear and a brand-new toothbrush.

"Oh, Zach, thank you. It's just what I always wanted," she said. "And I have a gift for you."

She took me by the hand and led me into the bedroom.

The lights were low, and the light scent of her perfume was in the air. "I'm ready for my gift," I said. *Oh God, am I ready.*

She opened a dresser drawer. It was empty.

"Ta-da! It's all yours," she said, tossing the underwear and the toothbrush inside.

"Thank you," I said, wrapping my arms around her and pressing her close.

"Hold that thought," she said, breaking away. "Dinner is served."

I followed her into the kitchen, opened the wine, and poured two glasses.

"A toast," she said. "To the team of Jordan and MacDonald, best damn cops in the city."

I downed most of my drink and refilled my glass. "And to the team of Jordan and Robinson, best damn couple in the city." I took another big drink.

"Wow," she said. "You're really pounding that wine. Tough day?"

"No," I said. "Pretty great day, actually. But I plan to spend a long romantic evening with the woman I love, and if Cates calls, I want to make sure I have enough alcohol in my bloodstream to be able to tell her I'm too liquored up to protect or serve."

She kissed me again, lit the candles, and set two steaming plates of lasagna on the table.

We sat down. "And what happens if Kylie calls?" she said, her dark eyes playing with me.

"She won't. She drove to Atlantic City to bring Spence home. In fact"—I raised my glass—"here's to MacDonald and Harrington: together again, at last."

"But what if she does call?" Cheryl said. "I know you. You can't say no to Kylie."

"You're right," I said. "If she calls, I can't say no."

I stood up, took her by the hand, and walked her back to the bedroom. I opened my new dresser drawer, buried my cell phone beneath the underwear, shut the drawer, pulled her out of the room, closed the bedroom door, and the two of us went back and sat down at the table.

I took one more sip of my wine. "Now," I said,

sliding my fork onto the tender pasta and inhaling the intoxicating aroma of perfectly seasoned meat, cheese, and tomatoes, "where were we before we were so rudely interrupted?"

ACKNOWLEDGMENTS

The authors would like to thank NYPD detectives Sal Catapano, Daniel Corcoran, Kevin Gieras, Brian O'Donnell, and Thomas Mays; NYPD transit bureau officer J. C. Myska; Dr. John Froude; Dr. Lawrence Dresdale; Dan Fennessey; Richard Villante; Robert Chaloner; Mike Winfield Danehy; Brian Sobie; Lani Crescenzi; Marina Savina; Gerri Gomperts; Bob Beatty; Mel Berger; and Jason Wood for their help in making this work of fiction ring true.

ABOUT THE AUTHORS

JAMES PATTERSON holds the Guinness World Record for the most number one *New York Times* bestsellers. He is a tireless champion of the power of books and reading, exemplified by his new children's book imprint, JIMMY Patterson, whose mission is simple: he wants every kid who finishes a JIMMY book to say "Please give me another book." He has donated more than one million books to students and soldiers and has over four hundred James Patterson Teacher Education Scholarships at twenty-four colleges and universities. He has also donated millions to independent bookstores and school libraries. James will be investing his proceeds from the sales of JIMMY Patterson books into pro-reading initiatives.

MARSHALL KARP has written for stage, screen, and TV and is the author of the Lomax and Biggs series. He is also the coauthor, with James Patterson, of the other books in the NYPD Red series.

BOOKS BY
JAMES PATTERSON

FEATURING ALEX CROSS

Cross Justice • *Hope to Die* • *Cross My Heart* • *Alex Cross, Run* • *Merry Christmas, Alex Cross* • *Kill Alex Cross* • *Cross Fire* • *I, Alex Cross* • *Alex Cross's Trial* (with Richard DiLallo) • *Cross Country* • *Double Cross* • *Cross* (also published as *Alex Cross*) • *Mary, Mary* • *London Bridges* • *The Big Bad Wolf* • *Four Blind Mice* • *Violets Are Blue* • *Roses Are Red* • *Pop Goes the Weasel* • *Cat & Mouse* • *Jack & Jill* • *Kiss the Girls* • *Along Came a Spider*

THE WOMEN'S MURDER CLUB

14th Deadly Sin (with Maxine Paetro) • *Unlucky 13* (with Maxine Paetro) • *12th of Never* (with Maxine Paetro) • *11th Hour* (with Maxine Paetro) • *10th Anniversary* (with Maxine Paetro) • *The 9th Judgment* (with Maxine Paetro) • *The 8th Confession* (with Maxine Paetro) • *7th Heaven* (with Maxine Paetro) • *The 6th Target* (with Maxine Paetro) • *The 5th Horseman* (with Maxine Paetro) • *4th of July* (with Maxine Paetro) • *3rd Degree* (with Andrew Gross) • *2nd Chance* (with Andrew Gross) • *1st to Die*

FEATURING MICHAEL BENNETT

Alert (with Michael Ledwidge) • *Burn* (with Michael Ledwidge) • *Gone* (with Michael Ledwidge) • *I, Michael Bennett* (with Michael Ledwidge) • *Tick Tock* (with Michael Ledwidge) • *Worst Case* (with Michael Ledwidge) • *Run for Your Life* (with Michael Ledwidge) • *Step on a Crack* (with Michael Ledwidge)

THE PRIVATE NOVELS

Private Vegas (with Maxine Paetro) • *Private India: City on Fire* (with Ashwin Sanghi) • *Private Down Under* (with Michael White) • *Private L.A.* (with Mark Sullivan) • *Private Berlin* (with Mark Sullivan) • *Private London* (with Mark Pearson) • *Private Games* (with Mark Sullivan) • *Private: #1 Suspect* (with Maxine Paetro) • *Private* (with Maxine Paetro)

NYPD RED NOVELS

NYPD Red 4 (with Marshall Karp) • *NYPD Red 3* (with Marshall Karp) • *NYPD Red 2* (with Marshall Karp) • *NYPD Red* (with Marshall Karp)

SUMMER NOVELS

Second Honeymoon (with Howard Roughan) • *Now You See Her* (with Michael Ledwidge) • *Swimsuit* (with Maxine Paetro) • *Sail* (with Howard Roughan) • *Beach Road* (with Peter de Jonge) • *Lifeguard* (with Andrew Gross) • *Honeymoon* (with Howard Roughan) • *The Beach House* (with Peter de Jonge)

STAND-ALONE BOOKS

The Murder House (with David Ellis) • *Truth or Die* (with Howard Roughan) • *Miracle at Augusta* (with Peter de Jonge) • *Invisible* (with David Ellis) • *First Love* (with Emily Raymond) • *Mistress* (with David Ellis) • *Zoo* (with Michael Ledwidge) • *Guilty Wives* (with David Ellis) • *The Christmas Wedding* (with Richard DiLallo) • *Kill Me If You Can* (with Marshall Karp) • *Toys* (with Neil McMahon) • *Don't Blink* (with Howard Roughan) • *The Postcard Killers* (with Liza Marklund) • *The Murder of King Tut* (with Martin Dugard) • *Against Medical Advice* (with Hal Friedman) • *Sundays at Tiffany's* (with Gabrielle Charbonnet) • *You've Been Warned* (with Howard Roughan) • *The Quickie* (with Michael Ledwidge) • *Judge & Jury* (with Andrew Gross) • *Sam's Letters to Jennifer* • *The Lake House* • *The Jester* (with Andrew Gross) • *Suzanne's Diary for Nicholas* • *Cradle and All* • *When the Wind Blows* • *Miracle on the 17th Green* (with

Peter de Jonge) • *Hide & Seek* • *The Midnight Club* •
Black Friday (originally published as *Black Market*) •
See How They Run • *Season of the Machete* • *The Thomas
Berryman Number*

FOR READERS OF ALL AGES

Maximum Ride

Maximum Ride Forever • *Nevermore: The Final
Maximum Ride Adventure* • *Angel: A Maximum Ride
Novel* • *Fang: A Maximum Ride Novel* • *Max: A
Maximum Ride Novel* • *The Final Warning: A
Maximum Ride Novel* • *Saving the World and Other
Extreme Sports: A Maximum Ride Novel* • *School's
Out—Forever: A Maximum Ride Novel* • *The Angel
Experiment: A Maximum Ride Novel*

Daniel X

Daniel X: Lights Out (with Chris Grabenstein) •
Daniel X: Armageddon (with Chris Grabenstein) •
Daniel X: Game Over (with Ned Rust) • *Daniel X:
Demons and Druids* (with Adam Sadler) • *Daniel X:
Watch the Skies* (with Ned Rust) • *The Dangerous
Days of Daniel X* (with Michael Ledwidge)

Witch & Wizard

Witch & Wizard: The Lost (with Emily Raymond) •
Witch & Wizard: The Kiss (with Jill Dembowski) •
Witch & Wizard: The Fire (with Jill Dembowski) •

Witch & Wizard: The Gift (with Ned Rust) • *Witch & Wizard* (with Gabrielle Charbonnet)

Confessions

Confessions: The Murder of an Angel (with Maxine Paetro) • *Confessions: The Paris Mysteries* (with Maxine Paetro) • *Confessions: The Private School Murders* (with Maxine Paetro) • *Confessions of a Murder Suspect* (with Maxine Paetro)

Middle School

Middle School: Just My Rotten Luck (with Chris Tebbetts, illustrated by Laura Park) • *Middle School: Save Rafe!* (with Chris Tebbetts, illustrated by Laura Park) • *Middle School: Ultimate Showdown* (with Julia Bergen, illustrated by Alec Longstreth) • *Middle School: How I Survived Bullies, Broccoli, and Snake Hill* (with Chris Tebbetts, illustrated by Laura Park) • *Middle School: My Brother Is a Big, Fat Liar* (with Lisa Papademetriou, illustrated by Neil Swaab) • *Middle School: Get Me Out of Here!* (with Chris Tebbetts, illustrated by Laura Park) • *Middle School, The Worst Years of My Life* (with Chris Tebbetts, illustrated by Laura Park)

I Funny

I Funny TV: A Middle School Story (with Chris Grabenstein, illustrated by Laura Park) • *I Totally Funniest: A Middle School Story* (with Chris Grabenstein, illustrated by Laura Park) • *I Even*

Funnier: A Middle School Story (with Chris Grabenstein, illustrated by Laura Park) • *I Funny: A Middle School Story* (with Chris Grabenstein, illustrated by Laura Park)

Treasure Hunters

Treasure Hunters: Secret of the Forbidden City (with Chris Grabenstein, illustrated by Juliana Neufeld) • *Treasure Hunters: Danger Down the Nile* (with Chris Grabenstein, illustrated by Juliana Neufeld) • *Treasure Hunters* (with Chris Grabenstein, illustrated by Juliana Neufeld)

OTHER BOOKS FOR READERS OF ALL AGES

House of Robots: Robots Go Wild! (with Chris Grabenstein, illustrated by Juliana Neufeld) • *Public School Superhero* (with Chris Tebbetts, illustrated by Cory Thomas) • *House of Robots* (with Chris Grabenstein, illustrated by Juliana Neufeld) • *Homeroom Diaries* (with Lisa Papademetriou, illustrated by Keino) • *Med Head* (with Hal Friedman) • *santaKid* (illustrated by Michael Garland)

For previews and information about the author, visit JamesPatterson.com, or find him on Facebook or at your app store.